ROYAL REFUGEE

Book 1 in the *Lost Crown* series

Lorena Angell

OTHER BOOKS BY LORENA ANGELL

Lost Crown series

Royal Refugee, bk 1
Royal Resistance, bk 2
Royal Redemption, bk 3

The Unaltered series

A Diamond in My Pocket, bk 1
A Diamond in My Heart, bk 2
The Diamond of Freedom, bk 3
The Diamond Bearers' Destiny, bk 4
The Diamond Bearer's Secret, bk 5
The Diamond Bearers' Rising, bk 6
(Books 7-10 coming soon)

For more titles by Lorena Angell visit
http://lorenaangell.com

CONTENTS

CHAPTER 1

Ekaterina Cvetkovski

As she lay on the cold gurney, feigning unconsciousness, Ekaterina Cvetkovski listened to the two men—one who had repeatedly beaten her over the course of a few months, and the other who'd consistently nursed her back to life—as they discussed her frail condition. A tingle of hope spread through her body, temporarily lessening the pain on her back and in her ribs, as she thought about what would come next. Hope was a rare commodity for Ekaterina, something she didn't like to allow into her mind. Pain, however, helped her stay focused on the calculated escape plan. She wouldn't let hope interfere with what would be her last chance for freedom.

"I don't care if she has to be wheeled in on this gurney. She only needs to live long enough to become my son's wife—that, and I would prefer she produced an heir," President Boris Kochev grumbled. He cleared his throat and continued. "Nevertheless, her royal name will be enough to give me the support I need. Why isn't she responding to the medications, Jovan?"

"I don't know, sir. She seems to have lost the will to live," Dr. Jovan Ilievski replied matter-of-factly.

"Are you sure the fluids in her IV drip are strong enough? Maybe she needs more nutrition?"

"I'm confident in the IV drip, sir. I only wish we'd found out sooner she was purposely starving herself."

"What is it going to take to get her to accept her responsibility and stop this foolishness?" President Kochev asked.

"Perhaps the wedding should be delayed."

"No. We are four days away from securing everything. I'm not going to let one ingrate . . ." President Kochev trailed off, then let out a frustrated grunt. "I have to go explain her absence to the guests at the engagement celebration. Keep me informed of her progress, Jovan."

The door to the palace Infirmary slammed shut behind him, and Ekaterina winced as she took in a deep breath and opened her eyes. She watched as Dr. Ilievski hurried over to the door, opened it slightly, and peered out. He closed it and said, "Now, Princess Ekaterina. Quickly, there isn't much time." Dr. Ilievski rushed into the nearby supply room.

"Jovan, please don't call me Princess." Ekaterina pushed back the blanket and swung her legs over the edge of the bed to sit up. Her body ached nearly everywhere, and her head swam upon sitting. She pulled off her hospital gown, under which she wore a tee-shirt, bra, and underwear.

Dr. Ilievski came out of the supply room with a pile of clothing. He stopped and looked her over with his brows pulled together. "Are you sure you're okay?" he asked. She nodded, willing herself not to faint. She would only get one shot at this, no matter how terrible she felt.

He brought the clothing over and dumped everything next to her, grabbed a button-up shirt, and helped her thread her arms through the sleeves. A fresh jolt of pain as he brushed against a bruise on her shoulder made her bite her lip.

"You know the drill. We have only a couple of minutes," he said. Together they attached the buttons. Her fingers trembled as she tucked each button through their holes. "I don't know why Kochev was so late with his visit tonight. He's put us off track. Any second now, palace staff and guests are going to start pouring through the door, wanting my help. You should have been gone thirty minutes ago." He handed her a pair of pants and held onto her arm for balance while she pulled them on. "The plane you're supposed to already be on is scheduled to leave in ten minutes. They damn well better wait for you."

"Thank you, Jovan," she said as she tugged and wiggled into the jeans. Then she put on a second pair of jeans over the first. He had to help her with those as her weak muscles protested the effort.

Jovan cleared his throat and let out a sigh as he motioned to her legs. "Your bruises and most of your marks will go away with time." Even though his face displayed a stern expression, Ekaterina heard the sorrow in his voice.

Deciphering Jovan's emotions had taken Ekaterina a while, but she felt much more comfortable around him than when she'd first met him four months ago. His strong jaw and piercing eyes had a way of letting her know when she'd messed up, but they could also convey compassion when he'd look upon the abuse marks covering her body, delivered by Boris Kochev. Jovan's ability to keep a poker face was probably why he'd been able to retain Boris Kochev's approval.

As Jovan helped her squeeze her double-socked feet into hiking boots and began tying them for her, Ekaterina thought about the events leading up to the first time she'd met the doctor and how she hadn't been impressed. Her father's unexpected death left her an orphan with nowhere else to go. President Kochev attended the funeral of Emil Cvetkovski, his trusted advisor, where he made Ekaterina an offer of assistance. She could live in the palace, be surrounded with protection from those who sought to do her harm, until she figured out what she wanted next in her life. To the public who witnessed his altruistic offer, he looked generous, and taking Emil's daughter under his wing made sense, at least that's what she figured everyone thought.

She'd resided peacefully in the palace for four days before learning exactly what Boris was all about, and the abuse he was capable of issuing. Disillusioned and broken, she was brought to Dr. Ilievski, who didn't appear to care one way or the other if she survived. She couldn't have been more unimpressed with his mannerism and what seemed to be a lack of compassion.

Over time, she learned Jovan was a good man who'd been tricked into servitude at the palace. Rather than rebelling or trying to run, he'd chosen to remain and help the not-so-fortunates, like herself. He and her had much in common, even though Jovan was twelve years her senior. They related on many topics, and with the number of times she'd found herself in the Infirmary, she and Jovan had formed a solid friendship.

She closed her eyes and gritted her teeth at the pain while Jovan tightened the laces on the boots.

"Are you sure you're all right?" Jovan asked as he stood and straightened his horn-rimmed glasses. He handed her a military hat with a brim. "You look faint."

"I'm fine," she lied. Ekaterina moved to where she could see her image in the tall mirror across the room. The layers of clothing made her look like she'd gained back the weight she'd lost since arriving at the palace. If only she could as easily fix her sallow face and sunken eyes. She bit down on the hat's brim with her teeth, then twisted her long hair to form a bun on top of her head, before placing the hat firmly atop to hold her hair in place.

"Do you have enough strength to make it out to the gate?"

"I feel infused with energy," she lied. "I'm minutes away from freedom." Ekaterina knew she might not live much longer, but whether she remained and died at the palace, or boarded the underground's smuggling plane and died, she'd be free.

Escape was preferable, death acceptable.

With a grimace on his face, Dr. Ilievski helped Ekaterina into a large military jacket. Her layers of clothing made the task difficult, but not impossible. He pulled a fake mustache from his lab coat pocket and removed the paper from the adhesive. He faced her and gently pressed the mustache above her top lip. Unexpectedly, he pulled her into an embrace.

"Please be safe," he whispered in her ear.

"Thank you for everything, Dr. Ilievski—Jovan," she said into his chest and he released his comforting hold. Ekaterina placed her hand on the side of his face and looked into his eyes. "Without you, I would have completely given up hope."

Jovan reached out and gently took her hand in his, brought it to his mouth, and kissed the back of her hand. "I'm honored to have helped you, Ekaterina. Do you remember everything I told you about which surveillance cameras are active, and where you need to go?"

She nodded.

"The cab driver has your other coat and hat in the vehicle. Take care, and," he paused briefly, "this isn't something I thought I'd ever say, but, I hope to never see you again."

Ekaterina gave the doctor another nod, too afraid to speak, mainly to keep her tears at bay.

Dr. Ilievski left her side and peeked out the door once again. He motioned for her to join him. She crept up behind him. "Go now," he instructed and pushed her out the door.

She looked back. "Goodbye, Jovan." Her throat constricted, and she suddenly felt very alone.

Ekaterina hurried down the empty corridor, keeping her eyes open and alert for palace staff or soldiers. Jovan had given her an escape route and ensured her path would be clear. She didn't know how he could make such promises, but so far, he'd been successful.

As she approached the door to the staff's break room, she truly hoped there was an outdoor exit like Jovan promised. She'd passed the room many times before. She'd even glimpsed inside, but she never saw a window or exterior door, so she'd ruled it out as a possible escape option.

Ekaterina entered the break room, acting as if she was supposed to be there. She half expected to find other staff members inside, but the room appeared empty. Through what looked like a closet, an exit door stood at the end, just as the doctor had said. Ekaterina pressed both her hands on the horizontal bar and pushed hard, opening the door. Bitter cold wind with stinging snowflakes whipped her face.

Nothing had ever felt so good.

Once outside the building, she hurried across the parking lot to the rear service entrance gate. Her eyes darted left and right and she hustled as fast as her injured body would let her. At any second this escape attempt could be thwarted. Like the last one. She didn't think she would survive another beating from President Kochev, especially since she hadn't eaten much in days. Miraculously, no employees or guards appeared along the way. A yellow cab waited for her just beyond the gate to take her to the airport. She opened the back-passenger door and climbed inside.

"Good evening, Ms. Cvetkovski," the driver said with an accent she'd only heard from her chamber maid—the accent of the neighboring country, Svobodia. Ekaterina hoped she'd soon be hearing nothing but that accent from now on. Excitement coursed through her like electricity. Freedom was so near.

"Buckle up, please. The roads are difficult, and we're in a hurry."

She had no doubt the roads would be slick tonight. The raging snowstorm had started earlier in the day, casting not only a dark cloud over the city, but also her hopes for escape. Ekaterina looked to her left and found the oversized coat and wool hat on the seat Jovan had promised would be there. She let out a sigh of relief to see the coat she'd worked so hard on, preparing it for fleeing.

A few days prior, when Jovan informed her he secured her a spot on the next defectors' airplane, Ekaterina took to inflating baggies and attaching them inside the liner of her coat to both disguise her physical appearance and to be able to transport a few precious belongings with her across the border. Some of the personal items sealed in the bags were the locket containing the only photos of her mother and father; her lineage documents, proving she was in line for the throne should President Kochev ever be overthrown; and two dried rose buds: one from each of her parent's funeral bouquets. Additionally, Ekaterina had several baggies stuffed with money to pay for lodging in Crosser homes, and relocation expenses. Handing the coat over to Jovan, knowing he would give it to strangers from the Insurgent underground, was one of the toughest things she'd ever done.

She quietly inspected the bags to insure all the contents were accounted for. A hot tear escaped and rolled down her cheek when she identified each object. She felt grateful yet confused. Why would the underground help her like this when not too long ago they had made an assassination attempt on her.

Regardless, they'd decided to help her now, and she couldn't worry about why. She took off the military hat and felt her fake mustache slide a bit on her face. She paused, then pulled it off. The last thing she needed was to have it half on her face while she boarded the plane.

With quick movements she stuffed her hair up into the wool cap, then pulled the earflaps down and tied the strings securely under her chin. She struggled to remove the military jacket with the lap belt holding her in place and the tight fit of the material against her layers of clothing. She would have to wait until she was out of the car to switch coats.

The cab driver said nothing else, and for most of the hectic ride she stared out the window. The dim glow of the streetlights did little to illuminate the roads. Snowflakes fell so fast and thick that they blanketed the incandescent lights. As the cab turned up a narrow street away from the main roads, the wintry white world plunged into darkness, lit only by the faint beams from the snow-covered headlights. He turned again and drove toward a large, lighted area. Ekaterina could make out the shapes of airplane hangars. They'd reached the airport, entering through a back door of sorts. Away from the main terminal, a cargo plane was being prepared for flight. They drove directly to the plane. Several people were scurrying around as a line of passengers boarded.

"Here you are, Ms. Cvetkovski. Good luck." The driver looked at her in the rear-view mirror.

She said nothing in return. She unlatched her seatbelt and slipped quietly from the cab, tossing the military jacket into the back seat. The cold air sliced through her multi-layers of clothing as she pushed her arms into the big coat and attached the fasteners with shaky fingers. Then she walked swiftly through the snow to her escape, the sharp air hurting her lungs with each breath. She approached the idling plane sitting on the tarmac with uncertainty and dread shooting through her body and settling in the pit of her stomach like an anvil. The airplane looked as if it had been towed in from the airplane graveyard and given a bogus stamp of approval. Several mismatching panels had been bolted on, and thick rust covered the seams and screws.

It can't be too dangerous, she thought. The pilot and co-pilot must have been satisfied enough with its condition to agree to fly it. The people ahead of her boarded. Surely, they noticed the precarious condition of the plane, too, and yet they chose to climb the stairs.

The integrity of the plane wasn't the only thing that bothered Ekaterina. The wicked blizzard conditions and limited visibility, not to mention the build-up of ice on the wings, brought additional concern. Even if the airplane could get off the ground, would it be able to maintain altitude?

Ekaterina felt torn. The dilapidated plane symbolized her potential freedom from the dominating presence of the Kochev family in her life, but it also epitomized where she believed her life was headed right now—death. Maybe the two were the same.

Yet, she'd never felt so free.

These people must feel the same: they'd rather take their chances now than stay in their current dire situations.

She took her place in line as a fierce wind gust blew snow in her face. The plastic bags inside her coat acted as an insulation barrier against the bitter cold—an unexpected plus. If only she had a facemask to protect all her exposed skin.

Firm hands gripped Ekaterina's shoulders without warning. She panicked and fought to get away, thinking she was being seized and that President Kochev had found her.

"Whoa! I'm trying to help you!" A female spoke loudly because of the roar of the engines.

Ekaterina turned and found an older woman holding a parachute.

"You're going to need this if you want to live," the woman said, then moved closer and motioned for Ekaterina to put her arms in the straps.

Thoughts raced through her mind, one of which was Jovan hadn't told her she'd need a parachute. She glanced around and found other people already wearing them.

"Young lady, this plane is leaving soon. I recommend if you're on it, you wear this."

She turned around so the lady could put the pack on her back. As the straps were tightened, a couple baggies popped beneath the tension. The lady eyed Ekaterina curiously at the odd noises, then quickly tied a bright orange bandana around Ekaterina's upper arm. Ekaterina touched the bright cloth briefly and swallowed her remaining doubts, before she was hustled onto the plane.

As one of the last defectors to board, Ekaterina sat on the bench stretching down the pilot's side of the fuselage. She stared straight ahead at the boxes and crates filling the other half of the plane. Straps, cords, and netting stretched this way and that, holding the cargo in place. She really hoped the crew had done a good job of securing the cargo because if the load shifted, her legs might be smashed, and if she survived this escape attempt, she'd need them to run.

In the past, some Crossers who'd been captured and brought back to Bregot had given their first-hand accounts of the horrors of defecting. Some said the Crosser homes were abusive and robbed them of all their money. Others said they were chased down by the Toparti police who then demanded all their money before returning them to Bregot. Ekaterina didn't know what to expect, but anything had to be better than her life now.

Leaning forward, she glanced down the bench at the other twenty or so passengers, all daring to escape from Bregot. No one looked at her. Several fellow defectors breathed rapidly—clouds of frozen breath lingered in front of them—obviously nervous about fleeing their home country and the oppression and despair, but none fleeing for the same reason as her. She was sure of that.

Ekaterina leaned back against the side of the plane and pulled her earflaps tighter to keep her identity secret. If anyone knew they were on the same flight as the last remaining royal member of the ousted government, they might choose to kick her off. Or they might opt to wait for the next flight, one that wouldn't be as likely to have President Boris Kochev's missiles locked on target. Perhaps she should have figured out a way to have kept the fake mustache on.

The wall rumbled against her back, which ached and stung

from the last set of lashings she'd received from Boris. After having failed time and again to escape from her impending marriage to Vladimir, she became depressed. Her will to rebel left. Boris thought a good lashing would pull her out of her depressed state. It hadn't.

The engines revved louder, and the plane shook. They started to roll forward. A man stood in the doorway of the cockpit and yelled instructions. His high-pitched voice competed with the roar of the plane.

"Your chute opens with the cord on your left shoulder. When you jump, count to five, and then pull your chute. If it fails, pull the backup chute with the cord under your arm. Remember to roll when you hit the ice to prevent it from breaking. If you go through the ice, release your pack using these clasps and swim for your life."

Ekaterina's breaths came in ragged gulps. Landing on ice? Swimming? She hadn't been prepared for any of this. She could hardly stand as it was. Keeping her eyes closed, she tried to remain calm, but her chest constricted with fear. Her heart thumped like thundering hooves at a racetrack. The plane taxied to the end of the runway and then accelerated abruptly. She frantically gripped at the edges of the bench. Stiff wind pushed against the plane, resisting its attempt to go airborne as if the wind itself operated under the control of Boris Kochev, like everything else in Bregot. The nose of the plane angled upward, and the tires left the ground. The dip and sway made Ekaterina sick to her stomach. The plane bounced as it pushed forward through the storm, climbing unsteadily in altitude. The right wing dipped as they cornered north toward Svobodia, the only country bordering Bregot.

The small country of Bregot descended from the main continent as a southern peninsula extending into the sea. The two countries were separated by the Modry Mountain Range, which formed an impassable border over thirty miles wide separating freedom from tyranny. The only road cutting through the mountains was closely guarded with a gated border, plus multiple checkpoints, which eliminated the option of fleeing the country by vehicle. Hiking through the mountains had its own perils. If one survived the harsh wilderness and wild animals, one would still need to have advanced mountain-climbing skills to navigate up and over the treacherous peaks. The coastal waters around Bregot were heavily patrolled by Kochev's naval forces, so escape by boat was difficult as well. The only other option was flying, not that it was much safer.

The expense involved in fleeing the country truly shocked Ekaterina. Air traffic controllers needed a lot of money to persuade them to turn their heads while a covert mission took place on their watch. Airport guards also accepted bribe money. The meager wages they received from Boris Kochev were hardly enough to support their families, who like most of the citizens of Bregot, lived in poverty.

And the expense didn't end there. Once Ekaterina arrived in Svobodia, she would need to pay a Crosser home to take her in and care for her until she felt healthy enough to leave.

Over the course of several years, the Insurgents had connected with a network of Crosser homes just over the border in Svobodia—high-security safe-houses run by families who made it their business to guard and protect defectors from Bregot and help them become integrated into Svobodian society. Ekaterina hoped she'd be so fortunate to end up in a reputable home. Still, she'd rather try her luck with freedom and hope for the best.

Most people in Bregot couldn't afford to escape the ruthless rule of Boris Kochev. The only reason Ekaterina could do so was because of her father's life insurance policy—a policy funded by one of Kochev's banks. In a round-about way, she realized, Kochev was inadvertently funding her escape.

An even greater irony painfully flashed through her mind: her father's life insurance money was being used to fund the flight that might very well take her to her death. Hot tears stung her eyes. She missed her father dearly.

Ekaterina's left hand changed grips and held the leather strap above her head, and her right hand clutched a vomit bag. The turbulence from the storm was enough to test even the strongest of stomachs. Several other defectors had already used their bags, and she feared she would lose the battle with her stomach as well.

She pushed her thoughts back to the reasons she'd fled— anything to reassure her this voyage would be worth it. She remembered her father's funeral and how the small gathering of mourners was interrupted by the cavalcade of armored vehicles bringing Boris to the service to pay his respects to Emil Cvetkovski.

Ekaterina had eyed Boris warily through the service. Mere days before her father's death, he had asked her if she would consider marrying Boris's son, Vladimir. She and Vladimir had attended school together and she despised him. He was arrogant, cruel, and possessive. She'd laughed at the proposal and her father cautioned her, reminding her about how much power Boris had. She remembered the fear in her father's eyes when she once again declined.

Three days later, he'd died of a heart attack, even though he'd never had any medical issues before.

After the services, Boris spoke with Ekaterina and offered her residency at the palace. "There have been threats made against your life, Ekaterina," he said loudly enough so that everyone could hear his exaggerated concern for her well-being. "I've known you since you were a little girl, and I consider you like my daughter. Please come to the palace where I can keep you safe until we can eliminate the threats against you." He looked around to make sure the assembled mourners were listening.

"What about my home?"

"I'll have all your things brought to you in the palace."

Wrapped up in her grief and with nowhere else to go, she agreed.

Ekaterina remembered the first few days of palace life. She was pampered and all her needs were cared for. Her lodgings at the palace were exquisite, with several handmaids appointed to her. She saw Vladimir only twice, in passing. However, she ran into Vladimir's friend Risto Petkovski quite often.

Another classmate, Risto and Vladimir went together like stink on a skunk—wherever Vladimir was, Risto remained close by. Risto had relentlessly pursued Ekaterina romantically since she was fourteen. She knew Risto very well and didn't want anything to do with him or Vladimir. But that didn't stop Risto from trying to win her attentions.

She thought about the monumental event between her and Risto that took place four days after she'd arrived at the palace.

Risto had found her walking the hall and pulled her into the vacant dining hall.

"Risto, what are you doing?" she remembered asking, twisting her arm free from his grasp.

"I have to talk to you," he insisted.

"About what?" She folded her arms across her chest.

"I can get you out of here. I can help you escape."

"Escape? I'm not trapped."

His reaction to her words scared her. "Of course you are!" Then he massaged his temples as if they hurt and closed his eyes. "I shouldn't have told him. I feel like it's my fault."

"What are you talking about? What's your fault?" Ekaterina found it surprising Risto could feel at fault for anything or could feel at all, for that matter.

Footsteps outside in the hall caused Risto to freeze in his spot until the steps faded away. He closed the gap between them and grabbed both her shoulders, pulling her face close to his. "He wouldn't have wanted you if he didn't know I did. I should have kept my mouth shut. They warned me. I screwed up, but I can make it better. Leave with me and I'll keep you safe."

"Who warned you? What are you talking about?"

"We have to hurry, Ekaterina." The urgency in his voice made the hair on her neck stand on alert.

"I'm not going anywhere with you." She broke free and moved away, putting distance between them.

"Vladimir only wants to marry you because I wanted you first."

"What?" She whirled around and faced him, not believing what she heard.

"He doesn't truly want you. Your life will be unhappy with him, and when he gets tired of you, he'll move on to someone else, discarding you like an empty milk jug."

"That doesn't matter. I don't have any interest in being Vladimir's anything." She walked toward the other door.

He crossed the room in quick steps and spun her around by the shoulders. His fingertips dug into her skin. "You're not taking me seriously, Ekaterina. Listen! You're a prisoner here. I can help you escape, but you have to trust me."

Her voice shook. "I don't know what you're talking about. I'm not a prisoner. Leave me alone."

President Boris Kochev, along with his entourage, entered the dining room and stopped abruptly upon seeing the two of them so close. Risto quickly released his grip and stepped back. Boris bellowed, "What's going on in here?" His eyes moved from her to Risto with a heated anger.

She turned her back to Risto. "Nothing. We were just having a discussion. But we're done now, aren't we, Risto?" She looked over her shoulder.

"Oh yes, we're done."

Ekaterina's skin crawled with the way he enunciated each word.

Risto continued. "Ekaterina asked me how to escape from the palace, and I strongly advised her against it."

Astounded, her eyes darted back to Boris, who approached and stood directly in front of her. Voice cracking, she insisted, "That's not true! He's lying! He came to me with—"

Boris cut her off by slapping her across the face with the back of his hand. She stumbled backwards into Risto, who caught her under her arms. Her eyes instantly filled with moisture. She gained her own footing once again and pushed Risto away.

Boris stepped closer to her. "You are nothing but an insolent, unappreciative girl who has yet to learn her place. I shall take it upon myself to teach you." He turned to his guards and flicked his hand toward the door. "Take her to the blue room."

Ekaterina remembered the long walk to the blue room. Not completely sure of what to expect, yet somehow knowing all the same, Ekaterina chose to occupy her mind with thoughts of Risto's offer and subsequent betrayal. He'd said so many things that didn't make sense. Why was he so determined to get her out of the palace? And then why turn against her?

The guards directed Ekaterina down to the basement, or more appropriately, the dungeon. The blue room was situated down a barren hall with no windows. The room had pads on the walls and chains hanging from the ceiling.

Once Boris arrived, he spoke as if he'd memorized his speech. "You are here, alive, because of me," he said. "And this is how you thank me? By trying to run. I have cushioned your life since you were seven years old, ever since your parents came out of hiding, and gave you every opportunity to live a privileged life. You should be grateful. And you will be. You'll get to live as Vladimir's wife and help cement our place in history. So, if you think for a second you can leave here, think again! Now, I will teach you your place until it sinks into your unappreciative mind."

She didn't remember too much after that except pain like she'd never felt before. Bruises swelled across her arms and back over the few days. She was kept in the blue room where Dr. Ilievski cared for her while she healed and the bruises faded. All the while plans for the wedding rolled forward without her consent as did Ekaterina's resolve to find a way to escape.

In the weeks that followed, Ekaterina attempted to escape twice, which only led to additional beatings and lectures and her permissible roaming area reduced to only a couple of rooms. The third round of beatings had broken her spirit. She began to accept that she'd never escape and decided to stop eating, to just let herself die.

However, Dr. Ilievski intervened, unable to stand seeing her waste away.

He gave her hope.

Now, sitting on the hard bench of the airplane, Ekaterina reached to her upper left arm and tightened the knot of the orange bandana—the color of a border Crosser. She knew how it worked. She knew what to expect, but it still left her uneasy. Once on the ground in Svobodia, assuming she was still alive, she would need to make her way to the town of Toparti, located on the lake's northern shore. There she would have to wait on the side of the road until someone came for her. The orange bandana needed to be in full view. Hopefully a caregiver would come by to pick her up. Hopefully they would be good caregivers.

The pilot yelled over the speaker, "Folks, we are nearing the drop-off point. Good luck and God bless."

A rush of frozen air forced its way through the cargo hold. Ekaterina leaned forward to glance down the bench and saw those near the other end were already standing and moving toward the opened door at the other end of the plane. Everyone around her stood in preparation. She stood, too, and began moving forward in line. Ekaterina's heart raced with trepidation. One by one, everyone ahead of her jumped out of the plane.

Her turn came. Bravely, she stood in front of the door, a black hole in the side of the plane. The unbearably cold wind felt like glass shards cutting into the exposed flesh of her face. The assistant patted her back and placed the ripcord into Ekaterina's hand. She took a deep breath and reminded herself once again she would rather die than be married to Vladimir Kochev. She leapt out into the blackness, counted to five, and pulled the cord.

The jolt of her chute opening sent her stomach to her toes in a nauseating lurch. Ekaterina clutched the chute straps and prayed as she descended through the blinding flurry of snow and icy wind. She hoped she'd be able to see the ground before it hit her feet so she could roll as she'd been instructed, but she struggled to keep her eyes open against the biting wind. Then, the raging elements around her lessened. She opened her eyes and saw she'd broken through the underside of the clouds. The lights of the town named Toparti shown like a beacon of hope, calling her, offering her the freedom she'd thirsted for ever since she'd become imprisoned at the palace. At her current rate of travel, she estimated she'd land near the shore of the lake unless the wind changed direction. Having been one of the last to jump, she'd also be closer to shore—an unexpected bonus.

The ground was coming up fast, and she could see the ice. Strange movement on the ice caught her attention. No, not on the ice—*in* the ice. The other jumpers had broken through the ice!

No! No! Ekaterina wanted to be back on the plane. She wanted to be anywhere but here at this moment. The ice wasn't thick enough! Her feet connected with the ice in a spot still intact. She attempted the rolling technique, but the force cracked the ice and she plunged into the freezing water. So cold! So black. No air!

Her lungs seized from the bitter cold of the water. She couldn't breathe if she'd wanted to. She kicked frantically to resurface and used her parachute cords as a guide to reach the hole in the ice her body had created. The chute was still on top of the ice. Hopefully she wouldn't pull it under. When her head broke through the surface of the lake, she took a sharp intake of frozen air and coughed violently, then screamed for help as she continued to kick to stay afloat, her weak muscles protesting every movement. The eerie shrieks and screams of other Crossers nearby filled the night sky.

Ekaterina's body felt heavy and she shook uncontrollably. But she was alive. She clumsily pulled on the cords of her chute, hoping to be able to use it as a rope to get out of the water. The ice was too thin to support her weight and cracked beneath her elbows, piece by piece. If she couldn't get up on the ice, she at least needed to get to shore. Adrenaline coursed through her and, using her elbows, she frantically pounded at the ice, breaking it apart, pushing it out of the way to allow her to advance toward shore.

Ahead, with the illumination of the streetlights, she saw Crossers emerge from the ice and stumble up the shore and to the road. Headlights cut through the falling snow and a vehicle came to a stop by the Crossers who'd made it out of the lake.

"Here! I'm here!" Ekaterina yelled and waved her arms. She slipped under the water again after taking her elbows off the ice. The air pockets inside her coat helped to give her buoyancy, but not quite enough to keep her head above water. Kicking again, she resurfaced and bobbed to the ice shelf again, sputtering water out of her mouth and coughing violently. She pulled again on the parachute chords but to her horror, the snagged parachute detached from the outcropping of ice that had been her lifeline. The vehicle drove away without seeing her.

If she wanted to live, she had to get out of the water and up to the road. She continued to kick to stay afloat and banged her elbows on the ice to break it. Her adrenaline waned and her muscles felt sluggish. The ice thickness increased as she neared shore and she suspected it would hold her weight, unfortunately she didn't have anything to pull herself up with. On the plus side, her body didn't seem to be cold anymore. In fact, she felt warm—almost hot. And she was incredibly tired.

The yells and screams of the other Crossers had subsided. Her kicking was all but a standstill now, and she felt so tired and lethargic, but she was close to the bank of the lake. Her foot struck something hard. Ground. She had reached the shallow depths. Now if only she could stand up and climb on the ice. She was so weak, so tired. If she could just rest a little first, then she'd have enough strength to get out of the lake. The last thought that crossed her mind was of her father. He had a smile on his face.

Konstantin Andonov

"Did she make the plane?" Konstantin Andonov asked, an unlit cigar clenched between his teeth. He held the telephone receiver to his ear with his shoulder while he rummaged through the desk drawer to find his lighter.

"Yes, Mr. Andonov," the voice on the phone said. "I dropped her off just in time. I should tell you, though, I had to eliminate one of the gate guards. He hadn't been affected by the drug, and I couldn't risk him seeing Ekaterina leave. He'd have sounded the alarm."

"Were you seen on camera?"

"Doubtful. The snow had covered the lens."

"Good. What about the body?"

"I put him in the taxi trunk and dropped him at the graveyard."

"You did your job well, son. Stop by and I'll give you your payment." Konstantin hung up the phone and sat back in his chair with his lighter and puffed the cigar as he lit the end. Swirls of smoke hung in the air.

Kral sat in a chair across the room, dressed in his palace uniform. He leaned forward and put his elbows on his knees. "Was it a successful departure, Mr. Andonov?"

"Yes. The plane crossed the border undetected."

"Do you need me to take care of a body?"

Konstantin nodded. "A guard at the rear service gate had to be taken out. He's at the graveyard."

Kral sneered. "We should have just killed Ekaterina while we had her unguarded in the taxi. Boris will find her and bring her back."

"He will. But I want the good doctor to join our side, so we're playing the doctor's game."

Kral stood. "I'll take care of the body." He straightened his uniform and left the room.

Konstantin settled into his chair with his cigar and an overload of thoughts. If the earlier assassination attempts on the princess had been successful, he would have never discovered that Boris Kochev's personal physician, Dr. Ilievski, worked against him. No, this was a beautiful discovery, and would be used to the best advantage of the underground.

Kral was right, though. Boris would find the princess eventually, and yes, she would have to die, but not until the doctor had joined them. Kral would have to get that through his head and stay focused in his position at the palace.

CHAPTER 2

Ivan Lazarov

Ivan Lazarov drove through the streets of Toparti, palms beating the steering wheel in time to the song on the radio. The roads were covered with a good layer of snow and growing increasingly dangerous as the blizzard raged on. He let out a compassionate "Oooh, man!" as he passed a vehicle that had slid off the road. The tune on his radio blared out "Another One Bites the Dust" by *Queen,* and Ivan chuckled at the irony.

He directed his focus back to the task at hand: looking for the distinctive fluorescent orange color, the sign of a Crosser. He had already picked up four, all male, and delivered them to his family's home. They still had room for two more if he could find anyone else.

Ivan had been born and raised in Toparti and lived with his parents, his older brother Luka, and his grandmother on his father's side. His family operated a Crosser home, hiding under the guise of a Bed-and-Breakfast, helping those who dared try to flee the oppressive regime to the south. Their home was equipped to house, feed, and transport border Crossers until the individuals could apply for asylum or assume new identities. There wasn't a regular schedule of when people would arrive needing assistance, only the chatter across the HAM radio airwaves—spoken in cryptic language—indicated when another load was on the way.

Earlier in the day, Ivan learned more Crossers would be coming that night. His mood headed south and hadn't much changed through the afternoon and evening. He'd had the better part of the day to dwell on his mundane life. The older he became, the more of his time was occupied with Crossers—pick up the

Crossers, hide the Crossers, shop for supplies for the Crossers, drive the Crossers to Severni, scout for more Crossers. He was tired of it. At nearly twenty years of age he wished he could get out of the house, to move on from his tedious life. That, or at least be given a more important role in caring for Crossers, like his older brother Luka.

A few weeks ago, he expressed his frustrations to his mother, Elena. "When will they stop coming?" he whined. "When do we get to live a normal life?"

"Shame on you, Ivan!" Elena snapped back. "The least we can do for those unfortunate souls is offer them aid. Without us, they would die in that Godforsaken country. You need to stop thinking about yourself."

His stomach knotted up with her rebuke. "I'm sorry, Mom."

She exhaled and looked at the floor. "No, I'm sorry, Ivan. I shouldn't expect you to feel the same way your father and I do. You have every right to choose the direction your own life will go and decide if you want something different for yourself. We made our choice long ago to help the defectors because we understand their situation, but that doesn't have to be your life's path."

"Yeah, right. Everyone in this family has helped Crossers. If I decide not to, then I'll be looked down on, won't I?"

"No, sweetheart."

Ivan had a soft spot for his mother, and he loved it when she called him sweetheart, but he knew she was placating him.

She continued. "You shouldn't do something out of obligation. If your heart isn't in it, you can't effectively protect a Crosser."

"But how will I ever know unless I'm given more responsibilities?"

"Responsibilities come when you care enough to deal with them. I don't mean to pressure you, and I'm certainly not trying to push you out of the house, but have you thought any more about college?"

Ivan rolled his eyes and shifted on his feet in annoyance. "I don't know if I want to do more school."

"You could get a job. Or you're always welcome to stay here and continue working with us just as you've always done."

"As errand runner and Crosser-picker-upper, I know." He let out an exasperated sigh. "I don't know what I want yet."

She placed a hand on his arm. "Take your time. Luka didn't fully decide to help with Crossers till two years ago, and he's twenty-six. He had a couple jobs during that time to figure out what he truly wanted to do."

Ivan knew better than to complain, but it didn't stop him from wishing for a different life, something more like what his friend next door, Anton Gulevski, had. Anton's family had been their neighbors for over ten years, and they had hit it off right away when Anton moved in. Ivan remembered feeling envious of his friend on many occasions, especially when chores were top priority. Anton didn't have nearly as many duties around his house and he was free to be a kid and careless teen. He didn't have to keep secrets or constantly share his house with strangers. Ivan felt like he'd missed out on a normal childhood. He just wanted to hang out at home, bum around a bit, but some Crosser priority always got in the way.

When Anton told Ivan his family was going to start housing Crossers a few months back, Ivan opened up and admitted his family was already doing so. Up to that point, Ivan had only been allowed to tell Anton the "Bed-and-Breakfast" cover story. Ivan felt an intense need to warn Anton of how much his life was going to change because of his family's choice to operate the same type of business.

"Dude, you can kiss your freedom goodbye," Ivan told Anton. "Think about how many times you've invited me to go somewhere with you, but I couldn't because of one reason or another. All those reasons were Crosser related. And now your parents are dumping that on your shoulders, too."

Anton was the only person who seemed to understand Ivan's situation and frustrations. Ivan couldn't gripe to his parents about feeling useless and wanting more independence, or they'd tell him to stop being selfish, like his mother had already told him. He couldn't talk to his older brother Luka about his worries about being unprepared for adulthood without being chided about being immature. He only had Anton to unload on, and Anton was a good listener. Ivan felt relieved being able to open up to Anton and it gave him the support he needed in his out-of-control world—the world where his life didn't seem to be his own.

Ivan and Anton often talked about their futures. They both wanted to get away from Toparti and the gloom and doom and sheer boredom abounding there. They wanted to go as far north as they could and perhaps attend one of the universities up there. Maybe they would become doctors or lawyers or anything that would give them a real life. However, neither wanted to admit they were too chicken to venture out on their own and too scared to want to apply to college.

For the present evening, however, Ivan's life involved one thing: locating and picking up Crossers. He drove slowly along the road, looking down to the edge of the iced-over Lebed Lake. The landscape was dark except where the streetlights illuminated the ground and lake shore. Then he saw it. A bright orange bandana out on the ice—well, attached to someone on the ice.

Ivan stopped his car and got out. From where he stood, he could tell the person was submerged in the ice up to their armpits. He couldn't see a face, only a heavy wool cap with earflaps. The blowing snow made it difficult to see much of anything else. He knew he'd have to go out on the ice to retrieve the Crosser, something he didn't want to do, but was prepared for. He hustled to the back of the car and retrieved a rope and an axe. He fastened the axe to his waistband, then tied the rope to the car's front bumper and ran down to the lake's edge, uncoiling the rope as he ran.

"Hello there," he called out. "Are you okay? Hello?"

No response. Ivan wrapped the other end of the rope around his waist and tied it off. He needed to be prepared just in case he went through the ice, like the Crosser. The mostly submerged person was about fifteen feet from the shore. Ivan stepped on the ice to test his weight. *So far, so good,* he thought. He took another step and heard the ice crack, which prompted him to lie down to distribute his weight more evenly, then he belly-crawled out to the motionless form. He pulled the axe from his waistband and gently broke the ice around the Crosser, then heaved and pulled. As the body came up and out of the lake, the ice cracked underneath again.

His breath caught in his throat. Ivan knew the water wasn't deep here, but the last thing he wanted to do was fall in. His jeans would weigh a ton if they got wet, but at least he'd be able to pull himself out with the rope. He inched backwards and tried again. Slowly but surely, he extracted the body from the lake, and pulled the person to shore.

With such a large, wetted coat, Ivan expected the Crosser to be heavy. He would most likely have to drag the body to his car. But when he braced his legs to pull, he was surprised at the Crosser's light weight. This person probably weighed around a hundred pounds, either a very small man or more likely a teenager.

Ivan repositioned and scooped the Crosser up off the ground and carried them up to his vehicle. Small puffs of air came from the Crosser's lips, but the timing seemed erratic. Time was of the essence. His Crosser needed to be warmed up immediately. Ivan struggled for a few minutes to maneuver the Crosser in the car, but once he had, he untied the rope from the bumper and shoved it in the back seat, not taking the time to untie it from his waist.

When he got home, he jumped out of the car and began untying the rope from his waist.

His mother came out to meet him, her lips pulled tight with a grimace. "Ivan, Luka just brought in two more," she said. "We don't have room for this one. All the cots are taken."

Ivan's mouth fell open and his head twitched back and forth briefly. "Why was Luka picking up Crossers?" he asked. "That's *my* job."

"We got word some of them had fallen through the ice. I sent him out to help."

"But you'd already sent *me* to pick up two more. Did you think I wouldn't bring any back?" Bitterness and anger rose within him. She obviously didn't understand the level of rescue effort he'd done to retrieve the last one from the lake.

Elena tilted her head. "I hoped he'd find you and help you, but he must have gone the other direction and found two right away."

"Well, what am I supposed to do with this one? I can't very well put him back where I found him! He's nearly frozen to death. We have to do something."

"Maybe your father can call over to the Gulevskis to see if they can take him."

"That's not fair. Have Luka send one of *his* away."

"They are already set up inside."

Anger welled up inside of him. He felt like his mother hadn't even thought he'd bring someone home and now Luka got priority. "No! I pulled him from the lake. *I'll* take care of him in *my* room." Ivan's heart pounded in his ears. No way was anyone going to take this Crosser.

"Ivan," his mother said with a note of concern, "you're not trained to care for Crossers."

"How hard can it be?"

"It can be *very* hard, Ivan."

Some of the steam left him as the chill of the air seeped into his bones. "Then you can teach me. On the job training." He attempted a weak smile, hoping his mother would give him a chance. "He needs help now, Mom. I can do this."

She stared at him for what seemed like an eternity. "Okay, let's go," she said abruptly. She helped him haul the Crosser into the house. They went through the back door and into the kitchen, instead of heading downstairs to the hidden bedrooms.

Ivan and his mother carried the lightweight Crosser through the swinging door and into the dining room, then across the living room to Ivan's bedroom. Ivan pushed open the door with his backside, and they carefully laid the stiff, frozen person on the hardwood floor.

"Get those clothes off quickly. I'll get some warm blankets," Elena said, then left the room.

Ivan took a deep breath. He would show everyone, and himself, he was ready to handle larger responsibilities.

Crossers always came in layers—layers of clothing, that is. They didn't bring bags or suitcases. They wore all their clothing, layer upon layer. The mass of clothing also helped to keep them warm in the frigid temperatures, unless they fell through the ice and got wet, in which case it could be the death of them.

Ivan turned on a small portable heater, blowing warm air on the unfortunate frozen soul. He removed the hiking boots and two pairs of socks. He opened the coat fasteners and eased each arm out of the coat sleeves, then pulled the coat out from under the Crosser. He reached up to untie the strings of the bulky hat. His peripheral vision took in mounds under the shirt, and his brain was a tad bit slow in realizing he was seeing what looked like breasts. As his brain caught up with his actions of removing the hat, he was stunned to find a mass of long dark hair, wet of course. The realization of what he'd gotten himself into hit him in the gut like a sledgehammer.

A girl! And one about his own age, he guessed. Right away he noticed her striking facial features. High cheekbones, long lashes, delicately arched eyebrows, and dark circles under her eyes. She seemed a little thin. Nonetheless, she was stunning, the most beautiful girl Ivan had ever seen, even with skin nearly blue with cold.

Elena came back in with warm blankets. "What's taking you so long? Oh! My goodness!" Her words paused only momentarily, then she snapped out, "Well, get on with it, Ivan. She's dying on you." Then as quick as she entered the room, she left.

Ivan came back to his senses and began removing her pants, one wet pair at a time. At least she was only wearing two pairs. But the second pair was harder to remove. They wouldn't come off her slender hips without bringing her panties down with them. He fought by holding the elastic band of the underwear with one hand and pulling the waistband of the pants down, inch by inch.

Then he covered her legs with a fresh warm blanket, but not before noticing all the bruises. There were bruises everywhere in assorted colors: dark blue and purple, yellow and green. He moved up to remove her shirts. The outer one was a button-up, long-sleeved shirt. The second was a tee-shirt which was harder to remove off her body. He left her wet bra on and covered her with another warm blanket. Then he scooped up her freezing cold body and laid her on the bed.

He covered her with more warm blankets and tucked them all around her body. His mother came back in and saw what he was doing.

"No, Ivan, blankets won't be enough. She's frozen solid. She needs body heat."

Ivan looked at his mother and was surprised at what she implied. He had learned long ago that the best way to warm a person suffering from hypothermia was with another warm body, flesh on flesh, but this was not something he was prepared for. He shook his head. "I'm not going to do that."

"She could die," his mother said.

"You want me to lay down naked next to a total stranger—a girl?"

"You wanted this, Ivan. It's either you, or I'll get Luka to do it. Body heat is the only thing that will save her."

"Can't you do it?"

"I have too many other things going on. Don't forget, we have six other Crossers in this house. You volunteered for this, remember? If you're not up to handling her, I'll have her sent somewhere else."

Ivan heard the stress in his mother's voice and conceded. "Okay, I'll do it." He took off all his clothes, except his briefs, and climbed into the bed.

His mother stood right by the bed, issuing orders. "Now put your arms around her. Hold her tight so she'll absorb your body heat."

"Mom!"

"Turn her on her side and form your body to hers. Come on. This is not a game."

"Do you have to stand there and tell me how to cuddle? This is embarrassing enough as it is."

"This is not about *you*, Ivan! And it has nothing to do with 'cuddling.' This isn't a romantic trist. You are like a doctor and this Crosser is your patient. Male or female, old or young, Crossers must be treated the same. Sharing your body heat is the difference between life and death for this girl. You wanted to learn how to care for Crossers. This is step one. Don't let your Crosser die." She began gathering up the wet clothing from the floor.

Ivan sobered up. His mother was right. This girl needed to live. As Ivan rolled the Crosser on her side so he could conform his body next to hers, he discovered crisscrossed scars and lashings on her back. Stunned, he choked out, "Mom, wait, look at this!"

She came back to the bed and leaned over to examine the injuries. "Oh dear! How horrible! What an awful . . . from the look of the scars, I'd say she's been whipped several different times. She has fresh wounds across old scars." She reached over and ran her finger over the girl's back. "This is just sickening. I hope she makes it through the night so we can find out what happened to her."

"Yeah," he said, barely more than a whisper.

His mother left to go put the wet clothing and more blankets in the dryer to warm. Ivan looked a little longer at the scars, and a deep compassion filled his soul. Who would do such a horrible thing to a human being? Her face had been spared any injury, he'd noticed. But why?

Then a different thought entered his mind. This girl must be a strong individual to withstand this kind of treatment. Clearly, she wanted to escape the abusive life she had over there, and that's why she boarded the Crosser plane to flee. If he hadn't found her in the lake, she would have died. Of course, there was still the possibility of that happening. He fit his body close to hers, wrapped his arm around her to pull her next to him, and adjusted the mass of blankets over them. She felt like an ice cube.

His mother kept bringing in warm blankets every half hour or so and switching them out. After a few hours, the girl started to have shiver fits. They would come on suddenly and became violent, and then they were gone. Ivan's mother told him it was a good sign. She was warming up.

Ivan knew he would normally be overheated with all the freshly warmed blankets his mother kept piling on them, but he had a hard enough time keeping warm himself. Then he realized he was being selfish and felt guilty for only thinking about his own comfort. He wasn't the one teetering on the edge of death. His comfort came second, her survival demanded it.

During the night, Ivan dozed off periodically but woke up whenever the girl shivered or moaned. Once he drifted into a fleeting dream of walking out on the frozen lake in the middle of the blizzard. The muted buzz of an airplane engine echoed in the distance. The snow whipped around him and stung his face. He stepped forward and heard the ice crack beneath his feet. He felt himself slipping down, down into the water. He was pulled helplessly into the suffocating darkness. He awoke with a jolt and a racing heart.

Elena came in to check on them again at 6:00 am.

Ivan quietly whispered, trying not to wake the girl, "How are the other Crossers?"

"Fine, all things considered. This one is in the most critical condition of the Crossers we have. Apparently, Crossers were landing on top of one another in the lake and crawling over each other to get up on the ice. It's upsetting beyond measure to know that good people can be driven to such extremes because of one loathsome man. All they wanted was freedom from tyranny."

Boris Kochev

Boris Kochev opened his eyes to the ringing phone next to his bed. The bright morning sunlight hurt, making him squint as another wave of nausea rolled through his body.

"What?" he barked into the phone.

"Pardon me for calling so early, sir," Dr. Ilievski said. He didn't sound like he was in any better shape. "Did you have Ekaterina moved?"

"No. Why?"

"She's not here, sir."

"What are you talking about?" Boris' voice thundered into the phone.

"She's not in the Infirmary."

"Well, where is she?"

"I don't know. Perhaps you could have security pull up the surveillance tapes. All I know is my clinic became flooded with sick staff members last night and I lost track of her. I didn't even realize she was gone."

Boris slammed down the phone. "Get me Vladimir," he ordered his room attendant.

Moments later, Vladimir appeared in his father's room. "You asked to see me?" Vladimir still had a green tinge to his skin and looked as if he wasn't finished being sick.

"When was the last time you saw Ekaterina?"

"Yesterday, why?"

"She's gone."

His eyes widen. "She died?"

"No. She's gone, Vladimir. She's missing."

Vladimir's jaw dropped and his eyes narrowed. "I'll go ask Risto."

"He's still here?"

"Yes. He became ill like everyone else so he stayed in a guest room."

"Go find her, Vladimir. You know how important she is to us."

"Yes, Father, I do."

Boris picked up the phone and issued the order to close the border, even though he knew she could already be across. She would have been taken to Svobodia or beyond. They would need to start the search in Toparti. The wedding was only three days away. She must be found.

Boris considered that if Risto was still at the palace, then he wasn't helping her flee like she accused him of doing months back. Boris hadn't forgotten her words and he'd kept a close eye on Risto ever since, but he hadn't seen any reason to believe her over him. Still, something about Risto bothered Boris every time he saw him.

Vladimir Kochev

Vladimir stumbled into Risto's room and found him sleeping beside the toilet in the bathroom. "Risto, wake up! Where's Ekaterina?"

"Huh?" Risto mumbled.

"She's disappeared. Do you know where she is?"

"What? No. She was too sick to run."

"I ordered the guards to conduct a search, but everyone seems to be moving in slow motion from this illness."

Risto sat up quickly and threw up in the toilet.

Vladimir left the room in disgust. "Where did you go, Ekaterina?" he muttered as he looked out the window at the mounds of fresh snow, feeling incredibly peeved for being tricked by a girl. He'd believed, like his father, she was too weak to escape. Now, once word got out, everyone would know she'd run away from him. Vladimir could imagine the gossip from the people. They would know she didn't want to marry him. The embarrassment he felt because of her enraged him to the core. She would pay for this!

CHAPTER 3

Ekaterina

Ekaterina's senses came back to her one at a time. Smell returned first, as she became aware of delicious aromas filling her nose—coffee, eggs, and baking bread. Hearing came next, but all she could hear were distant muted voices and the occasional clank of kitchen utensils. She felt the soft warm bed under her and the mound of blankets on top of her. She knew she was lying on her side with something heavy and warm draped over her waist. She opened her eyes and saw a plain white wall. A clock with a popular sports team logo sat on a bedside table and showed the time as 8:58 a.m. She couldn't remember how she got out of the lake or came to be in the bed. Maybe she was dreaming.

Maybe she was dead.

A shudder ran through her body, confirming she was alive—and cold. To her alarm, the heavy warm object on her waist moved. She held her breath. Cautiously, she lifted the mass of blankets and looked underneath to discover she was only wearing her panties and bra and that the thing draped over her waist was an arm. An obviously male arm.

Her heart rate tripled. Panic seized her lungs in realization that the rumors about Crosser homes were true. What had happened? What had he done to her? The panic holding her lungs hostage turned to anger—anger at herself, anger at the man who felt he could take liberties with her while she was unconscious.

Ekaterina shoved his arm aside and began kicking her feet and flailing her arms to free herself from the layers of blankets. Her sudden struggle awoke the man, who sat up abruptly. He raised his hands with his palms out and his fingers splayed, but she just wanted to get far away.

"Hey, it's okay. Calm down," he said.

She stumbled out of the bed and fell to the floor as pain ripped through her left ankle and foot, causing her to let out a shriek. She pulled her legs to her chest and wrapped one arm around her knees. The other arm moved in a defensive manner, trying to decide which part of her she should block from his view.

The male jumped from the bed and approached her, clothed only with underwear. His size and bulk of lean muscles told her he could overpower her with little effort.

"St-tay away f-from me!" she yelled. Her chattering teeth and shivering made it difficult for her to speak.

"I'm not going to hurt you," he said, stepping closer.

Ekaterina scooted away from him toward the corner, her injured foot screaming in protest. "Where am I, and why am I und-d-dressed? What did you do to me? And wh-who are you?" She couldn't spit the questions out fast enough.

He smiled and sat down on the floor at arm's length away from her, to which she scooted back another inch. "You're in Svobodia," he explained. "You were on the Crosser plane last night, remember? I picked you up out of the iced lake and brought you to my house. You were unconscious and frozen to the bone. I had to . . . I was only warming you up with my body heat."

She glared at him, not knowing if she could believe him. Her eyes darted around the room, looking for a way to escape, but her injured ankle and unknown location made her realize leaving would be impossible. She gulped down her breaths and trembled. She was trapped again.

"Nothing happened, I swear. My name is Ivan. Are you hurt?"

"What kind of question is th-that? Of course, I'm hurt!" She didn't know what else to say to the dark-haired, shirtless, pants-less man. However, upon closer inspection, she determined his age wouldn't be much more than hers. "Obviously you are too young to be in charge. Bring me someone I can talk to."

Ivan frowned and pushed himself off the floor. "Fine." He pulled a blanket off the bed, tossing it at her feet. He walked over to the dresser, took out a pair of jogging pants, and put them on. Then he pulled out a tee-shirt and lobbed it to her. The shirt landed on her head. She pulled it off her face and looked at him in confusion. Without another word, he left the room.

His insensitive attitude irritated Ekaterina as she yanked the large shirt over her head and pushed in her arms. She stood, balanced on one foot, and hopped to the bed, but lost her balance and tumbled into the mass of blankets in pain. At least she could crawl back under the layers of bedding to get warm. She heard voices outside the door. In walked Ivan and an older, shorter woman. They stood over the bed and looked at her.

"Nice to see you awake, honey," the woman said. "I'm Elena, Ivan's mother. Where do you hurt?"

"I'll be fine. It's nothing." Her words came short and curt. She felt better knowing there was a woman in the house, but her gut still rumbled with distrust.

Ivan let out a loud breath, then said, "You were just sitting on the floor holding your leg. It's not nothing."

Ekaterina narrowed her eyes as she stared him down. After a moment, she said, "My foot hurts."

"Any other pain?" Elena asked with a soothing tone as she lifted the blankets to look at her foot.

Ekaterina thought for a second. Plenty of places on her body hurt, and her ribs still ached, but nothing like the pain in her foot. "Just some aches. Nothing bad."

Ivan shook his head and turned his back to her with his hands on his hips, clearly frustrated. His move showed Ekaterina more of his imposing form and . . . perhaps immaturity.

"Are you hungry?" Elena adjusted the bedding.

Ekaterina nodded.

Ivan stepped out of the room momentarily and came back with a tray of food that must have been sitting just outside the door. The woman helped her sit up. After Ivan made sure the legs of the tray were locked in place, he leaned forward and set the tray in her lap. His nearness to her body made her uncomfortable and she pressed her body into the pillows a few millimeters and held her breath. Her move made him look at her. Ivan's face was so close to hers she could see the black ring around his brown irises. They stared at each other briefly then he straightened his body and stepped away.

Ekaterina let out her held breath carefully. She still didn't know if she was safe at this location and from the looks on Ivan's and the woman's faces, they seemed just as unsure about her.

Ekaterina nodded and said timidly, "Thank you for the food, Elena."

Elena smiled and her shoulders dropped. "What would you like us to call you?"

"What do you mean?" Ekaterina angled her head.

"Defectors never use their real name, dear. So, what name would you like us to call you by?"

"Kat—um—Katia."

"Okay, Katia. We're happy to have you in our home and will do our best to protect you until you can be moved north."

"Thank you."

"We'll step out now and let you eat your breakfast. I'll find you some comfortable pants to wear," Elena said and ushered Ivan out the door.

Ekaterina had not planned to use the name "Katia." It just fell out of her mouth when asked. She should have used a different name, like Rosa or Dafina or Olga or anything not so close to her real name, but her mind had turned to mush after the events of the morning. Her mind went back to her father. He was always full of one-line aphorisms, deep with meaning like "You can't change the past" or "Living in the past makes you ignore the present and prepares for a bad future," but her favorite was "Stop should-ing all over yourself." She decided not to regret the name she blurted out. Instead, she would view the new name as a symbol of the dramatic change in her life.

She looked at the warm plate of food and stopped for a moment to appreciate the fact she still lived. She had survived the jump somehow, and her future was now in her own hands, not in the Kochevs'. She dug in: fried potatoes, toast, and some type of warm cream sauce over scrambled eggs, with a glass of milk. Though famished, she found she couldn't eat much of the heavy meal before feeling terribly full. She didn't want to make herself sick by overeating. Her foot throbbed and she wished Ivan and Elena would come back to give her something for the pain.

While she waited, she looked around the bedroom and scrutinized her surroundings. To her left was the door, a dresser, and double doors that she assumed opened to a closet. The wall at the foot of the bed was solid white, with a window in the corner. White sheer curtains partially obstructed the view, but still allowed light in. Ekaterina figured she could fit through the window if she needed to escape. A cushioned armchair positioned next to the window would make it easier to get out. The bed and two end tables were the only items along the last wall. The table next to her held a small lamp and the alarm clock she'd seen earlier. No pictures, posters, or anything else to personalize the area. The dark waxed hardwood floor completed the emotionless room.

About thirty minutes later, when she'd just about drifted off to sleep, Ivan returned. "Are you finished with that?" He pointed to the tray. Ekaterina nodded and handed it to him. His hands brushed hers as he took the tray and she instinctively jerked away. Ivan scrambled to prevent remaining contents from dumping into her lap. He let out a sigh of relief after successfully keeping everything on the tray.

She looked up into his dark eyes and said, "I'm sorry."

"Don't be. I'll be more careful."

He left the room and Ekaterina let out a defeated sigh. She couldn't help being on edge, and she couldn't quite determine if she really needed to be, after hearing all the terrible stories about Crosser homes. Ivan and his mother didn't fit the description she figured she'd find after fleeing her country. Ekaterina decided to ask a few questions to try to determine what kind of home she'd landed in.

Ivan returned and stood near her feet. "Do you need to, um, you know, use the bathroom?" His eyes darted around the room rather than meeting hers as he asked the question.

She shook her head, then said, "Look, Ivan, I'm sorry for panicking. It's only that I woke up so disoriented and . . ."

"Hey, it's okay. You don't need to apologize." Ivan cracked a smile on one side of his mouth.

She looked down at her hands. "Your other Crossers probably don't give you this much trouble."

"I don't know. I've never done this before."

She met his eyes. "Isn't this a Crosser home?" she stuttered.

He shuffled back and forth on his feet. "Yes, but I'm not . . . I've never taken care of . . . well, someone like you."

"I don't understand." Her mouth went dry. Was this a new Crosser home? Would they be able to care for her?

"Everyone in the family has a different task. My job is to pick up Crossers after a drop. I found you and brought you here. The other beds in the house were already full, and it was either take you somewhere else or put you in my own bed."

"You've never taken care of a girl before?"

"*Anyone.* I've never taken care of anyone. That's Luka's job. My brother. I'm the pick-up guy."

"But you said the beds were full. Why did you—"

"I didn't know my mom sent Luka out to help. The beds were full by the time I brought you back."

Ekaterina took note of the rising frustration in his voice and paused her questions. She needed time to calm herself as well. His answers, or lack thereof, were causing her adrenaline to spike. Taking a deep breath, she looked out the window at the bright sunlight. "There was a bad storm last night."

"Yeah," he exhaled, "it was a total blizzard. They told me a plane was flying in, and I wondered who would fly through such a mess. They must have had some valuable 'cargo' on board." He wiggled his fingers for air quotes.

Ekaterina cleared her throat and returned her focus to him. "So, I made it to the road for you to find me, right?"

"No. I found you stuck in the ice, about fifteen feet into the lake."

Her lungs deflated. "I never made it out of the lake?"

"Well, not on your own. But that's my job, remember?"

The reality became crystal clear to her—if not for Ivan, she'd be dead. "Thank you for saving me, and warming me," she said.

Ivan sat down on the bed beside her feet. "You know, Katia, you're not what I expected a Crosser to be like. I mean, you're polite, well, you know, now that you've calmed down."

She furrowed her brow. "Is that bad?"

"No. Luka has told me how rude Crossers can be. Unappreciative, even."

"Maybe they're not rude so much as scared. In my country, propaganda about the perils of crossing the border keeps many people from fleeing. Crosser homes are one of the things they portray as dangerous."

He smirked a little and dipped his chin. "And you're articulate and educated. You're *not* what I expected."

She changed the subject and looked beyond him. "Where are my clothes?"

"Why?"

"Well, don't I need to pay for my stay here?"

"Oh, right. My mom put your clothes in the dryer."

"Excuse me?" Her breath caught in her throat as the thought of her prized possessions being heated and tossed about. The baggies would surely melt. The photographs, too.

"Well, everything was soaking wet, you know."

"But my coat—"

"Your coat is hanging in the closet. It was too big to fit in the dryer."

Ekaterina let out a sigh and pressed her head back into her pillow.

He continued. "It was really hard to undress you, too. Wet clothes don't like to come off very easily."

She opened her eyes wide. "*You* undressed me? Not your mother?"

Ivan pursed his lips and stood abruptly from the bed. His cheeks flushed a bit as he spoke. "No offense, but you're just another Crosser to us. You needed help, and we gave it. Does it really matter who undressed you? You're alive, aren't you?"

She knew her mouth had fallen open from his sudden change in attitude, but she didn't close it.

Ivan's chest expanded as he took a slow deep breath. "Look, you can rest assured I'm not a bad guy. I'm here to protect you, not hurt you, like . . . like other people have."

She slammed her mouth shut. He must have seen the marks on her back and the bruises everywhere else. The thought of him examining her body without her knowledge caused her cheeks to heat. She reminded herself what he said—that's how they treated all of them, like Crossers, not people. She pushed the conversation in a different direction. "Would you bring me my coat?"

He moved to the closet doors and opened one side, then removed her coat from a hangar. "It's still quite wet." He brought the coat to her.

She pulled on the stitching holding the liner to the outer shell of her coat and ripped it open, exposing the webbing of inflated baggies.

Ivan moved closer. "Oh, I wondered why you looked so big yet weighed so little. And, those probably helped save your life in the water," he said, pointing to the baggies. "While you were eating, my father said they pulled twelve bodies from the lake this morning. Guess they weren't as lucky."

Her mind went immediately to the plane ride. She could picture the anxious faces of the other passengers, people just like her who only wanted freedom from tyranny. Her eyes watered with the understanding that she would have died, too, if not for Ivan. "They only wanted freedom," she said. "I guess they got it."

She wiped her eyes and refocused on the task at hand. "How

much do I owe you to stay here? I know I'm supposed to pay right away, but obviously I couldn't when I got here," she said as she punctured a bag containing money.

"I, uh, don't know. How much you got?" he teased.

"That's not funny. Go ask your mother," she said sternly. Once the words were out of her mouth, his smile dropped, his posture went rigid, and his eyes narrowed. Then he left the room.

Ekaterina knew her tone was strong, but she didn't like him joking about her father's life insurance money. She was only able to pay for the Crosser home because of her father's death. She looked at the stack of large bills. Together with the three other bundles still hidden in her coat, she would use the money to start her new life. She was unsure if applying for asylum cost money. Hopefully the stay at Ivan's house wouldn't eat up too much.

She closed her eyes and relaxed. Her mind was still a little disoriented and her foot throbbed mercilessly, but she was across the border, away from Boris and Vladimir. The question was whether she was far enough away from their reach.

Ivan

Ivan left the room in a huff and stalked into the kitchen, muttering to himself, "Go ask your mother?" Part of him didn't like how she understood he didn't know what he was doing. Another part didn't like the fact that *he* didn't know what he was doing. If he'd been included in more of the Crosser-housing business up to this point, maybe he wouldn't have looked like an inexperienced kid.

He found his mother in the kitchen and asked, "What's our fee?"

She set cups down on a tray. "Why are you angry?"

"I'm not."

"What's going on?" She put her hands on her hips and glared at him.

"Nothing. What's our fee?"

"How is it you don't know the answer to that?"

"Uh, because no one's ever told me." You've *never told me.*

"Fifty."

"That's it?"

"Ivan, they've already had to pay so much to get here. We

don't need to fleece them for any more than what it takes to provide care."

"It just seems like a pitiful amount of money, all things considering."

"This operation has never been about the money. How are you handling your Crosser?"

His answer came with a grunt. "Fine."

Elena folded her arms across her chest. "Maybe Luka should take over now."

"What? No. I'm handling her just fine."

"According to what? You're acting too emotionally. This is why I haven't given you responsibilities in caring for Crossers."

"Well, I'm going to prove you wrong."

"I hope so. Because if I don't see an improvement in your mood, I'll have your father transfer her out of our house. Now, go tell her the fee and let her know the doctor will be coming by in a little while to examine her foot. We'll have a better idea once he comes as to how long she'll need medical care and when we can set up transport."

Ivan turned on his heel and walked back to his room, feeling even angrier. When he pushed open the door, his eyes connected with Katia's. She raised her eyebrows. He closed the door and said, "We charge fifty. Can you afford it?"

She frowned. "Does that also include asylum papers? I thought I'd be staying while papers were submitted and a new identity was set up for me. And what about transport away from here?"

"Are you joking?" he scoffed. Then he realized he didn't actually know the answer. He'd have to ask his mother, again.

Her eyes narrowed. "I just want to make sure you aren't going to randomly jack up the price with some hidden fees."

"We're not going to do that. Who do you think we are?"

"I've heard stories.

"About us?"

"No, yes, Crosser homes in general."

"Have you seen anything here to make you think those stories are true?"

"No, but the stories are scary. You don't know what I've been through. I just want to be safe. And these other Crossers. What if they can't pay? Would you leave them where you found them?"

He crossed his arms and bit the inside of his cheek. After a quick breath, he said, "We can't save everyone, Katia. There are more Crossers dumped on us than beds in this town—like last night. We're struggling to keep up with the constant stream of refugees. We care for them and feed them. How else can we pay for all that? Some Crossers skip out or steal. We have to be cautious, too."

Her eyes lit with fire. "Well, don't worry, I can pay." She dug her fingers into an envelope and pulled out the money, then thrust her hand forward.

Ivan snatched the cash from her and turned to leave, saying over his shoulder, "A doctor will be here later today to look at your foot." He slammed the door behind him before she could ask if she had to pay for that, too. He immediately regretted it. His mother had been right, saying he was too emotional, but Katia's words got under his skin. How could she think they wouldn't help people if they could?

Ivan entered the kitchen and gave his mother the money.

"Good," Elena replied. "Take the warm blankets to her and bring back the others to be re-warmed. I'll be in shortly to check her temperature."

Before Ivan could leave the kitchen, he heard his brother's voice shouting from downstairs.

"Ma, there's room down here for the extra Crosser. We can double up in one bed. Ivan doesn't know what he's doing and he's too hotheaded to deal with one."

Elena responded, "We'll consider it, Luka."

"No!" Ivan snarled. "I said I'd care for her and I will." He turned, with the pile of blankets in his arms, and headed back to his room. His frustration soared through the roof. Had he been taught more along the way about how to care for Crossers and the business end of things, he wouldn't be in this situation, feeling inadequate and defensive. His mother didn't seem to have any faith in him. His brother definitely didn't. And his Crosser saw him as a child. A deep sense of pride filled his chest. He'd show them all. He'd carve out his niche in the whole operation, even if he didn't know whether he wanted to continue. The short walk to his bedroom gave him little time to try to readjust his emotions before facing Katia again.

Elena Lazarov

After chopping up the last of their supply of carrots and pulling out some frozen chicken breasts to thaw, Elena entered Ivan's room and instantly picked up on the heavy tension. Ivan stood to the side, leaning against the closet door, his arms folded across his chest, his head hanging. She walked over to Katia and placed her hand on her forehead.

"You're still cold. Lift your tongue, dear." Elena rapidly waved a thermometer back and forth to bring the mercury level down. Katia followed her instructions and clamped down on the glass stick. Elena turned to Ivan. "What's the matter?"

He straightened up and dropped his hands to his sides. "What makes you think something's the matter?"

Elena looked back to Katia and found her staring at Ivan with question in her eye. Elena ordered Ivan over her shoulder. "Take the cold blankets to the dryer and then tend to the dishes."

Ivan left the room with the blankets.

With the thermometer between her teeth, Katia said to Elena, "I'm shorry, I shink I made him upshet."

"Keep your mouth closed, dear. He's never been personally responsible for a Crosser before. He's in training. But, don't worry. I've kept a close eye on your recovery and if any complications arose, I would have taken over your care. Now, if you're comfortable with him being your caregiver, I'd like to have him continue to train with you." Elena sat on the edge of the bed and removed the thermometer, giving Katia a chance to speak.

"That's fine. I wasn't very grateful, maybe that's what upset him," Katia said.

Elena squinted at the mercury. "Ninety-six. Better, but you've got a long way to go still. As for you worrying about upsetting Ivan, don't. He needs to learn stay focused on you and not on his emotions." She readjusted the blankets then stood and walked toward the door. She paused. "I'll have him bring in some warm soup for you and some ointment for your back."

"Ointment?"

"Your back, dear. It looked terribly painful last night when he turned you on your side."

Katia's face reddened. "Some ointment would be wonderful. Thank you."

Elena went to the kitchen, where she found Ivan emptying

the dish drainer. "Ivan, sit down. I need to talk to you." She motioned to the table and pulled out a chair for herself.

"I know what you're going to say." He took his own seat and sat, hard.

"And what's that?" She stared directly at him.

"You're going to say she'd be in better hands with Luka."

"Would she?"

Ivan brought his gaze level with hers. "I said I'd care for her, and I will."

"Be careful now. Don't commit to this if all you're trying to do is one-up Luka—or prove something to me, for that matter."

"I'm not."

"All right, then you need to clear your head and get down to business. You said you want to learn how to care for Crossers. Step one is there's absolutely no room for egotism, pride, or self-pity when it comes to Crosser care."

"I thought step one was not letting your Crosser die," he lightly joked.

Elena's voice lowered. She needed to impress upon him the seriousness of what he'd volunteered to do. "This isn't funny, Ivan. You need to deal with your own personal issues in private and not involve your Crosser. Do you understand?" Ivan's shocked expression at her bluntness was answer enough. "Step two is gathering information. We don't know anything about this girl. We don't know how much trouble she's in. Those injuries looked severe. Is anyone after her? Is our house a target? This is information you need to find out to make sure we aren't in danger."

Ivan leaned forward and placed his elbows on the table, clasping his hands. "What's step three?"

"Keeping your relationship on a professional level." Elena stood and walked over to the medicine cupboard and pulled out some ointment. "Crossers come and go. Some make impressions on us, while others are quickly forgotten. It may sound harsh, but we can't care about each of them. They all have horrific stories and we could easily lose ourselves in their crises. Our job is to get them safely on their way." Elena pointed to the wall in the direction of Ivan's bedroom. "She will leave at some point. We'll probably never see her or hear from her again. You have to understand that, Ivan."

"I do."

"Good. I told her you'd bring in some ointment for her back.

You'll need to apply it for her. Also, give me a moment to warm up some broth. She's still cold and needs to keep her belly filled with warm liquids. Would you also get two pain pills from the cupboard and put them on the tray?" Elena patted her son's arm. "Just follow the three steps and you'll do fine."

CHAPTER 4

Ekaterina

Ekaterina lay in the bed, remembering the events of yesterday in the palace and how Dr. Ilievski helped her escape. She couldn't help but worry about him and his safety because if Boris discovered Dr. Ilievski had helped her, the punishment would be swift and ruthless.

Did Boris even know she'd left yet? A sudden panic enshrouded her. Boris was probably aware she was gone, out of his reach, and most likely ordering his guards around like a madman. She imagined his veins jutting out on his neck like she'd seen so many times before when he seethed with anger. His personnel were most likely searching the palace, the surveillance recordings probably being examined, and a plan to search, find, and extract her was no doubt being constructed.

She rubbed her forehead and looked around the room, identifying escape routes, needing to know she could flee if necessary. The window and the bedroom door were all she had. Beyond the door, she'd have to exit the house. But where would she go? How could she escape with her injured foot? Perhaps she should try to stand again to see if she could push past the pain. She pulled the blankets off her body and swung her legs to the side of the bed as she sat up. The motion sent twinges of sharp pain up her leg, making her wince and freeze.

The door opened unexpectedly. Ivan entered the bedroom carrying a tray containing assorted items. "What are you doing? Do you need something?" he asked.

Taking a deep breath, she replied, "No, I just wanted to try to—"

"Stand? I told you the doctor will be by later." Ivan set the tray on top of the dresser.

Ekaterina stared at him a moment, then pulled her legs back onto the bed, wincing at the pain.

He brought over a glass of water. "Here." He extended his other hand which held a couple of pills. "Some pain relief."

She took the glass of water and cradled it close to her chest and pointed at the pills. "What are those?" She knew her voice held a little too much doubt, but how could she not be suspicious of everything around her?

"Just a mild pain reliever. You don't have to take them." He started to pull his hand back until she reached forward and tried to grab the little pills from his hand. He cupped his hand to prevent them from falling. "Hang on," he said as he captured her wrist with his other hand.

She gasped and held her breath, not liking the firm hold he had on her wrist. Looking up at him, feeling vulnerable, she whispered as she began to shake, "Please let go of me."

Ivan's entire stance, his presence, his tone of voice changed instantly. He knelt beside the bed, still holding her wrist, but with less of a grip. "I'm not going to hurt you, Katia. I just don't want to drop these. Here." He rotated her wrist slowly, all the while releasing his grip, then set the pills in her palm. His fingertips lingered on her palm as his eyes met hers. "You're safe here. I promise."

She let out a burning breath and raised the water and pills to her mouth, clumsily drinking down the medicine. She handed the glass to Ivan who still knelt beside her.

He accepted it and stood, but didn't walk away. After a moment of silence, he said, "I'm sorry about earlier, about getting so upset, I mean."

"Me too. I understand that it can't be easy to have strangers constantly in and out of your house and always worried you might be caught. It's . . . it's really great that there are people like you to help."

A blush tinged his cheeks. "I haven't really been that great about it."

"Well, I guess we're both learning." She smiled.

He smiled back. "I have some warm broth for you." With his other hand, he moved more pillows behind her to support her back and shoulders. "Why don't you sit back and I'll bring it over."

"But I just ate all that other food. I'm not hungry."

"The broth will warm you from the inside. You need it."

His demeanor had changed so rapidly back to pleasant, and while she welcomed the change, she struggled to figure him out. Ekaterina sat back and pulled the blankets to her chin. She eyed him closely as he traded the water for the mug of steaming liquid on the tray.

"Here you go," he said.

She took the mug with both hands.

"How's your foot feeling?"

She tried to wiggle it, but the movement brought pain. "It hurts."

He nodded. "I think you were already injured when I brought you here last night. Probably when you hit the ice. I don't think you hurt it when you bolted out of bed this morning."

"I remember kicking the ground near shore and feeling some pain." She sipped the broth carefully, the warmth of the liquid soothing her throat and chest.

Ivan moved to the chair by the window and sat down, his eyes remaining connected to hers. "Katia, what did you do in Bregot? What made you decide to become a Crosser?"

The question came from nowhere and the answer would reveal everything about her. A thousand concerns raced through her mind. Should she tell him? Should she gloss over the intensity of the situation? Could she trust him? How could she make that determination after only a few hours? She felt somewhat safe, so far. However, she thought she was safe enough in the palace after her father died—safe, until she wasn't

Looking at Ivan, watching him wrestle with his immaturity and desire to be useful and helpful, she concluded he wasn't like Boris or Vladimir or Risto. He let it be known right away how he felt. Vladimir and Risto were eerily calm when others became offended. Risto would take insult and internalize it, squeeze it, push it into a grudge mold, and then wait until an opportune time to hurl the grudge, a time when it would be unexpected and cause the most damage. Or Vladimir, who would be quick to anger, but at slights that weren't really there, believing everyone was against him. She couldn't truly know how either of them felt.

No, Ivan was genuine. Real. His emotions showed instantly. She wasn't confused by his actions, she decided, but her confusion came from seeing someone display real emotions in real time. How long had it been since she'd witnessed someone real? Not even Dr.

Ilievski was real all the time. She trusted the doctor, but saw so many different sides of him, his different acts, that she couldn't always tell who he was lying to or for who? The last honest person in her life she could remember was her father. She could always trust what he said. He didn't lie even when he probably should have.

Ivan spoke again. "I need to know why you're here—and how much danger you're in."

She paused, unsure of how much she should tell him. "I'm running from an arranged marriage that is supposed to take place in three days," she said.

"Oh. And how much danger does that put you in? You know, from running."

"Danger?" She laughed, then realized he was serious. "You have no idea."

"We've dealt with Crossers with bounties on their heads before. One Crosser even had a relative that worked in the palace."

Ekaterina couldn't believe her ears. Ivan and his family had no clue how much danger they could be in by simply housing her. They would not be prepared if Boris came looking for her. Fear crept through the pit of her stomach and what might happen to them, to Ivan, if Boris found them. They needed to know. But if they did, would they kick her out? Would she be too much of a liability?

Her anxiety fought against her desire to be safe. Finally, she let out a deep breath, knowing that if Ivan and his family stood a chance, they needed to know the truth.

"I am being forced to marry Vladimir Kochev."

"Who's that?"

"What? You don't know who Vladimir Kochev is?" *How could that be possible?*

"No." He scratched his head. "Is he related to Boris Kochev?"

She half-coughed out her answer. "Yes, Vladimir is his son."

Ivan's eyes opened wide, and she could see white all around his dark irises. "You're supposed to marry the dictator's son?"

"Yes." Katia was relieved to hear Ivan realized the intensity of the situation.

"I don't blame you for running." He nodded at her bruised body. "How did you get all those marks?"

"I wasn't as submissive as Boris thought I should be, so he decided to teach me lessons."

Ivan leaned forward in his chair. "Boris Kochev beat you?"

She squirmed, remembering the unpleasant moments. "He believed being submissive was a requirement if you lived in the palace."

"Did it work?"

She smiled at him. "I'm here, aren't I?" She drank more of her broth to busy her hands and hide her face.

Ivan stood and paced the floor with his hands on his hips. He seemed to be working things out in his head.

She tried to place the mug on the table next to the bed but struggled with reaching because of the pain of her whip marks on her back.

Ivan came over. "I'll take that for you. Oh, and I'm supposed to apply some cream to your marks."

Katia followed his body with her eyes as he placed the mug down and picked up the tube of ointment. She sat forward to make it easier for him to reach her back.

He got onto the bed and situated himself next to her. He eased her shirt up to expose her marred skin. Katia felt uneasy, but again, worked her mind around the fact Ivan wasn't like the other monsters in her life. Her spine still tightened at his impending touch.

"My God, Katia. This looks horrible. Does it hurt?" He gently spread the cool ointment on her skin.

"Not so much now." She tried to ignore the memories, but they came flooding back. "The first time I was whipped, it felt like slashes of fire. The second time was actually worse because the first wounds weren't even healed yet. The third time, like hot slaps. Maybe I'd gotten used to it. Don't get me wrong. It always brought tears to my eyes, but the pain didn't last as long." Without realizing it, her own tears slid down her cheeks, half from the painful memories, the other half at the relief of Ivan's tender touch.

Ivan

Ivan was glad his face wasn't visible at that moment. His eyes watered with compassion for Katia and he felt all new anger for the malevolent dictator he'd heard so much about. Every Crosser passing through their house was fleeing the oppressive life Boris Kochev had blanketed on the people. Ivan had somehow never identified with the pain and misery these people had suffered through—until now, until Katia. She arrived with a roadmap of abuse striped all over her body, abuse delivered at the hands of Kochev personally. Her reaction when he grabbed her wrist tore him apart. She was frightened of him probably the same way she'd feared her abuser, and that hurt more than anything. He hadn't ever injured anyone with malice, especially not a female. His parents had taught him better than that.

He applied more salve to her marks, knowing she'd have lasting scars for the rest of her life. He gently pulled her shirt back down into place, and she leaned back against the pillows.

He stood and set the ointment on top of his dresser, then wiped his hands on a towel and turned to her. "Can I ask you a dumb question?"

"Sure." She pulled the blankets up to her chin.

"Why didn't you run away sooner?"

"I tried twice, but each attempt was unsuccessful. I didn't have a place to hide. No one would take me in for fear of Boris Kochev's wrath coming down on them. Plus, both times I got caught, the beatings were more brutal. Then I gave up. If it weren't for the help I received on the inside, I wouldn't be here today."

"Yeah, you'd be over there, about to marry Vladimir."

"No, I would have made sure I never married him."

"What do you mean?"

"You know what I mean."

"End your life?" He gaped.

She looked down at her hands and twisted and pulled the loose threads of the blanket. "If you think about it, getting on that plane and knowing I might die in the jump was itself a form of suicide, but dying was better than staying in Bregot." Her eyes met his and she sat up a little straighter as if her spirits were buoyed with bravery. "I will *not* have children brought up by Vladimir Kochev or his father. I lived in that terrible, toxic household for four months and wouldn't wish that experience on anyone. You've seen my back, what I went through. It broke me."

"I'm sorry." He paused to let her calm down. He wondered if he would have kept fighting. He thought he would, but really couldn't imagine going through that many beatings and being forced to marry someone he despised. "Where are your parents?" he asked, changing the subject.

"Dead."

He mentally scolded himself. "I'm sorry. Any siblings?"

"No." She shivered with her answer.

Ivan picked up the space heater and set it on the table next to her and plugged it in. "I'm going to go get you more warm blankets. I'll be right back." He grabbed the tray from the dresser top and left the room.

As he pushed the swinging door open into the kitchen, he heard his father's voice.

"I've never seen anything like it before. And so soon after a drop." Michal sat at the kitchen table with Ivan's mother, Elena, and grandmother, Mira.

"How many did you see?" Elena asked.

"At least six cars. They stick out like sore thumbs, too. You'd think after all this time they'd try to disguise themselves a little better. Our methods have evolved over the years, but theirs haven't."

"That's to our advantage," Elena said. "We always know what to expect."

"I agree," Mira added, "and because they do things the same as always, you were able to spot them earlier than usual."

"The question remains, who are they looking for? And why?" Michal asked.

Mira said, "Luka has learned that three of his six are from the Insurgent underground. Two more are businessmen, and the other one is a commercial pilot. Luka figures the heat on their heads is minimal."

Michal added, "Minimal or not, we can't let our guard down."

Ivan sat down at the table, nervous about his new-found knowledge. He felt a little odd, like he was betraying Katia, but he knew his family needed to know the truth. "I found out about Katia. She's supposed to marry Boris Kochev's son in three days. Well, she's being forced to marry him. Of course, she doesn't want to. Boris is responsible for all her injuries."

Elena stood abruptly and began pacing the kitchen. The tension in her voice rose appreciably. "Oh dear! She's the one. They're after *her*. This is not good, not good at all. We have to move her. She's too hot. We're risking too much. I shouldn't have let Ivan take her in."

"Mom—" Ivan protested, but his father cut him off.

Michal rose from his chair and pulled Elena into a comforting embrace. "We can't move her now. Roadblocks are in place. She'll have to stay here until everything calms down."

Elena looked directly at Ivan. "Not with you."

"What?"

"Your room is too close to the front door. You have no escape route." She paused, then said, "Plus, you have no experience. She should be moved down with the other Crossers."

Michal shook his head. "No, she's who they are after. There's no sense in placing all the Crossers in danger by putting her with them. Besides, if I was a Crosser on the run and found out one of the others was Vladimir Kochev's future bride, I'd turn her in."

"No, you wouldn't," Michal's mother shamed him.

"The person I am wouldn't. But Crossers think in a different way. They're fleeing for their lives and if one among them brings too much danger or risk, they turn on each other. If we put Katia down there, well, I am not going to take that chance. We'll store Katia's belongings in the crawlspace under Ivan's room. They can hide there, too, if they need to."

"What if we're raided?" Elena's voice shook as she spoke. "They'll be looking for trap doors, and the one in Ivan's closet is too obvious."

"Looks like I have a good excuse to finally finish working on it, then," said Michal. "I'll make sure its undetectable and blends in with the existing woodwork. We'll keep blankets and warm clothing in a box down there, just in case."

"And some non-perishable food," Elena added.

Grandma Mira addressed Ivan. "Nothing should be left in your room to indicate she's here, Ivan. If they suspect anything, they'll tear this house apart looking for her, and no amount of master-carpentry will keep you hidden."

"No problem. My room already looks empty as it is since I need to keep it that way so we can 'claim' it as our Bed-and-Breakfast room." Ivan stood and moved toward the clothes dryer for more blankets. He listened as his father summed up the situation.

Michal said, "We all need to act as if nothing is out of the ordinary, yet with a thought for everyone's safety. No heroics, or else we risk failure." He directed his words to Ivan. "You'll help me gather the materials to work on your closet floor after the doctor stops by."

* * *

Ivan stood in front of the closet doors and watched Dr. Stefan Khristov evaluate Katia. His father observed from the chair by the window. Katia lay perfectly still, staring at the ceiling while the doctor inspected her foot.

Ivan couldn't believe how she didn't complain during the inspection. He knew it must hurt. But she apparently braced herself against the pain. Her strength astonished him, especially since she looked so small and frail. Ivan found the quality endearing. A sense of protectiveness arose within him and he became determined to ensure she never have to go through that type of pain again.

"I can't be sure without an x-ray," Dr. Khristov said to Katia. "But if it's broken, it's probably no more than a hairline fracture. I think once wrapped in a splint, and if you keep your weight off it for a couple of weeks, it will heal on its own." Dr. Khristov began applying a splint and bandages. When he finished, he reached in his bag and pulled out a bottle of pills and handed them to Elena. "These are stronger than what she's already taken and will help with the pain."

"I can pay for the pills," Katia said, reaching for her coat.

Elena shushed her. "Don't worry about it. It's taken care of."

Michal stood and said, "Elena, would you stay with her for a few minutes? I need Ivan to come with me."

"Of course."

Ivan followed Dr. Khristov and his father to the kitchen where the doctor's vehicle was parked out the back door.

"What do I owe you, Stefan?" Michal asked.

"Just the usual house-call fee. Michal, what happened to her? She has some pretty severe contusions on her calves that I can tell aren't related to the foot injury."

Michal opened his wallet and pulled out the money needed. Ivan knew they'd recently received another donation from a previous Crosser they'd helped a while back. "Thank you" donations were always welcomed, but never expected. Michal said, "We don't know for sure, but whatever it was, she's away from it now."

"Did you hear about the posted Crosser reward?"

Ivan sputtered, "Reward?"

"Yes. Someone very important was on that plane last night and Kochev wants them back. A female."

Michal let out a breath. "Is there a description?"

"No. Only a gender." Dr. Khristov stepped closer to Michal. "I think you're going to have to pay me a little more for my silence."

Ivan's breath caught in his throat. Was Dr. Khristov trying to blackmail his father? He thought the doctor and his father were better friends than that.

Dr. Khristov reached his hand forward and placed it on Michal's shoulder. With a gentle squeeze, he said, "When I say pay me, I mean with a plate of Elena's cookies. They're worth a lot more to me than any reward Kochev is offering."

Michal's head fell forward. "Don't scare me like that, Stefan."

Dr. Khristov lightly slapped Michal's cheek and stepped back. "I'm sure all those dark-windowed cars haven't escaped your attention, Michal."

"I saw them." Michal nodded to Ivan and said, "Get the doctor his cookies, would you?"

Ivan continued to listen as he loaded up a plate for his dad's friend.

"Any raids yet?" Dr. Khristov asked.

"No."

"I don't understand why you put your family in danger. It certainly isn't for the money because I know what you charge Crossers. You could ask for a lot more and they would pay it. So why do you do it?"

"Kochev's soldiers killed my father, Stefan, but only because they missed their target: my mother."

"Are you kidding? I've never heard that before. When did that happen?" Dr. Khristov exclaimed.

Ivan secured the cookies with plastic wrap and brought the plate to the doctor. He knew his father was about to launch into the over-told family history story of his grandfather's death being the catalyst for housing Crossers. Ivan wouldn't ever openly admit it, but this was his least favorite bedtime story.

Michal's tone dropped a notch as he said, "I was quite young when my mother was dismissed from her position at the palace during the takeover of the Kochev family. She had been an irritation for Aleksandar Kochev, and almost prevented the ousting of the royal family. Kochev ordered her death, only they missed because my father took the bullet. He died protecting her." Michal's voice cracked and he took a moment before he spoke again. "Well, it stuck with me so much that I've defied Kochev ever since. I'll keep doing what I'm doing, helping as many people who wish to flee, until I'm stopped."

"I'm sorry for your loss. Someday, I want to hear more about your parents. But for now, I'll take these cookies with a better understanding of what drives you, Michal." Dr. Khristov smiled and clasped Michal's hand in a firm shake while holding the cookie plate in his other. He nodded at Ivan and left the house.

The room fell silent for a moment. Michal cleared his throat. "Come on, Ivan. Let's get the supplies for the floor."

Ivan followed his father out to the garage where the woodworking supplies were stored. He felt as if a cloudy veil had been lifted from his mind. His father's emotional retelling of Grandpa Lazarov's death hit a chord that Ivan hadn't ever felt in all the times he'd heard the story. Either Ivan hadn't paid attention, or he hadn't ever heard it told quite that way. Whatever it was, Grandpa Lazarov sacrificed his life for his wife. He died protecting her.

Why hadn't Ivan cared about Bregot before now? Clearly, his parents and Luka were devoted to helping Crossers. Why had it taken Ivan so long to understand and accept that true evil existed a mere thirty miles to the south?

Images of Katia's battered, bruised body came into his mind as his father loaded wood slats onto his outstretched arms. She knew how bad the conditions were across the border and did what she had to do to escape. She had no one. No parents. No living family. Ivan wondered how that would feel.

"Are you listening to me?" Michal's voice cut through his thoughts.

"Sorry, what?" Ivan looked up at his father.

"I said, thank you for not saying anything to Dr. Khristov about Katia being engaged to Vladimir. You and I know why a reward would be offered. He doesn't. Take those planks inside and keep your head on straight. Time is not on our side."

Ivan carefully carried the planks into his bedroom avoiding the doorframe. Katia wasn't in the bed which alarmed him. "Mom?" he hollered.

Elena entered his room moments later. "Wait, Ivan," she said. "Let me spread a covering on the floor first before you put those down." She pulled one blanket off the bed and flipped it open across the bare wood floor.

"Where's Katia?"

"In the bathroom."

Ivan set the boards down and dusted off his hands. He saw his grandmother helping Katia back into the room, giving her support while she limped on her splint.

"How's the foot?" he asked.

Katia responded, "This really helps keep the pain manageable. I can almost walk on it."

Grandma Mira shook her head. "Don't do that yet, dear. You may only have a hairline fracture now, but if you walk on it you could break it, then you'd be in a world of hurt."

Ivan helped his grandma get Katia back into bed. Katia watched his every move, which made him nervous.

"Thank you," Katia said. "What are the boards for?"

"We're going to work on the trap door to make it blend into the rest of the floor."

Michal entered the room as Katia asked, "What if a raid happens before you're finished?"

No one answered. Everyone only exchanged tense expressions.

Michal cleared his throat roughly. "Let's get to work."

CHAPTER 5

Boris

"Sir, General Brankov is here to see you."

Boris sat in his office chair with his head pressed into the headrest. He'd watched the surveillance footage from the night before and had become more frustrated to find two crucial cameras didn't have footage. The camera in the corridor outside the Infirmary still displayed static, and the camera by the service gate was covered with snow, blocking the view.

The general walked in and Boris didn't wait for him to be seated before asking, "When will the surveillance be fixed outside the Infirmary? How many weeks has it been?"

"It's next on the docket."

"Why is it taking so long?"

"The electricians didn't pass the background check. I'm bringing in a team from Svobodia who do not have ties to the Insurgents." General Brankov sat in the chair across from Boris.

"I want a camera inside the Infirmary as well and I want it done yesterday. Maybe we could have seen her acting suspiciously and prevented her escape."

"Might I suggest surveillance in the kitchen, too, sir? I think someone poisoned the food and made everyone ill."

"Yes. That too. You lucked out, General. Your absence last night saved you from all this."

"I wish I'd been here. I like to think I could have spotted her fleeing."

"Was your family event a success?"

"Yes. Thank you for asking." General Brankov paused, then asked, "Sir, what do you plan to do concerning the princess's disappearance?"

"Besides find her and beat some sense into her?"

"I meant publicly. I've overheard talk about her missing."

"I want you to put a halt to the whispers, Brankov! Tell everyone she's been moved to a private room for recuperation. Have Jovan support this story. I don't want anyone thinking she's left the palace. Do you understand?"

"Yes, sir."

Ivan

"All right, Ivan. This should do the trick," Michal said. "This lever here releases the locking mechanism." He demonstrated, pulling the lever, and the trap door swung downward into the crawlspace. "Once you're down, push the door up to close it, and slide the latch from the underside to secure it. Closing the door from up here is a little trickier. You have to push this handle on the wall and secure the lock with the same lever used to open it."

Ivan looked at the floor of his closet in amazement. The trap door was completely invisible to the naked eye, blending seamlessly into the hardwood floor as if it were part of the floor. The lever had been brilliantly installed on the side of the shelving unit directly above the trap door, appearing like another part of the shelving. If there was a raid, Ivan would be able to hide Katia quickly and effectively.

"Now give it a try," Michal said.

Ivan pulled the lever and quickly jumped down the hole to the dirt ground and closed the door in a matter of a few seconds. He realized with Katia's injury it would take longer. Ivan kneeled on the ground so his head didn't hit the floor joists or the single lightbulb hanging near the trapdoor, then he scanned the area under the house. Narrow vents on three of the walls allowed a small amount of light to spill in from outside, along with some cool air, into the four-foot high area. While his father had worked on the craftsmanship of the door, his mother brought boxes of supplies and handed them down to Ivan for placement in the crawlspace. He moved them to the far corner under the living room. The boxes contained clothing, bedding, and non-perishable foods. She also provided a covered bucket for waste and garbage. Should they ever have to use the crawlspace, it was well equipped to handle them for a couple of days, if need be.

Satisfied with the job, Ivan boosted himself up into his room and closed the trapdoor.

His father said, "Help me clean this up, and don't forget to chop wood and fill the wood boxes before this evening."

"Okay. At least now we can hide if we're raided."

His father scooped up an armful of tools and left the room.

Ivan surveyed the work, feeling a sense of pride. The desire he'd often had to leave and make a different life for himself, one that didn't include Crossers, diminished. He couldn't wait to tell Anton. He had finally been promoted to caregiver.

Ekaterina

After they were alone, Ekaterina asked Ivan, "Are you raided often?"

"We've had a few. They've all been successful though."

"What do you mean?"

"None of our Crossers were discovered."

Ekaterina felt relieved to hear this. Even though she knew her situation made everything more dangerous, it was nice to know this family had a successful record in keeping their Crossers hidden.

"How did you escape the palace?" Ivan's question brought her attention back.

"After failing with my own attempts to escape, I felt I would never be able to get out, so I decided to starve myself. I became weaker and weaker, and of course Boris couldn't stand to see me, the last Cvetkovski, slipping out of his reach. So, he ordered the palace physician, Dr. Ilievski, to hook me up to an IV and nourish my body against my will. Dr. Ilievski couldn't stand to see what Boris had done to me, so he put his own life at risk to help me escape. He made the arrangements to get me out of the palace and onto the plane. I couldn't have done it otherwise."

"Sheez. Wait. What do you mean the last Cvetkovski?"

"I'm the last of my family line. The ousted queen was a Cvetkovski and was well liked by my people. In fact, Bregotians still like the idea of the Cvetkovski family leading the country. That's why Boris felt the public would like him better if his son married a Cvetkovski."

"Wait a minute. Are you saying you're a member of the former royal family? You're a princess?"

"Well, technically, yes." Ekaterina recognized the dazed look in his eyes as he took in the new information and compiled a misconception of her. She'd seen the look many times in her life. People were quick to jump to conclusions that she came from privilege and wealth whenever the word "royal" was mentioned. Ivan seemed to be no different in that respect. She wished her life could have been more royal instead of spending the first seven years of her life in the Underground, poor, scared, and malnourished. "Anyway," she hastily continued, "Dr. Ilievski told me a plane would be taking off with a load of Crossers as soon as the lake froze over. I would need to eat and regain my strength if I wanted to be on it. He would continue to portray my condition to Boris as ailing and poor in the hopes of delaying the wedding, although in the end nothing would delay it, even if I was wheelchair bound. Dr. Ilievski told me that when the plane was ready to fly, he would add some kind of drug to the evening meal and make everyone in the palace sick. Like a bad case of stomach flu. That, and with the help of a disguise and cooperating Insurgents within the palace, I'd hopefully be able to sneak out undetected. It worked. The gate wasn't even guarded when I walked out."

"So, what did he put the drug in?"

"I don't know the details. He said he'd taint as much of the whole meal as possible."

"What did he use?"

"No idea. But it worked."

"Well, it obviously didn't take Boris long to realize you were gone."

"He's completely obsessed. I think the threat of a coup is huge. Not a day went by that Boris didn't look in on me. The marriage was supposed to appease my people, strengthen his rule. Now that I'm gone, he'll have to figure out something else."

"Or more likely, he'll do everything he can to hunt you down and find you." He filled his arms with wood scraps and moved toward the door. "I need to . . . I'll be back in a minute," he said and left the room.

Ivan

She's a princess! Ivan's mind raced a mile a minute. He'd saved a princess. He'd rubbed salve on a princess' back. There was a princess in his bed and he'd slept next to her. He stopped walking and leaned against the wall while he took a deep breath to try to calm down. His parents needed to know this information. Part of him worried they'd want to move her from his care. He didn't want that. Katia was his Crosser. His responsibility. Yes, he could do this.

Ivan found his father first, of which he was glad. After his mother's reaction to finding out Katia was intended to marry Boris's son, she'd probably have a heart attack with this news.

"Dad, I need to talk to you."

"Okay."

Ivan didn't know how to say it gingerly, so he blurted it out. "Katia is a princess."

"What?"

"That's why Boris wants her so much. She is the last known princess of the previous royalty. Her marriage with his son is supposed to strengthen his rule."

Michal rubbed his chin.

Ivan continued. "She was able to escape because the palace doctor put something in the food that made everyone sick. No one noticed her leaving."

Michal's eyebrows shot upward. "This may cause issues with getting her new identification papers and transporting her . . . if someone recognizes her . . . we may need a new plan to get her out of here. I'll let the others know. We'll figure something out."

Ivan nodded and swallowed hard. After his father left the kitchen, he poured a cup of hot cocoa for Katia and grabbed a couple of fresh-baked cookies on his way to his room. At the bedroom door, he paused and took a cleansing breath, then went in and set the cocoa on the side table. He turned to Katia and handed her a cookie.

"So, what's the verdict?" she asked, her voice unsteady. "Are you sending me on my way?"

"No, sorry. You're stuck with me." He chuckled. "If the doorbell rings, we'll scurry down the hole." He motioned to the closet.

She took a small bite of her cookie. "We should practice."

"Going down the hole?" he asked.

She nodded.

"I don't . . . well it couldn't hurt, or maybe it will hurt, you at least."

She straightened her back and shot him a serious look. "I think we should. It may be awkward with my foot and I don't want to lose time if someone shows up."

"But you're not supposed to walk on it."

"Ivan, if they come for me, my injury is the least of my worries. Besides, the extra pain medicine the doctor gave me is working now."

He set his cookie down and said, "All right, um, if we hear the doorbell, we should move quickly. So, here we go." He poked his finger at the empty air in front of him and said, "Ding dong."

She quickly dropped her cookie and swung her legs over the edge of the bed. She hopped and limped to the closet, and he grabbed her arm to try to help.

"I'm okay. Just open the door, Ivan."

"Oh, right." He fumbled with the lever. The door dropped open, then he turned to her. "Do you want me to help you down? Or should I go down first? I mean, we're not both going to fit in the opening at the same time."

Letting out a huff, she said, "Honestly, it's a good thing we're practicing, because if this were a real raid, I'd be captured already." She turned and hopped away.

"Where are you going?"

"Let's start over."

Ivan closed the trap door and walked back over to the bed. "Maybe we should plan this out better. How about if the doorbell rings, I run to the lever and drop myself down the hole and wait for you. You can sit down and put your feet in first, and I'll ease you down to prevent you from hurting your foot."

"Yes, that sounds good. Ding dong!" She sounded, and they both jumped into action. Ivan flipped the lever and dropped down the hole, then turned around to help catch Katia. She made it to the opening just as he was ready to help her down, but she sat down and dropped her feet and her body down in one fluid action, catching Ivan off guard. He scrambled, grasping any part of her to try to slow her descent. His hands slid under her shirt and up her sides to her armpits. Her tee-shirt bunched up across her chest. He let go of her, admittedly embarrassed, yet relieved he'd caught her before she crashed to the ground.

She remained calm. "Close the door, Ivan."

He pushed the door up and secured the latch, feeling embarrassed about the accidental skin contact. He turned to see her sit on the ground and pull her shirt hem back down where it should be. When she began massaging her foot through the splint, he instantly moved in front of her. "Did I hurt you? I'm sorry. I didn't mean for my hands to—"

"I'm fine. Let's do it again. That was too slow."

"You came down way too fast. I wasn't ready." They both got up. Ivan opened the trap door, relieved she didn't seem bothered by his clumsiness. He climbed out and turned around to help her. She stood on her good leg, but the bedroom floor was at the level of her shoulders, and she didn't have the leverage to boost herself up and out.

"I can't get up." She looked sheepishly at Ivan. "You'll have to help me."

He reached under her arms and pulled her up out of the hole. As he did so, his feet slipped, and he fell on his back, with Katia landing on top of him with a thud. At least he kept her from hurting her foot, and his body made for a softer landing than the hardwood floor.

She lifted her head off his chest and looked him in the eyes. The moment hung in the air, and he felt heat race through his body.

"Um, maybe you should boost me out of the hole first, next time," she said quietly, still lying on top of him.

"Yep, I was thinking the same thing. Wanna do it again?" He cocked a smile.

"Yes."

She moved off him and pushed herself up halfway. Ivan stood and helped her upright and gave her balance as she hopped toward her side of the bed. He noticed she was breathing rapidly, like him.

"You forgot to close the trap door," she said, pointing toward the closet. He attended to the door and came back to sit on his side of the bed, but before he'd completely sat, she made the doorbell sound.

"Ding dong!"

They both smoothly hustled over to the closet, and Ivan slipped down the hole. Katia sat on the edge and put in her feet and paused for a half second, giving him enough time to place his hands on her thighs. As she inched forward, he slid his hands up to her waist, then he lowered her to the ground using himself as a supporting slide. At least his hands didn't lift her shirt, but this was much more exciting, having her slide down the entire length of his body to the dirt floor. He closed the trap door and sat down beside her, trying to hide his rapid breathing, not wanting his feelings to be known. "Better?"

"Yes, much better," she answered, looking over at him.

Ivan watched her face in the dim light of the crawlspace. He watched a smile start with her eyes and progress down to her mouth. He had the incredible urge to kiss her, but his mother's words of "not professional" echoed in his mind.

He stood up to put some distance between them and popped open the trap door again. This time he held her waist and boosted her up till her top half was lying on the bedroom floor. As he moved his hands down to just above her knees, he worried about hurting her wounds and bruises that he knew covered her legs. With care, he boosted her out of the hole, then he jumped out to find her sitting on the floor by the closet.

"That was definitely better on the way down," she said, "and that's what we need to work on. Getting back out isn't s-so urgent." A shiver shot through her body.

"Are you cold?"

"Mmm hmm."

Ivan reached over to the pile of blankets and grabbed a thick one. He scooted closer to her and draped it over her shoulders, securing it around her neck. "We can try again once you've warmed up a bit."

She started to get up on her own but struggled to keep the blanket in place and not put any weight on her foot. Ivan quickly came to her aid and offered his arm as balancing support while she stood on one foot. His eyes met hers and locked in place. He felt her soften against him, trusting that he'd hold her up. Momentarily, he imagined always being there to support her and what that might feel like. He swallowed hard to get control of his thoughts, then turned and helped her over to the bed, all the while reminding himself, she was royalty.

Ekaterina

Something felt different. Somewhere, while being supported by Ivan, Ekaterina noticed a change. She didn't want to feel anything. She needed to stay detached. Her life depended on eventually leaving this house and starting a new life.

A free life.

She slowly moved away from him and once again got comfortable on the bed, snuggling back under the warm blankets. Ivan took a seat in the corner armchair, his elbow on the armrest and his hand massaging his cheek. "What kind of a man is Boris's son?"

"Vladimir? Terrible." She picked up her cookie and took another bite.

"In what way?"

"In all ways. He's selfish, cruel, and unforgiving. He'll make a horrible ruler someday."

"Is he dangerous? You know, physically abusive?"

She thought about it for a moment. "He's never hurt me, but I think he's fully capable of it. His anger is more internal—he has more pride. I've seen a glint in his eyes on a couple occasions that lead me to believe the pain he'd inflict would be more personal. Boris, on the other hand, was very . . . detached. It was just part of the job to him."

"How old are you, Katia?"

"Eighteen. What about you?"

"Nineteen, almost twenty."

"How long has your family been helping Crossers?"

"All my life," he said on an exhale.

"You don't sound thrilled about it."

"Well, you know. All I do is pick up Crossers after a drop and run daily errands."

"I'd say that's a pretty heavy responsibility. If you hadn't found me, I'd be . . ." she trailed off.

Ivan leaned forward, putting his elbows on his knees and resting his chin in his palms.

"Are you wondering whether you should have pulled me out of the ice?" she asked.

"No, not at all. I rescued a stranded Crosser because that's what I do. I didn't know who you were or what you were fleeing. I only knew you would die if I didn't do something."

She flinched at the word "die," even though she had resigned herself to the idea that death would have been far better than staying in Bregot. "That's good," she said, "because many more people will be fleeing my country, and they will need your help. Boris's reign is a terrible ordeal, but it will eventually come to an end. Then it will get even worse when Vladimir takes over. Your family and the good they offer will always be needed. In fact, I would love to be in the position to help Crossers from my country. I just don't see how it will ever be possible."

"Oh, you never know."

"How many Crosser homes are there in this town, Ivan?"

"I honestly have no idea. We don't divulge too much, even to each other, in case we get interrogated by the authorities. But from what my parents say, the numbers are dwindling from when I was a boy. It might have a lot to do with the fact that the border has tighter security, or the risk is too high. There aren't enough homes to sustain the number of Crossers."

"More will come," Ekaterina said matter-of-factly. "The crossing methods will need to be refined to accommodate more refugees. A system needs to be established that will help facilitate those who want out of the country."

Their conversation was interrupted by the sound of the doorbell out in the living room. For one terrifying second they just looked at each other. Then they both sprang from their seats and bolted for the trap door. Like a well-oiled machine, Ivan dropped down through the hole and helped ease her down under the house. He closed the trap door carefully.

Ekaterina held her breath and together they listened to the muted voices as footsteps walked above them. Ivan wrapped his arm around her and helped her sit on the ground. He knelt in front of her and held her close. She looked Ivan in the eye with a silent prayer. His expression of absolute terror burned itself into her mind.

The footsteps above walked toward Ivan's bedroom door and entered his room. Ekaterina let out an involuntary gasp, and Ivan wrapped both arms around her, pulling her against his body.

The lever was pushed, and the door dropped with a thud. Ekaterina pressed her face into Ivan's chest, and his arms wrapped around her even tighter. He swiveled around to shield her from the opening. Their bodies trembled together.

CHAPTER 6

Ivan

"Ivan?" His father's voice filled the crawlspace, and then Michal's face appeared through the hole.

"Dad? What's wrong?"

"Nothing's wrong. Anton is here to see you. He's in the kitchen."

Ivan let out a huge sigh of relief and lowered his head so that his mouth rested on the top of Katia's head. He inhaled the sweet smell of her hair and let his eyes close for a moment. She still had a death-grip around his middle, and his arms were wrapped tightly around her, too. He brought up one hand and placed it gently on the back of her head.

"It's all right," he said tenderly. "Let's go back up." He felt her loosen her grip, but she didn't look up at him. He helped her hop toward the trap door.

Michal reached down to Katia and lifted her out of the hole.

Ivan followed and closed the trap door once he was out. He brushed himself off and glanced over at Katia, who sat quietly on the bed. The intensity of her look made his stomach flip.

Michal said, "I'll stay with her." He motioned to the floor at Ivan's feet. "Bring a broom when you return."

Ivan glanced down and saw the dirt they'd tracked up from the crawlspace. He turned to Katia and found her eyes glued to him. He wanted to talk to her, make sure she was okay, but he realized his father still watched, so he gave her a nod and left the room.

Ekaterina

Ekaterina lay back on the bed after Ivan left the room. She didn't want him to leave. Her fingers still tingled from gripping him so hard. She hadn't felt that terrified since the moment she'd boarded the plane. Except then, she had no one but herself to make it through the fear. Now . . .

Michal stood by the window. "Any problems getting under the house?" he asked without looking at her.

She forced herself to calm down. The doorbell had been a false alarm. She was safe. "No. We practiced."

He turned his gaze in her direction, "Really?" His eyebrow went up and Ekaterina saw the resemblance between father and son.

"It was a good thing we did. The first try was a blunder."

"You should know I've heard the search is on for you." He turned his attention back to the window and stared outside as if he were looking for something.

The blood left her face, and her breath stalled somewhere in her lower gut. She hadn't even been in Svobodia a full twenty-four hours, and she was already being hunted. The doorbell could have easily been Boris or one of his goons.

He continued, "No raids yet. They're looking for sightings or tips first. You being royalty is not something we're used to. The highest-ranking individual we've helped was a top military official, but that was years ago. I don't know what to expect concerning you."

"Would your government be able to help me?"

"Not immediately. Normally you could apply for asylum, but that would put you on the radar for Boris. I know there are traitors who would love to profit from sharing knowledge like that."

She looked at her hands. "It scared me to be under the house," she said quietly. "There's no way out. When you opened the hatch door I thought 'this is it, they've found me.' It was almost as bad as being kept in the dungeon back at the palace, just waiting for Boris to come."

His expression softened. "I've been thinking about that. I'll work on something else for you. Until then, you'll probably have to spend a little time under there."

"Ivan is a good protector." Her simple statement reddened her cheeks. She could still feel his strong arms wrapped firmly around her, smell his masculine scent, even though his own body trembled with fear.

"Ivan told me you said the whole palace was poisoned." He looked at her with his head tilted to the side.

She nodded.

"How?"

"It was in the food, but I don't know what was used. Dr. Ilievski is an extremely smart man."

"He sounds like he's on our side. Although, I don't know how one person could pull off something like that."

"Dr. Ilievski is my friend, but even I don't fully understand all his connections."

Michal's attention fell on the half-eaten cookie on the bed. "Is that yours?"

Ekaterina picked up the cookie and looked at Michal.

His eyes went to the dresser top, where Ivan's half-eaten cookie sat. "Two half-eaten cookies in different parts of the room might lead someone to think there are two occupants in this room. I'll need to talk to Ivan about this. If this had been a raid, those would have raised a question about your presence."

Ekaterina nodded her head in understanding.

He smiled and, once again, Ekaterina saw the resemblance to Ivan. "We will make sure everything gets covered. I promise."

Ivan

"Hey, man. What's up?" Ivan said as he pushed the door to the kitchen open. His heart pounded in his chest. He could still feel an echo of Katia's death-grip around his middle as if her fear was seared into his skin.

Anton nodded. "Hey, Ivan." He had already helped himself to the jar of cookies and had a couple on a napkin in front of him at the table.

Ivan thought that to be a good idea and grabbed himself another cookie.

"Did you hear? Our home was raided early this morning," Anton said in a hushed whisper as he got up and retrieved two glasses from the cupboard. "They were looking for a young girl. We picked up a male Crosser last night, but we could only take one because of our remodeling. Did you guys get any new ones last night?" Anton set the glasses on the table then opened the fridge and nonchalantly pulled out a carton of milk as if he lived there.

Ivan sat at the table. "Seven."

"Whoa, you're not equipped to handle seven, are you?" Anton poured milk into his own glass and pushed the carton toward Ivan.

"No. We put the extra one in my room."

"Any young girls?"

Ivan had been told repeatedly to be careful about what he told others about the Crossers, if anything at all. "Secrecy is a top priority in the house and is of crucial importance for everyone's safety," his father had told him. Ivan had confided in Anton in the past, but on that day, sitting in the not-so-private kitchen, he didn't dare openly admit too much about Katia for fear of being overheard by a family member. He wanted to tell his friend all about how intense it was to be down in the crawlspace, fearing for his and his Crosser's life, scared he wouldn't be able to protect her—protect the princess. Instead, Ivan answered, "Just males this time." Then stuffed a cookie in his mouth and poured a half glass of milk.

"Oh. Well, don't be surprised if you get raided, too. They broke my Walkman while tearing through the place. It ticked me off. But what was really weird was they didn't even care about the Crosser we had. They were only looking for a girl."

"Thanks for the heads up."

"So," Anton said, taking a big bite of his cookie, "do you want to go with me to *Sophia's*? I hear there's a new waitress and she's real cute. We could go check her out?"

"Sorry man, I have duties here."

"They've got PacMan," Anton said, obviously trying to persuade Ivan.

"Normally I would, but I am actually in charge of my Crosser, first one to be exact."

"Moving up in the world, are we?"

"Something like that."

Ivan's mother entered the kitchen.

"Well, I better get going. Wouldn't want you slackin' on your new job. See you around." Anton lightly punched Ivan in the shoulder and left the kitchen through the back door.

When the door closed, Elena asked, "Haven't seen Anton in a while."

"He wanted to hang out. I told him I couldn't because I'm learning how to care for Crossers." Ivan stood and put the milk away, then cleared the table. He waited for his mother to chastise him on revealing too much information. She didn't say anything. He asked, "Do we have any extra rugs or carpet samples to put down in the crawlspace to wipe our feet? We tracked dirt into my room."

"You could take the rug around the toilet and the covering for the tank for now until we figure something else out. How's everything going with Katia?"

"Good." He paused. "But can we tell people we know to use the back door and not ring the bell? One heart attack a day is my limit."

"That was good practice for you and her to get under the house. How did Katia handle it?"

"She was pretty scared. I felt bad for her."

"Well, that's understandable. You've seen her scars and bruises. You know what kind of pain she'd be in if she went back, both mental and physical."

"I know. Is dinner about ready?" Ivan grabbed the broom from the closet.

Elena checked inside the oven. "Soon. I'll bring it to you."

Ivan returned to the bedroom and cleaned up the dirt. Then he took the small carpeted pieces from the bathroom, opened the trap door, and climbed down to arrange them near the entrance. He also took a thick blanket from one of the supply boxes and spread it out like he would for a picnic. This way, if they had to come down again, they would at least be able to sit comfortably.

His father remained in the room while Ivan readied the crawlspace. Ivan took the broom back to the kitchen and poured himself a cup of cocoa and returned to his room to relieve his father.

Michal pointed to Ivan's half-eaten cookie on the dresser. "Ivan, two cookies and two mugs of cocoa indicate two individuals. Please, for both your sakes, use more caution. You shouldn't eat in here with your Crosser anymore."

"All right." Ivan's head hung low as he berated himself. He hadn't even thought about what it might look like to raiders.

Michal took the second cup and left the room.

Ivan brought Katia the other mug.

"I'll eat my cookie to get rid of the evidence." She smiled, then asked before taking a bite, "What did your friend want?"

"He told me they were raided this morning looking for a

female Crosser. I assume he meant you."

The cookie stopped moving towards her mouth. "But your father said there weren't any raids happening yet."

"He did? Hmm. Maybe he doesn't know about the raid at Anton's house."

"Should you tell him?"

"I will." He sat in the armchair and slumped against the back, legs apart and feet far in front. "You know, being down there was pretty intense, wasn't it?"

Her eyes dropped to her mug. She answered back in a barely audible whisper, "Yes. Thank you for protecting me."

Ivan rose quickly from his seat and turned his back to her while he looked out the window. "Well, I didn't really need to protect you. Not exactly. It was just my dad, well, Anton, I mean. So, you don't need to thank me."

"You didn't know that at the time." A moment of silence passed. "Is something wrong, Ivan?"

He turned to look at her but didn't know how to voice the thoughts racing through his mind. He walked over to the dresser and rubbed the back of his neck with both hands, then turned around and faced her. "When we were down there, I realized I've never been responsible for anyone other than myself. I wanted to run. I wanted to throw my hands up and say, 'I give up', say 'I changed my mind, I don't want to care for a Crosser.' But you hugged me so tightly out of fear and . . ." He sat down on the edge of the bed next to her feet. "I worry that I won't be able to protect you well enough. And then my dad goes and points out my lack of forethought with the cookies and cocoa and the fact that I carelessly put you at risk."

Katia's voice was soft and vulnerable. "I thought maybe you were thinking I'm . . . that I'm not worth the risk your family is taking."

His eyebrows shot up. "That's not at all what I think. I feel like I'm not the right person to be protecting you. If I don't do my job right, you could be captured and beaten by that S-O-B again. I can't let that happen to you because of my inexperience."

"It's normal to be afraid. I think you're being too hard on yourself. When the trap door opened, you put yourself between me and the potential danger. If this is your first time protecting anyone, I'd say you have a natural ability."

He walked over to the closet. "I didn't fully understand the enormity of your situation until we were in that position." He didn't know what he would do if something happened to her because he couldn't handle the situation.

A gentle knock sounded on his door. Ivan opened it and let in his mother who carried a tray of food. He watched Katia as she looked at the big pile of food on the one plate, along with a fork, knife, spoon, and large glass of milk. Her eyes met his and he smiled.

After his mother left the room Katia said, "I can't eat all this."

"It's enough for both of us. You know, we have to keep the pretenses that only one person is in this room. So, the question is, do you want the fork or the spoon?"

"Spoon."

"Do you want the top half or the bottom half of the milk?"

"Neither. I'll take the milk on the right side." She dragged her fingertip down the side of the glass and smiled.

Ivan couldn't help but laugh.

Boris

The phone call for Boris left him irritated. His "eyes" in Svobodia hadn't come up with anything yet, other than a planeload of defectors had fled the night before and no one at the airport seemed to know anything about it. Several of the defectors had died in the freezing water of Lebed Lake before they could be retrieved. Ekaterina must have been on that plane. But did she survive? Would they have to drag the lake to confirm her death? She must have had connections with someone in Svobodia to know when the plane was going to leave. And it seemed just a little too coincidental that a wave of stomach flu swept through the palace the same night she left. He seethed as he thought about her lying to him.

Boris picked up the phone and dialed the Infirmary.

"Dr. Ilievski here."

"I want to know what kind of virus or contamination made us all sick," Boris barked.

Dr. Ilievski responded in his usual professional manner. "I've been running blood tests on many of the staff, along with my own. The same results keep coming up."

"And what is that?"

"Nothing. I'm not detecting any virus consistent across all blood samples, although Violeta in the kitchen is pregnant and doesn't know it yet, but other than that, there are no foreign toxins or chemicals to indicate poison. However, there are a few additives that can be added to food to cause the kind of intense stomach upset we experienced, yet it would not show up in a blood sample. I'm still looking into it."

"Fine." Boris took a deep breath and let it out slowly. "Jovan, you were sure Ekaterina was too weak to flee. How come you couldn't see how strong she was?"

"I've asked myself that at least a hundred times. How indeed? You saw her yourself, sir. Did she look like she could do cartwheels to you?"

"No. She definitely deceived us. Who has she been talking with while in your care?"

"When she was awake and coherent, she talked to many people who came into the clinic. I think I know where you're going with this. You think she had an informant. I'd like to point out that she didn't eat any of the food last night. It's possible she knew something we didn't. But my question is, how do you even begin to root out the informant?"

"I want to know the name of every palace employee, guard, maid, butler, cook, and egg collector who did not get sick. That's where we'll start the investigation."

"I'll start making a list, sir."

"Has anyone questioned her whereabouts?"

"A couple of employees asked where she is. I told them she's resting in a private room, as you instructed."

"Good."

Boris hung up the phone and decided to put a halt to all nighttime flights out of the country. Any airplane trying to fly after dark would be shot down. He'd also have teams search any plane leaving from Bregot during the day. End of story. Also, no one could know that Ekaterina had escaped the palace. If he had any hope of succeeding with this plan, it had to appear as if she still resided here of her own will.

Boris didn't worry too much about damage control as he felt he had a firm hold on the media. What he did worry about was the anticipated impending wedding set to take place in three days without a bride.

Boris's assistant entered his office. "Sir, General Brankov is here to see you."

"Send him in."

General Brankov entered and positioned his tall, lanky form before Boris with a nervousness that didn't go unnoticed. "Sir, have you come up with an explanation about Ekaterina's absence?" the general asked.

"No one knows she's disappeared."

"Well, assuming she hasn't been located in time for the wedding, I'm wondering what you plan to tell the press?"

"Vladimir will find her before the wedding."

"What if he doesn't?"

Boris's anger began to rise.

"Sir, if I may, I have an idea of how you can deal with everything. You could say the wedding is delayed because of viable threats to her safety and will continue when the threats can be nullified. Of course, it won't be necessary if she's found and returned in time, but if not, I think this excuse would be sufficient to satisfy the people."

Boris rubbed his chin in heavy contemplation. "That sounds good. Alert the press."

"Yes sir." General Brankov saluted and left the room.

Boris leaned back in his chair and inhaled deeply. Relief settled over him. What would he do without his trusted personnel? General Brankov had come up with plausible propaganda, and Boris knew people were usually weak-minded and believed whatever they were told.

Ivan

The rest of the evening played out uneventfully. Katia slept off and on, and Ivan sat in the bedroom armchair, pondering his life prior to last night, when he drove around looking for Crossers and feeling sorry for himself. He had wished for more responsibility, but now that he had it, he wasn't sure he wanted the job. He'd been so focused on proving he could do it, he didn't think about the consequences if he failed.

If he surrendered the responsibility of his Crosser to someone else, what would happen to her? Would she be moved to a different home? Would she be cared for properly? Would that person understand the severity of her situation? He didn't know. And he didn't want to give her away on the chance someone else couldn't take care of her.

Determination filled him. No, he was her guardian, and he planned on doing his job.

Elena and Mira came in to tend to Katia's wounds and help her change clothes. Ivan moved out to the living room to give them privacy. His father sat on the couch with floor plans of their home spread out on the coffee table.

"Ivan, I'm going make an exit from your crawlspace. I plan on digging under the foundation in the northeast corner and merging into the existing tunnel." Michal went on to explain the logistics of the engineering for the upcoming project, which utilized his degree in civil engineering. Ivan tried to listen and understand, but his thoughts kept wandering to Katia.

"How long do you think it will take to complete the digging?" Ivan asked.

"Two to three days, perhaps a week if we experience a cave-in. I plan on reinforcing the ceiling with boards as I go. The excavated dirt will be spread inside the crawlspace and not hauled out."

"Sounds good. Dad, did you know the Gulevskis were raided this morning?"

Michal looked up from the papers on the table. "No. Did Anton tell you that?"

"Yes. He said they were looking for a young girl."

"I didn't ask the Gulevskis if they were raided. I assumed because of their remodeling project they wouldn't be taking Crossers right now."

"He said they took in one man."

"Hmm. Well, expect the worst then. Did you tell Anton about Katia?"

"No. I said we only had males, but I did tell him I have one in my room."

"Ivan, what have I told you about that?"

Immediately Ivan regretted telling his father even that much. "I know, Dad. I didn't tell him about the trap door or about Katia. Is it really that bad what I told him? He already knows we house Crossers just like they do. Besides, he told me about their Crosser."

"They're new to this business. We aren't. I don't like it when others ask questions about our home. It makes me nervous."

"This is Anton, Dad. He's my friend, not some—"

"Sharing information is dangerous. We've learned how to avoid Boris' troops because some of our Crossers were former troops who told us about their methods. They shared valuable information that we use against Boris. Likewise, anything shared about our family could be used against us."

"Are you saying Anton is a spy?"

"No, I'm saying no one should be told how we do things here, or it could give our enemies the edge they need. What if Anton was interrogated and pressured for intel? He might reveal what you told him to protect *his* family. The same goes for us. If we don't know anything about Anton's family, we can't reveal anything if questioned."

Ivan began to realize the dangerousness of exposure, even if accidental. He made a mental note to tell Anton they shouldn't share information anymore.

Michal continued. "Active searches are already underway for her. Normally we have a couple days after a drop before that happens. The roadblocks are already up. Private investigators are prowling and it's only been one day."

"Do you think we're under surveillance?"

"Not yet. There's no evidence of that."

"Then we could move her. Why don't we take her to the cabin?" Ivan thought his idea was good. He watched for his father's reaction.

"Because it's not a safe house." He let out a heavy sigh. "It's on a dead-end road. The supplies are limited, so a long-term stay is not possible. Besides, someone might see her if we take her out of the house at this point."

"We could hide her, cover her up."

"She'd be found when they searched the car at the roadblock."

"Why does our country even allow Boris to put up roadblocks?"

His father paused. "It's complicated. I'm not sure you've noticed, but we live in a very divided town. Some people support Crossers, but others do not. Those that don't would rather see roadblocks, which capture illegal Crossers, than protest Boris's overreach. Plenty of individuals in this town secretly work for Boris. That includes some of the police. So, when a blockade is set up to capture illegal Crossers, police and townspeople alike support it."

"This is frustrating, Dad. She is being hunted. She needs to get out of here. What about the tunnel? Could we keep her in there? At least she'd have a way out if we were raided."

"Do you know how difficult it was to build that tunnel, Ivan? It took months, and I will not have it all ruined because of some accidental noise like coughing or sneezing. That's all it would take, and the tunnel would be discovered. It's not very deep under the surface. Besides, the tunnel is only accessible through Luka's room which is full of Crossers who cannot know about Katia."

Ivan slouched into the couch.

"Look, Ivan" Michal continued, "I know you're worried and you should be. We all are. This is why we plan to connect the crawlspace under your room to the tunnel, so if there's a raid, Katia can have an escape route. But we will not use it unless we're raided. I assume you know the evacuation protocol?"

"We only flee through the tunnel during an actual raid," he recited.

"Yes. When all eyes are trained on our windows and doors, we escape underground."

"What about the roadblocks?"

"Even with all the local police and public support, the Bregotian patrol usually don't linger once a raid is initiated. The roadblocks dismantle and all parties flee for the border before the federal authorities arrive. As for you, I need you to be patient and alert. We will stick to the plan, start excavating the tunnel tomorrow, all with the goal of getting Katia transferred somewhere safer while she applies for asylum."

The last part of his father's sentence really struck Ivan: "get Katia transferred somewhere safer." He wanted her to be safe. He did. But the thought of sending her off brought a heaviness to his chest.

Ivan's mother joined them and sat by Michal. "Ivan, you'll need to sleep in the bed with Katia. Even though she's warmed up, now, we can't have evidence of you sleeping somewhere other than your bed. Raiders would see that as proof we're housing someone in your room. Besides, it would be easier to straighten the bedding before going under the house versus picking up bedding off the floor or from the couch."

Michal nodded in support.

Ivan swallowed hard.

CHAPTER 7

Ivan

Ivan lay still as stone on the bed facing the back of Katia's head. The awkwardness of the situation was far worse than he'd imagined. After being down in the crawlspace, feeling her body pressed close against his, he couldn't get his mind off her. On top of that, the whole revelation she was a princess expected to marry Boris Kochev's son had his stomach in knots.

She lay beside him sleeping soundly. The past twenty-four hours had clearly taken its toll on her, and she had crashed after her bath. At least her body temperature was back to normal, and Ivan felt relieved she could finally relax enough to sleep so soundly.

Katia rolled over in her sleep and turned her head toward Ivan. Their faces were mere inches apart. The small amount of light spilling into the room illuminated her face, highlighting her bone structure. With a gentle movement, he brushed a few strands of hair off her face, being careful not to disturb her much needed sleep. His thoughts revisited the earlier conversation with his father where he was reminded Katia would be leaving soon—off to start a new life. His mother had said most Crossers never contact the family again. Would that be the case with Katia? Would she simply disappear, move on, never to be heard from again?

Ivan was torn. He wanted Katia to be able to be free and live a carefree life, but he also didn't want to lose her. She was his first Crosser.

* * *

Ivan awoke to a growling stomach. He opened his eyes and

found Katia staring back at him. Her hair was spread on her pillow in wavy piles.

"Good morning, Ivan." She smiled.

Ivan became intensely aware of his heartbeat. He rolled away from her, sat up, and stretched his back. "Did you sleep well?"

"Yes. Surprisingly. I thought I might have bad dreams or something, but I felt really comfortable."

He couldn't help feeling elated that sleeping next to him made her feel that way. "How are you doing this morning? How's the foot pain?"

"About the same, I think. I haven't taken any pain pills yet."

"Not a problem. I'll grab you a glass of water." Ivan's hand had barely grabbed the doorknob when the doorbell rang.

His heart leapt into his throat. Katia shot straight up and scooted off the bed, pulling the covers back into position. He had the trap door opened and had climbed down the hole before she made it to him. He helped her down and closed the door. His parents were right to have him sleep in the bed with Katia. They were able to scuttle quickly and hopefully not leave a trace behind of a Crosser.

"Let's sit over on the blanket," he whispered and guided her over, ignoring the pounding of his heartbeat, which hadn't had a chance to slow down since waking up. He opened the box containing supplies and pulled out another blanket to wrap around her shoulders, then took a seat next to her, their shoulders touching. Slim shafts of light peeked through the vent on their right, lighting up motes of dust drifting to the ground under the footsteps. They sat in silence, listening to the mumbling voices above, trying to see if they could make out any words.

After a few minute,. the trap door dropped and Michal's voice sounded into the crawlspace. "All clear, you two. Come on out."

"What a way to start the day," Katia whispered, as Ivan helped her over to the opening.

"Not what I would've chosen," Ivan quipped.

"Maybe we could stay down here all day. It's nice to pretend we can just hide from the world."

Ivan didn't respond. His thoughts were frozen on her use of the word "we."

Once they were back up in the room, Ivan asked, "Who was at the door, Dad?"

"Salesmen, or so they said," his father said, holding a variety of tools piled into a deep bucket. "Time to dig, Ivan."

"What's happening?" Katia asked.

Ivan remembered she'd fallen asleep before he'd updated her on the plan. Before he could say anything, his father spoke.

"We're going to dig an exit from the crawl space, so you're not trapped down there."

Her eyes widened. "Oh."

"Can I get some breakfast first?"

"Make it fast. We need to get going on this."

* * *

By mid-afternoon, Ivan and Michal had made good progress digging towards the tunnel, but Katia finally voiced a frustration. The doorbell had rung three more times, with Elena waiting to help her into the crawlspace. Finally, Katia asked if she could simply stay down and no one balked at her idea.

By the end of the day, Michal and Ivan had dug down under the foundation of the house and installed supporting beams. Katia lay under a pile of blankets, having slept off and on throughout the day, her foot propped up on a stack of supplies.

Ivan dropped his shovel and wiped his brow. "I'd do better with a pick-axe and a teaspoon, Dad. I move a little dirt and hit another rock."

"Hey, you're not telling me anything I don't already know. I dug out the other tunnel."

"You have my empathy."

"Yes, well, I was much younger and in shape then." He twisted, his back cracking. "I say we hang it up for the day."

Ekaterina

Ivan and Ekaterina lay in bed that night, each silently staring up at the ceiling. Though she wouldn't admit it out loud, she was glad to be back in the soft bed. She thought about all the trouble Ivan's family had chosen to go through to help Crossers, to help her, and with so much risk. They'd be better off if she simply left.

"Ivan, can I ask you something?"

"Sure."

"Why doesn't your father just move me out of your home?

Wouldn't it be better than staying here, putting everyone in danger?"

"If we tried to move you, they'd find us. They have roadblocks in place. If they do think you're here, they'll raid, which means removing the roadblocks. That's when we can escape through the tunnel."

"It sounds risky."

"It is, but it works. They don't raid till they're certain of success. Once they bust into someone's home, the local authorities become involved. Boris's men don't want to be arrested, so when they raid, they do so quickly, and then retreat just as quick back across the border.

"And your family *chooses* to do this?"

"Yeah. Because we're good at it and we know how everything works, and because my dad and grandma have a score to settle with the Kochevs."

"And you? Why do you do it?"

Silence blanketed them and she wondered for a moment if he'd fallen asleep. Then he began to speak.

"I didn't understand all of it . . . before."

"Before what?"

"Before you."

Her skin tightened with excitement. "And now?"

"Now I can understand why fighting for this cause is worth it."

She felt flattered that she'd made such an impact on him, but began to realize, he'd made an impact on her, too. He'd proven men could be decent and trustworthy. "Tomorrow, I plan to stay in the crawlspace all day long," she said.

"If it makes you feel safer."

"I feel safe when I'm with you. If that's where you'll be, it's where I want to be, too." She held her breath and turned her face to look at him. He did the same and then slowly brushed the hair off her face. She didn't move, afraid at the tingling feeling she got as his fingertips traced across her skin.

He turned his head back towards the ceiling. "We should get some sleep."

"You don't think they'll raid us during the night?"

"Highly unlikely. They usually raid in the daylight, often at the crack of dawn, to make sure no one escapes. Get some rest, Katia." He closed his eyes and she stared for a moment at his face, lightly illuminated by touches of moonlight.

"Goodnight, Ivan."

Ivan

The next day started out with no new developments. Ivan was joined by Luka in the crawlspace, and together they continued working on the tunnel. Katia stayed down there as well, tired once again of the random visitors. Many people were crawling the neighborhood, searching for a female Crosser, and being under the house seemed like the best solution. She was curled up in a blanket by the boxes of supplies, reading a book Elena had lent her.

Ivan couldn't help but notice the way Luka surveilled Katia from head to toe, almost as if he was thinking, "All this for *her?*"

Once Ivan and Luka were down the tunnel and out of Katia's earshot, Luka bumped his shoulder into Ivan's. "She's real cute, Ivan."

"Shut up," Ivan hissed.

"Come on. You know I'm only jealous. I've never been in your situation, you know, sleeping in the same bed with a Crosser. Well, not a cute girl Crosser at least."

"Why are there so many damn rocks?" Ivan said, ignoring his brother. He reached down and wrapped his fingers around a rock twelve inches across and turned to haul it out of the tunnel.

"Just as I thought. You want another reason to go be with her."

Irritation welled up inside him. "What? It's a rock, Luka. And it's big. I'm taking it out of the tunnel so we don't trip on it."

"Mmm, hmm."

"Shut up." Ivan hauled the rock out to the crawlspace and heaved it into the growing pile. If his father's calculations were correct, they still had about four feet of earth to move before they would reach the other tunnel wall. Every four inches they progressed forward, they added a two-by-four wood plank to the ceiling with uprights for support, creating a space five feet tall and three feet wide.

Michal had begun forming the supporting archway on the inside wall of the existing tunnel. He needed to cut the upright beams and install a header for support. In order to work on the tunnel, Michal had to open the access in Luka's room, exposing the existence of the tunnel to the six Crossers, but the revelation couldn't be avoided, and for the princess's sake, needed to be done.

Luka wiped at his brow and said, "Ivan, hand me another upper beam."

Ivan searched through the small pile of lumber for a three-foot board but came up empty handed. "We're all out of upper beams. I'll go get more."

"No, I'll do it," Luka said. "You stay with Katia."

Ivan followed Luka up the ramp into the crawlspace. By the looks of Luka's posture, his back was probably aching as much as Ivan's.

Luka dropped the trap door open and climbed up into the bedroom, closing the door behind him. Ivan went to Katia and lay on the blanket to stretch his back. "We're out of upper beams. He's going to get more."

"How's the digging going?"

"Slow, but steady. We're almost there, I think."

"I wish my foot felt better. I'd help you dig, but I still can't fully stand," she said. She sat cross-legged next to his torso and rubbed the splint on her ankle. "It's feeling a lot better than yesterday. I can put some weight on it now. I've been practicing."

"That's not a good idea if it's broken." He looked over at her. He was about to say she didn't want to have a limp for the rest of her life because of being impatient with the healing process, but his mind stalled at the "rest of her life" part.

"What's wrong Ivan?"

"What do you mean?"

"You're looking at me like something is wrong."

"Oh sorry, I was just . . . thinking."

"Thin-king," she repeated, enunciating each syllable.

"Katia, what do you plan to do with your life once you're free?"

"Oh, wow. You were thinking a big question." She took a breath. "I don't know. I haven't thought about it that far."

"Maybe you should."

"You sound confident I'll be able to escape."

"Do you have doubts?"

"Frankly, yes, but not about escaping from your house. I worry about staying hidden long term. You don't know the Kochev family like I do. They don't ever stop. I'll probably have to flee to another country, except . . ."

"Except what?" He saw pain in her eyes.

They were interrupted by the trap door inching open and a piece of paper drifting down to the ground before it shut again. Ivan sat up and placed his hand on hers, then he went over to grab the piece of paper, which read, "Danger. Stay put. Men at the door."

"What is it, Ivan?" Katia whispered.

He turned his head toward her and placed his finger to his lips. Once he made it back to her, he handed her the note. She read it, her fingers trembling. Ivan hadn't heard the doorbell or any sounds of footsteps. He was scared but didn't want Katia to know. He silently indicated they should move away from the trapdoor and over to the boxes of supplies. Wrapping his arm around her waist for support, he helped her hobble over.

Ivan reached in a box and pulled out a different blanket, which he spread out on the ground behind the supplies, hoping the pile of boxes would shield them from view. He helped her sit down. Her body shook as she positioned herself on the blanket. He sat beside her, ready to lie flat if the trapdoor opened.

The dim light from the vent nearby reflected on the gathering moisture in her wide-open eyes, making his throat constrict. Her chin trembled and he wished he could comfort her, but he didn't know what to do.

Katia mouthed, "Raid?"

He shrugged, not wanting to elevate her fear. He wrapped his arm around her shoulders and pull her against his side in a comforting hug. She in turn slid her arm around his waist and brought her knees toward him, bringing their bodies closer together. He felt her warm breath against the edges of his collar, a sharp contrast to the cool temperature of the crawlspace.

Ivan's mind raced with the impossibilities of keeping her safe. They were trapped under the house. The exit wasn't completed. How was he supposed to protect her?

Seconds turned into minutes, and after several minutes of silence from above, he began to relax. Nothing was happening. No shouting, no stomping, nothing falling over or crashing and breaking. He ran his fingers over her shoulder, giving a little squeeze of reassurance. He felt the tips of her fingers respond in kind where they rested on his waist. The action made him feel suddenly different—tense, not because of the possible danger above, but because of the possible situation below.

He put his focus back on the happenings upstairs. Still, nothing sounded out of the ordinary. He pulled his head away slowly. She tilted hers upwards.

"Are we ok?" she whispered.

"I think so," he said, expecting she'd drop her hand from his waist, but she didn't. He brought his hand to her face and touched his fingers to her cheek, moving slowly to give her the opportunity to pull away if she was uncomfortable. She closed her eyes briefly, but didn't flinch. Then he felt her hand on his back pull him closer to her body as she tilted her chin up and connected her gaze with his.

Ivan leaned in. Their lips met, gently at first, making him wonder if she was only responding to thank him with a polite kiss. But when her kiss lingered, all the senses he had purposely closed off came fully awake. His curiosity of her needed to be explored, if only for a moment. He parted his lips, inviting her in, hoping she wouldn't turn tail and run the other way. On the contrary, she took the invitation and responded by bringing her other hand up to his jawline, returning the heated, passionate kiss.

He twisted his torso a little further toward her, not wanting to lose the intensity of the moment, but the movement caused his back to cry out from the odd angle. He let out a hiss and laid back, bringing her with him, supporting her body as she lay on her side. The momentary pause did nothing to dampen their excitement toward each other. The sweetness of her mouth and the incredible softness of her lips drove him crazy with desire.

"Is she hurt?" Luka's loud voice rumbled through the stillness of the crawlspace.

Panicked, Ivan sat up quickly and moved away at arm's length. "Whoa! Luka!"

"Yep, it's me. Is she hurt?"

"No," Ivan and Katia said at the same time with equal amounts of guilt in their voices.

"Well," Luka chuckled, "it looked like you were performing mouth-to-mouth on her, that's all."

Ivan and Katia glanced at each other, then back to Luka. Ivan couldn't believe his mind had completely blanked everything else out except for her. Evidently hers had too, or she would have heard the trap door open.

"Who was . . . you know, um . . . upstairs?" Ivan wondered if his hair was as messed up as Katia's or if his face was as red as it felt.

"Investigators." Luka's eyes focused on Katia, who propped

herself up on an elbow. "They were looking for you. They had a physical description and said a reward has been posted."

Katia exclaimed, "A reward? Like money?"

"A great deal of 'like money.' " Luka grinned. "Don't worry, I'm not going to turn you in. Not when I get to see a humongous display of innocent embarrassment. I'll leave you two alone so you can try to explain your awkward moment and say something like, 'I don't know what came over me' or 'I'm sorry about that; it won't happen again.' " Luka turned and moved to the tunnel.

Ivan took a deep cleansing breath and faced Katia. Before he could even formulate any words, she spoke first. "I wasn't going to say either of those things."

"Me neither. I'm only sorry I didn't hear him come down the hole."

"I didn't hear him either!" she whispered with her eyes wide open.

He pulled her up into a hug and caressed the back of her head. "That was even better than I could have dreamt." He kissed the top of her head. "I've got to go. Are you comfortable?"

She nodded and a relaxed smile crossed her face.

Ivan wrapped a blanket around her shoulders and headed to the tunnel where he found Luka already positioning an overhead board.

Luka looked over his shoulder and laughed. "Thought you'd never come."

"Drop it, Luka."

"Oh no, I can't do that." He jammed the upright into place to secure the top board, the turned around. "You see, you've made the biggest mistake ever where Crossers are concerned: never become attached to one. But it's just our little secret, right?"

"Shut up."

"It's common sense, little bro. Use your head. She'll be gone before you know it, and you'll be left here. It's called self-preservation, man."

"Is that how come you've never married? Self-preservation has helped you reach the ripe old age of twenty-six without a broken heart. Sheez, how do you do it?"

Luka stalked over to Ivan, more like he waddled, half bent over due to the low ceiling. "Don't begin to think you understand anything about me, 'cause you don't! And don't think you know more than me about complications that can come from getting too involved with a Crosser."

"All right." Ivan held his hands up in front of himself. "Relax."

"Yeah, right. I'll relax when we finish this and get her out of here."

Ekaterina

As Ekaterina watched Ivan as he disappeared into the tunnel, a plethora of emotions ran wild through her body. Yes, she'd kissed him. She shouldn't have. She'd wanted to. She didn't regret it. What had made her act so impulsively? What did it matter? He'd clearly liked it, just as she had, and yet she felt amazed by the amount of passion between the two of them.

For a moment she just wanted to relax and allow herself to imagine what life could possibly be like with Ivan Lazarov verses Vladimir Kochev. She already knew the answer even though she didn't really know Ivan yet. She didn't really know Vladimir either, but what she did know of him was enough.

Ivan was genuinely sweet and brave. He had an instinct to want to protect her from harm and she found that to be endearing.

The last thought lingered in her mind. What was she thinking? This unfortunate young man shouldn't be dragged into her life. He didn't deserve that. He was a good guy, an anomaly, at least in her world. If she managed to escape, she'd be on the run for the rest of her life. She didn't want to have anyone chained to that kind of ordeal. In truth, she wasn't even quite sure what that ordeal would be like.

Over the last two days, she'd watched Ivan closely, cataloging his reactions, his expressions, his tone of voice to different situations. She'd seen how determined he was to succeed with his first attempt to care for a Crosser, even if it was to simply prove to his parents and brother that he could shoulder the responsibility. He could do it. She felt certain. But was it really the life he would have chosen for himself? If he hadn't seen her in the ice, he wouldn't have brought home an extra refugee. He wouldn't have had to volunteer his room. He wouldn't have to be digging a tunnel.

But then she would never have met him.

Likewise, if she hadn't said no to the idea of marrying Vladimir, her entire life would have been different, too.

CHAPTER 8

Ivan

"Wait. Do you hear that?" Ivan asked Luka.

Luka stopped digging. "What?"

Ivan pointed to the dirt in front of them. "Dad. I mean, I heard a drill. Dad with a drill."

The unmistakable whirring fired up again sounding rather close. Luka said, "We're almost there. We need to be extra careful."

Ivan nodded and scooped the dirt and rocks Luka loosened from the dirt wall in front of them into the buckets. He turned and carried the fresh dirt back to the crawlspace where Katia lay on a bed of blankets. When she saw him emerge, she sat up.

"How is everything going in there?"

"Almost done, actually." Ivan took the buckets to the far corner and dumped the contents in the pile of excavated dirt. She smiled at him, causing his heart to triple its pace. His eyes were instinctually drawn to her mouth and her sweet smile

He entered the tunnel and found the last of the earth barrier was down, exposing his father on the other side.

Luka said, "Remove the rest of this dirt, Ivan."

His father jumped in. "No. It's getting late. Ivan you need to go stock the wood boxes with firewood. Luka, you can get this dirt."

"What about Katia?" Ivan asked.

"Take her up to your bedroom. Grandma will watch her while you chop wood.

Ivan wiped his hands on his thighs and left the tunnel. A sense of pride emboldened him, knowing he could now fully protect Katia. She wasn't trapped anymore. His eyes sought out hers in the dim crawlspace. When their gazes met, a fire ignited in his stomach.

"Come on, we're going back upstairs. The tunnel is complete." He reached her and offered his arm for balance.

She entwined her arm in his and hopped to the trapdoor. "I'm so relieved the tunnel is finished."

Ivan helped Katia up into the room where Grandma Mira waited. He was a little let down to see his grandma but only because he hoped he'd be able to kiss Katia again before going outside. Working in the tunnel hunched over all day had taken its toll, but not more than the emotional storm brewing in his gut. Ivan welcomed the extracurricular activity. He needed something to ground his thoughts. What better way than chopping the hell out of a pile of firewood to get his mind off the kiss. The memory still sent tingles through his body. Being around Katia was driving him crazy.

In the backyard, Ivan swung the axe hard, sinking it into the large log. He put his foot on the log and wobbled the axe free and chopped again, slicing the log in half. He continued attacking the round logs, turning them into halves and quarters, then stacking them against the garage, ready to be taken inside for the fireboxes.

"Whoa! What got into you, Ivan?" Anton peered over the fence with both arms folded across the top of the rail.

Ivan gave him a cursory glance, then slammed the axe down again, chopping a log in half. He threw it onto the pile. "Why do you ask?" he answered with a smile.

"All this pent-up anger you're taking out on innocent logs can't be good."

"Who said it was anger?"

"Isn't it?"

Ivan wiped his brow with his sleeve. "No. As a matter of fact, I'm feeling pretty good." He leaned the axe against the log and walked over to the fence. He pulled his leather gloves off one finger at a time. Adrenaline had reignited his energy, and with it, his excitement.

"Feeling good about what?"

"Can't a guy just feel good?" Ivan stretched his arms wide and tilted his head towards the sky.

Anton's eyes narrowed as he surveyed Ivan. "It's a girl. You have a girl! Don't you? I didn't even know you were dating anyone. Wait, is it the new waitress at the diner? Did you go without me?"

"No."

"So, when did you find time to meet someone?"

"Sometimes opportunities fall out of the sky."

"You sly dog." Anton lowered his brows and reached one hand forward to Ivan. He brushed Ivan's shoulder and said, "Why are you so dirty?"

"We're remodeling."

"So are we, but I'm not covered in dirt."

"Yours is sawdust. Mine is dirt."

"Huh. Well, whatever, you've got to spill about this girl."

Ivan leaned closer. His fingers twitched around the bundled gloves in his hands. He hadn't had news like this to share in so long. His whole life felt like it revolved around nothing but Crossers. For this one moment, he felt like a normal teenage guy. Besides, there wouldn't be any harm in telling Anton. He was his friend. "Can you keep a secret?"

"Do you have to ask? I've never told anyone about the things you've told me."

"Today I kissed a Crosser."

"You said you had all males in your house. Wait, did a girl show up? How old is she?"

Ivan shrugged his shoulders in answer, a glint in his eye.

"Come on, I need the details. My life has been so boring lately."

"I shouldn't even be telling you this much."

"Well, are you going to kiss her again?"

"Probably, if it feels right."

"What does that mean?"

"You know, if I sense she wants me to, then I will."

"I hate you, you know that? But I'm relieved you didn't go to *Sophia's* without me." Anton smiled. "Well, good luck with her," he said, then turned and walked to his house.

An hour later, exhausted and sweating from exertion, Ivan stood in the shower washing away the day's grime. He had a smile on his face that probably shouldn't be there. He scrubbed his face vigorously to try to rub it off, but it was no use. Ivan simply felt happy. He wondered if this is what love felt like.

Once he'd finished with his shower and had dressed again, he entered his room. Katia was lying on her back on the bed, beautiful as ever.

"You look refreshed," she said.

"I don't feel it. My whole body aches. What didn't hurt from digging hurts now from chopping wood, but not to worry. I'll live. How are you?"

"Tired of talking. Your Grandma is something else. She was full of questions about Bregot and Boris Kochev."

"What sort of information was she after?"

"I think she plans on investigating his death. If she can prove he was murdered, it would look bad for Boris Kochev."

"Do you think he *was* murdered?"

"I'm not positive, but Boris said things to me that have made me wonder, and he died shortly after I refused to marry Vladimir. I haven't had any way to investigate or prove anything, though."

"Well, if anyone can find out the truth, it's my Grandma. Maybe it would be enough to cause an overthrow of power," Ivan suggested.

"Anything is possible."

Michal Lazarov

Michal helped his wife clear the table after dinner with a sigh. They'd used the rest of their fresh vegetables with the meal so he'd soon have to do a grocery run. With so many Crossers, supplies went much faster. He didn't want to leave the house any more than necessary, especially with the increasing possibility of a raid. Plus, excessive shopping at a time like this would raise alarms. Bed-and-Breakfast season was in a lull until the ski resorts opened, so his usual explanation for large grocery purchases wouldn't work and would only leave the assumption his family was housing Crossers. And with the amount of the offered reward money, Michal assumed there'd be plenty of people willing to turn in anything suspicious.

Ivan brought the dinner tray to the kitchen and reported that Katia had fallen asleep. Michal waited for Ivan to leave the room then said, "Boris's presence is increasing."

Luka brought a plastic tub of dishes up from downstairs. "Hey, Dad. I called Nikola at *Sophia's* and he said a large truckload of soldiers arrived tonight. They only do that when they're ready to raid. Right?"

"I'm afraid so," Michal said with a heavy heart. "I may have said too much at the hardware store when I stopped in to buy more boards. The clerk was inquisitive, and my answers didn't seem to satisfy him. I worried he might alert the authorities to an unusual purchase. Apparently, he did."

"Don't beat yourself up," Luka said, "Buying lumber doesn't mean you're housing the missing female. Kochev's men wouldn't raid unless they know for certain she's here."

"That's how it's gone in the past, but we must be on our toes, always."

"Well, at least we finished the tunnel."

Michal nodded. "Luka, make sure each Crosser wears their shoes tonight while they sleep," Michal said, "and have their belongings close by for an easy, organized escape."

"Michal," Elena said worriedly, "we've never evacuated seven before. It's usually everything we can do to fit six."

"I've arranged for two vehicles. Ivan and Katia will take one car, and Luka will take the minivan with his six Crossers."

"What about Ivan?" Luka asked. "He doesn't know what to do or who to avoid."

"I'll give him instructions."

Luka added, "Plus, he's gone and fallen for his Crosser."

Elena paused while wiping off a dish. "I'm not surprised. I've seen the way they look at each other. It's unfortunate, but *you* understand how easy that can happen, Luka."

"Yeah, well, when I fell for my Crosser, we didn't have six others needing to be protected. Ivan's mind isn't clear. It's muddled with feelings. He'll botch this up," Luka said.

Michal jumped in. "All the more reason to keep Katia separate from the others. Should Ivan mess up, they'll capture her. Your Crossers won't be compromised. Ivan's young age should keep him safe. They'll think he's just helping, not in charge, so they'll know they won't get any information from him. They might toss him around a little, but he should be okay. But you never know. Maybe he won't get caught."

Elena said, "I think Ivan and Katia should sleep in the crawlspace tonight. The bedroom is so close to the front door. It's not like the Crosser room downstairs. If they stay in the crawlspace, they'll already be down below in the morning if a raid happens."

Michal nodded to Elena. "Go have them move, but take extra blankets. It will be considerably colder down there than his bedroom."

"Not to worry," Luka said wryly. "I'm sure he'll love the

opportunity to keep her warm."

"Knock off the jokes, Luka. This is serious."

"Sorry, Mom. I'll get everyone ready." Luka headed downstairs.

"I hope this is all worth it for one girl," Elena whispered.

Michal put his arm around her. "I know I've put our family through a lot. And I know I've let my anger about my father's death fuel us for a long time. But knowing that this girl's escape can guarantee that Boris' plan will fail makes me feel like I've finally accomplished the first step to bringing his family down." He kissed her on the cheek. "It won't bring my father back, but maybe it'll help keep what happened to him from happening to other families."

Elena gave him a gentle squeeze. "I just don't want it to damage our children like your father's death scarred you."

"Hopefully nothing will happen, and we'll get the girl out of here safe and sound."

Ivan

The instructions to sleep in the crawlspace had Ivan on edge. His mother acted calm and collected, but the undertones of this move signified an imminent raid. Both Ivan and Katia were dressed in blue jeans and two long-sleeved shirts each, for layered warmth, and wore their shoes to bed, with Katia's injured foot still in the splint.

Several additional blankets were added to the already large pile of bedding on the foam mattress that had been brought down for comfort and warmth. They were instructed to use only minimal light and even less talking.

Ivan's mother took him by the arm after Katia was situated under the house. "You need to be careful here," she said.

"I know."

"No, listen to me. The stage is set for a raid. It's going to happen. Don't be caught off guard, Ivan. Keep your mind focused."

"Mom—"

"Don't let yourself become consumed with her. You are her protector, not her boyfriend."

"Mom! I *know*." Luka must have told her about them kissing.

"Be ready at first light. If you're caught, don't fight. They'll take her and probably leave you alone."

"That's not going to happen."

"Don't be arrogant."

"Are we done here?" He hated being rude with his mother, but she wasn't giving him enough credit.

"No. I love you, Ivan, and I'm so proud of you."

Ivan didn't expect that. A lump caught in his throat. "I love you, too. Thank you. It will be all right, you'll see." He closed the trap door and went over to Katia. His mother's fear was something he hadn't seen before.

"What was that all about?"

He downplayed his concerns. "She's just worried. She's also afraid I'll be too distracted with you to notice a raid. As much as I'd like to get close with you again, we shouldn't. Luka was able to sneak right up on us. We can't afford for that to happen again."

"You're right."

"Escaping a raid is a precision-timed thing. If we leave too early or too late, we'll be caught, and as I've never done this before, it could get interesting."

"When is the right time to flee?"

"During the crashing and breaking."

"What does that mean?"

"Just what it sounds like: crashing and breaking. Raids always start quickly. They tear through the house looking for Crossers. The idea is to catch everyone off guard. So, when the damage is going on, we flee."

"Won't they see us leave?"

"No. The tunnel exits quite a long way away from our house. They monitor the doors and windows for escapees, but they don't know about our tunnel. When they raid and find nothing and no one was caught fleeing the home, they figure the Crossers were moved already or were never here, when we literally escaped under their feet."

Her face turned stony with determination. "Ivan, you asked me what I want to do once I'm free. I want to defy Boris Kochev by helping people flee the country. Help me survive this, Ivan. Help me to be able to help others."

"I'll do my best."

She smiled, then leaned toward him and kissed him tenderly on the lips. Not a passionate kiss like earlier, but a "thank you" kiss.

"Will it distract you too much if we sleep cuddled together?"

she asked.

"It's cold down here and we need to stay warm," he said with a wink.

They snuggled down into their warm bedding and Ivan let exhaustion overtake him

* * *

Ivan awoke at one point, with barely any light coming through the vent. He inhaled Katia's uniquely sweet scent and couldn't imagine being anywhere else. He heard soft footsteps overhead and figured his mother was up early to prepare breakfast. Katia stirred in her sleep, and Ivan held her tighter. Any second this serene setting might be shattered. Ivan couldn't believe he had wished for this responsibility. The thought of how simple his life had been prior to finding her made him shudder. His life would never be the same, but that wasn't a bad thing.

Elena

Elena lay in bed next to her husband as the first light from the impending dawn filtered into the room. Her mind raced. She thought about all the possibilities of the day and the dangers. What-ifs filled her soul. What if things went sour? What if someone was killed during a raid? What if Ivan was captured or harmed? Elena made the decision then and there to finally get out of this part of the housing Crossers. She had raised two boys to adulthood while hiding Bregotian defectors. Life hadn't been easy. *Their* lives hadn't been easy. She remembered one of the raids they'd endured. The boys were adolescents, not directly involved with the Crossers, thank goodness. In the early dawn hours, the front door smashed in and several men stormed their house. She remembered the yelling and screaming, the devastating panic as her boys were hauled out of their bedroom and held captive while the house was searched. Michal had stayed with the Crossers that night and used the tunnel to get them to safety. The Crossers were able to get away, but the boys were traumatized, which she believed was part of the reason Luka waited for so long to join the cause and why Ivan resisted.

Luka then experienced more devastation during the last two

years, having also been involved with a female Crosser. He'd tried to hide his emotional scars, but every now and then, she saw through her son's façade. What she saw was pain and longing.

Ivan, on the other hand, had been protected. Elena prided herself on having kept Ivan out of the Crosser loop. She kept him in the dark and didn't give him many responsibilities, all in the hope that he would be able to make a life for himself someday. If he chose to help Crossers, that was fine, if it was his own choice.

However, her intentions to protect Ivan had only upset him. He didn't feel like anyone believed in him or his abilities. Nothing could be further from the truth. She did scold him on occasion when he would verbalize his disinterest in helping Crossers, but in all honesty, she hoped he could figure out his own life.

And now it seemed he'd become involved with his own Crosser. Elena knew nothing good could come from this infatuation.

Elena heard a quiet knock on her bedroom door. It must be Mira. She slid out of bed and into her house slippers, then walked to the door. With a yawn, she opened it. Terror seized her. Mira wasn't in the doorway. Instead, she sat on the couch, taped stretched across her mouth and a gun pointed at her head.

Before Elena could even think, a man stepped into the doorway, whipped her around, and covered her mouth with a large, gloved hand.

Elena could barely breathe. She felt herself being pulled backwards, seeing the outline of her husband's sleeping body still lying in bed. She struggled and twisted in the man's grip, but his strength outmatched hers. As they passed Ivan's bedroom door, she strained her neck to see if any raiders were tearing apart his floor. She couldn't see anyone in his room. The decision to have Ivan and Katia sleep in the crawlspace for the night was probably the best one ever made. Hopefully, Ivan would hear the commotion and get out in time, except there wasn't any commotion yet.

Elena stomped on the ground while being dragged, hoping the noise would alert the rest of the household. Michal stirred, but too late. Three other men, all dressed in faded, green fatigues, had already charged into the room.

"Make another sound and I'll kill the old lady," a rough voice said into her ear.

The hand covering Elena's mouth pulled away and was quickly replaced with cold sticky tape before she could scream.

Her trembling hands were bound behind her with the same tape, then she was pushed onto the couch next to Mira, who was already restrained the same way.

Elena's thoughts skipped over to Luka. Had he heard her stomps in time and escaped with his Crossers? Elena's eyes met Mira's then switched over to the bedroom door to see three men hauling out Michal. He was deposited next to Elena on the couch with his mouth and hands already taped. Three other men stood behind the couch, shouldering guns aimed at each of their heads.

A large bulky figure stepped from the shadows by the front door. He walked over and stood in front of the couch. He bent forward and put his face in front of Elena's. His hot breath reeked of onion and beef. "We know she is here. You're hiding her." He moved to Michal and said, "I don't have a problem with you three, but I do have to report to my boss, who's outside right now, and he isn't very kind when he's angry." He straightened his back and moved in front of Mira. "Tell me where the girl is and everything will go smoothly. Try to hide her from me, and well, let's just say things will get . . . bumpy." The brutish-looking man threaded his fingers slowly into brass knuckles.

Tears rimmed her eyes. This wasn't usually how raids went. A horrible feeling rolled around in her gut that these men wouldn't want to leave any witnesses. Ever so softly, Elena felt Mira lean into her with her shoulder. Elena glanced over and Mira jerked her head toward the men.

Elena blinked and nearly missed Mira's quick movement from her seated position, striking like a cobra, ramming her body into brass-knuckles-man, and knocking him backward onto the coffee table. He smashed the glass fruit bowl with his back, and blood began to pool around his sides on the shattered tabletop. He howled in pain. Mira fell also and split her head open on the corner of the table. Two of the men behind the couch moved to help the fallen brute.

Knowing they'd only get one chance, Elena cast a quick look at Michal and with a shared nod, they launched themselves toward the other guards. Elena kicked the nearest man in the kneecap, doubling him over in pain. Michal plowed into the other, sending him flailing backwards into Ivan's bedroom door, slamming it open and into the wall behind.

CHAPTER 9

Ivan

Ivan bolted upright to the sound of loud footsteps and held his breath. He felt Katia stiffen next to him, her hand gripping his shoulder. Moments later, breaking glass and an eerie howl confirmed his fear.

They were being raided.

Muffled shouting and screams of pain along with what sounded like his bedroom door banging against the wall filtered through the floorboards. He looked at Katia, her eyes wide and alert.

"Time to go," he mouthed. He grabbed their jackets and helped Katia over to the tunnel entrance. She shook from head to toe, and Ivan's heart broke at her terror. He found it difficult to help her through the narrow tunnel and also keep the weight off her foot, but they managed one step at a time.

Once they were away from the noises, Katia paused under a lightbulb to catch her breath.

"Your family?" she mouthed.

Confliction pulled at his chest and he shook his head slowly. They were on their own.

Vladimir

Vladimir Kochev stood outside the Lazarov home, smoking a cigarette. His two personal bodyguards flanked him half a step behind and a truckload of soldiers stood guard around the perimeter of the home. He admired the view to the south. The Modry mountains framed the huge lake in front of him, and the enormous snow-topped mountain range behind almost made him feel insignificant.

Almost.

He listened to the raid going on behind him and smirked at the thought of finding Ekaterina. How dare she try to evade him. How dare she think she even could. No one got away from the Kochevs. No one! They'd find her and get her back to Bregot, and the postponed wedding would proceed at its originally scheduled time: four o'clock this afternoon.

"Sir," a voice came from behind him, "we've searched the home. She's not here."

"Yes, she is. Keep looking," Vladimir stated plainly.

"Tane needs medical attention, sir."

Vladimir didn't answer. He didn't need to. If Tane had allowed himself to be injured by these imbeciles, that was his problem.

Vladimir heard the door close behind him. The sun was thinking about making its presence known to the east, and a bluish-pink hue covered everything. *Once we're back to the palace,* Vladimir thought, *she's going to be married to me ASAP. No more waiting. She won't escape me.*

He waited several more minutes for the word they'd found her, but it never came. Flicking his cigarette in no particular direction, he whirled around and headed to the door, his escorts close behind. *If you want something done right, you have to do it yourself.*

Vladimir entered the home and found everyone adequately subdued. Three adults sat on the sofa, each bleeding in some way. The sight made him feel powerful. Anyone who thought they could defy him and hide Crossers deserved to be caught and made to suffer.

Tane lay on the floor in front of the couch.

"Get him out of here," Vladimir said to no one in particular. Two men stepped forward and pulled the injured man away.

"Sir, we've searched everywhere. The perimeter guards report that no one has left the premises during the raid. She's not here."

Vladimir turned to the collaborators. "I *know* you've been housing Ekaterina. Where is she?"

The tape was ripped off their mouths. The elderly lady

replied with a snide remark, "Thanks, honey, now I won't have to wax."

Vladimir backhanded her across the face. Old or not, no one talked to him that way.

The man spoke up, his voice full of strain. "Leave her alone! It's true we housed a female Crosser, but she's already gone. Once they leave our home, we don't know where they go."

"Liar!" Vladimir roared. One of Vladimir's guards, sporting a set of brass knuckles he'd taken off Tane, stormed over and punched the man in the gut. Vladimir liked the unspoken understanding he had with his men. They could almost read his mind. Almost. "I have it on good authority that your youngest son is housing Ekaterina. Where is his bedroom?"

The man's eyes flickered to the left. Vladimir followed his line of sight and walked over to the entrance of the room. Slowly, he investigated. Quite simple: a double bed, two end tables, a lone armchair in the corner by the window, and a closet. He looked in the closet to see organized shelves and compartments. Vladimir studied the wood floor in the closet and throughout the room for tell-tale signs of secret trap doors, but he didn't see anything. No strategically placed rugs. No unusual patterns to catch his eye. Vladimir left the room.

"Where did your son go?" Vladimir asked the man.

"He left already with the girl."

"Yes, but when?"

"Yesterday morning."

He frowned. "Your son was seen here late last night. I'm losing my patience with you, and when that happens, people start to die." He walked back over to the old lady.

"All right, all right!" the man conceded. "He left during the raid."

"Impossible. My guards have been watching and saw no one leave."

"I assure you, they did."

Vladimir began barking out orders, "Search every garage and woodshed in the near vicinity. They haven't gone far. Find them." He turned back to the three adults. "Defying Boris Kochev is a crime punishable by death."

"Only in Bregot," the old woman stated calmly. "Killing people in Svobodia because Bregotians escaped under Boris's nose will only encourage the anti-authoritarian governments to issue an investigation. I don't think your father wants that kind of publicity. Do you?"

Vladimir glared at the old lady. *Who did she think she was?* Vladimir thought. *Someday, when I'm in charge, I won't be afraid of killing traitors.*

Ivan

Ivan helped Katia through the tunnel with one arm around her waist and her arm over his shoulder. Once the ladder at the end of the tunnel came into view, Ivan let out a sigh of relief. He pointed up and put his finger to his lips to signify silence. The dim light from the last bulb on the line washed over her frightened face. She nodded in understanding.

Ivan reached up and unlatched the door and was about to push up when he heard footsteps and male voices above in the garage. His arm froze instinctively as well as his lungs, and he threw a worried glance to Katia. She'd heard the noise, obviously, and had her eyes trained on the trap door. He reached past her and twisted the light bulb over her head until it went out, leaving them in the dark. The nearest light bulb was barely visible.

He strained, listening to hear if it was Luka and the other Crossers who'd made it out before them, but the voices sounded rough and low, not matching anyone Ivan could identify. Besides, the Crossers wouldn't be so careless with noise. No, for some reason the raiders were already searching the outlying areas.

His mind raced, along with his panicked heart, worried about being found—but, worried more about Katia. How could he protect her if the tunnel was discovered? He had no weapons. They'd be slow moving to get back to the house because of her foot. Even if they made it back, what would they do there? If outbuildings were already being searched, that meant the escape window had closed.

The steps above faded and he heard a door shut.

Ivan felt around for the light bulb and twisted it back on. The low light washed over Katia's petrified face. He reached for her and pulled her close to his body for comfort. He whispered, trying his best to hardly make any sound, "It's the raiders. We can't leave yet."

Her body trembled in his arms, but he also felt her steel against him. She mouthed in return, "What now?"

Ivan took a deep breath and tried to think straight. "We wait."

She nodded her head and together they sat down in the dirt, with their backs against the boards that formed the wall, listening to any changes on the outside, any sign of a familiar voice or blissful silence so they could continue.

Ivan squeezed his eyes closed in the hopes of pushing back the tears that wanted to fill them. He didn't have time or the strength to worry about his parents, brother, and grandmother. All he could do was hope they were still alive.

Anton

Anton Gulevski was ushered into the Lazarov home, past the three adults on the sofa.

"You!" Michal exclaimed.

"Quiet! Or I'll retape your mouth," one of the guards ordered.

Anton averted his eyes, although he couldn't help notice the reddened puffiness on Mira's face. He hadn't expected anyone to get hurt. He just thought the guards would find the girl and take her and he'd get the reward money. And no one was ever supposed to know it was him who betrayed Ivan's family.

Entering the kitchen, Anton was brought to the table where Vladimir Kochev sat with a conceited, impatient expression plastered on his face. Anton had seen photos of him before, but they portrayed him as older and larger in stature. The guy before him didn't match the image in his mind of a "man of power", rather, more of spoiled rich kid.

"Sit." Vladimir pointed to the chair across the table. Anton sat. "She's not here," Vladimir said, drumming his never-seen-a-hard-day's-work fingertips lightly on the tabletop. "You said she was here."

"Well, you should have raided *last night*, when I discovered her presence," Anton stated, jutting his chin forward.

The two bodyguards beside Vladimir stiffened even more and stepped forward. Vladimir held up one hand, stopping them. "*You* probably tipped them off with your inept questioning," Vladimir scoffed.

"I gave you everything you needed to get her. No one said anything about hurting the family. Just give me my money and I'll be on my way."

Vladimir stood abruptly and reached across the table and grabbed Anton by the shirt.

"What the—?" Anton exclaimed, struggling in the grip.

"Your money is for the delivery of the girl. No girl, no cash."

"It's not my fault! I did everything I could!"

"Then I don't need you anymore." Vladimir's other hand moved toward Anton. Light glinted off a blade held in his hand.

Anton's chest seized in panic. This wasn't how everything was supposed to play out. "No, wait. Wait!" Anton stuttered, stalling for time. "I can still be useful."

The knife's movement paused. "How?" Vladimir asked, his eyes cold.

"I-I don't know where Ivan might have taken her, but I can give you some profile information about him." His voice wavered.

"Go on." Vladimir's eyebrow raised.

"He's nineteen and strong, both physically and mentally, but he's never taken care of a Crosser before. He won't know what to do or how long to stay away. He'll call home or make some other mistake. It's only a matter of time."

"How well do you know him?"

"Very well. He confided in me. He told me he and the girl kissed. That's how I found out. I informed one of your agents right away."

Vladimir's eyes turned dark. "They kissed? Did he have sex with her?"

"I-I don't think so. No. He would have said something. He was just excited about a kiss."

Vladimir released Anton and sat back into the chair, his shoulders dropping. "Good."

A man entered the kitchen with a radio in his hand. "Sir, we have to leave now. The authorities have been alerted."

Vladimir said to Anton as he stood and inserted the blade into a leather sheath on his belt, "I'll give you one more chance to receive your reward. I'm leaving three of my men here to guard the parents. You will stay in this house and answer every phone call and doorbell and you'll convince the police everything is fine in this household. Do whatever is necessary to quiet this with the authorities. Any other thoughts on any location where she might be, you send a guard to check it out. If the boy calls home, you tell him whatever it takes to find his location, and then call me." Vladimir flicked a card with a telephone number scribbled on it in

Anton's direction. "If you fail in any way, I'll be done with you, permanently."

Ivan

Ivan gently nudged Katia.

She sat up and looked around, blinking in confusion. "Is it time for us to leave?" she whispered.

He nodded, pointing at his watch, which read six o'clock.

She nodded in return and he helped her up. He positioned himself directly under the trap door to the garage and slowly pushed it up, peering out through the tiny crack. The only window in the garage faced the owner's home. The porch light spilled through the dusty window to give a small bit of light in the otherwise dark garage. Assorted yard tools hung in an organized fashion on the walls next to a rudimentary work bench covered with small baby food jars full of screws, nuts and bolts.

An old bicycle hung upside down from the rafters, just high enough that they didn't bump their heads on it. One vehicle had been backed into the two-car garage for a quick escape. Ivan assumed the empty vehicle parking spot was where Luka's get-away car had been parked. Luka must have fled with his Crossers in the night.

Not seeing anyone, he pushed the trap door all the way open. He climbed out and turned around to help Katia. She slowly climbed the ladder with her one good foot as he pulled her up.

Ivan assisted Katia into the front passenger side of the car. The cold vinyl seat protested under her weight. He fastened her seatbelt while she repositioned her legs, then gently closed her door. He hurried over to the garage door, lifted it open, wincing at the noise, and peered up and down the alley to make sure they were alone. Then he climbed in the driver's seat and fastened his belt.

"Here we go," he muttered as he turned the key, which he found underneath the floor mat. The ignition fired up and struggled to turn the engine over. Nothing. He let go of the key and tried again. Still nothing. He turned the key again and they listened as the engine failed to cooperate. His heart raced even faster. He tried it one more time, this time giving it a little gas, and finally the engine engaged. A thick exhaust cloud filled the garage as they pulled forward.

Ivan's eyes searched for guards and snipers, hoping they would be able to escape unnoticed. He thought about stopping to close the garage door, but feared the car engine might die, and after struggling to get it to start, he didn't want to risk anything. He drove to the end of the alley and applied the brakes, only to hear the engine sputter and die.

"No!" He batted at the steering wheel with his palm and turned the key again. The engine responded and fired up. The road was clear of cars, so he was able to turn without completely stopping as he gave the struggling engine gasoline to coax it along. If he gunned it too hard, the noise would be noticed. A noisy, smoking, speeding car would certainly draw the wrong attention. *What had Dad been thinking when he chose this car?*

"Where is everyone?" Katia asked as they drove through town.

"I don't know. It's a little eerie." He looked in his rear-view mirror and saw nothing behind him. The hair on the back of his neck raised.

"Where are we going?"

"My dad gave me directions to the safe-house in Severni. Luka and the other Crossers should be there."

"A safe-house?"

"Yes, that's where we're going to hide. Keep your eyes peeled for suspicious cars."

Ivan drove cautiously and turned onto the highway heading west. Severni lay forty-five miles away, up and over the mountain pass. Snowflakes fell with a purpose and the roads were covered with a fresh layer of snow. Ivan tried adjusting the headlights to see if brights offered better visibility than dims but was blinded by the illuminated wall of snowflakes. Dims were better.

Up ahead was the location where roadblocks were commonly set up. He knew the block should be gone, but what if it wasn't? What if they were about to be stopped? He didn't have a backup plan. The only thing he knew for certain was he didn't want Katia to be captured. As he approached the area, he let out a breath of relief. The roadblock was gone. He decided not to tell Katia of their good fortune for fear of making her worry about other blocks and hazards.

The outlet of Lebed Lake cut a rugged canyon through the hills to the west. The highway followed the small river for a couple of miles, then turned away and climbed the mountain with sharp switchbacks. The river continued into a deep canyon, which was excellent for white-water rafting. Ivan let his mind wander, anything to distract him from the intense fear he felt.

Anton and Ivan had rafted the majestic river many times. After heavy rains, the waterfalls on both sides of the canyon were breathtaking to behold. The best waterfall was fifteen miles down the canyon on the right, named Bulchinski Voal Falls, which fell dramatically off a cliff above. The river at that point was calm and deep, perfect for swimming.

Whenever Ivan rafted this river, he always knew where he was in relation to the highway because when they reached Bulchinski Voal Falls, he was directly south of the family's vacation cabin. Last summer, he and Anton hiked from the bridge that crossed the creek to the top of Bulchinski Voal Falls. The hike led mostly downhill, and the small creek was in a constant state of falling until it plunged over the edge of the canyon. In hindsight, it was an idiotic, dangerous venture on their part, one his mother would have chastised him for.

Ivan drove the precarious switchbacks in silence through the increasingly severe winter weather. The snow-covered road was difficult to navigate, with almost zero visibility due to the blowing snow. He increased the windshield wiper speed to double time to clear the wet snowflakes from the window.

"Are you warm enough?" he asked Katia, checking the warm air blowing through the vents.

"Yes. I'm just relieved we don't have to be out in this snowstorm." She turned her head away from Ivan and said, "I wonder what Boris told the people about me."

"What do you mean?"

"The wedding was supposed to take place this afternoon at four o'clock. He would have given an excuse, and I highly doubt he would've said I've escaped."

"Wow, you'd be married right now if you hadn't crossed the border." He cast a quick glance in her direction when she didn't respond and recalled their conversation about her making sure she wouldn't marry Vladimir. Ivan added, "I'm really glad you crossed the border, Katia."

Ivan saw the small bridge up ahead that arched over Bulchinski Voal Creek, just east of the road to the cabin. The car began to sputter again, even with the accelerator pressed. "You've got to be kidding me!" With one last jerk, the car died about a hundred feet from the turn-off. Ivan pulled over as far as he could to the side of the road before the car came to a complete stop. After trying repeatedly to restart the car with no success, his mind swirled in different directions, like the wind-driven snow outside. The nearest building he knew of was the family's cabin, but to say it was nearby was an understatement. They were faced with a long walk in a raging snowstorm. Ivan would need to carry Katia the distance as she wouldn't be able to hop all the way there. And, as his father had pointed out, the cabin wasn't prepared to be used as a safe location. Unfortunately, there was no other choice. But what to do about the car? He obviously couldn't leave it on the side of the road. He might as well hang a sign with a giant pointing arrow saying, "Escaped Crosser, that way."

Ivan noticed Katia's silence. She hadn't complained when the engine died, and she hadn't worried out loud about what they were going to do now. He appreciated the fact that she didn't demand answers, the likes of which he didn't have.

Turning to her, he said, "Some get-away car, huh?"

Her mouth formed a slight smile, but he could tell she was frightened.

He pointed forward. "Well, um . . . up ahead is a road to the right that leads to a cabin—my family's cabin. It's rustic, but we'd be out of the storm, although it's a bit of a hike to get there." He turned around, looking back down the road they had come up. "We can't leave the car here. I'll help you out, and then I'll use gravity to guide the car backwards as far down the hill as I can. Maybe I can ditch it down a steep embankment and out of sight."

She added to his thought, "The further away you can roll the car from us, the less likely anyone would piece together where we are."

"Right."

"But Ivan, even with our extra layers, we won't last long in this storm." She glanced down at her foot. "And, my ankle—"

"I'll carry you, Katia. Don't worry. We'll be at the cabin in no time, warming up to a crackling fire. You'll see." He jumped out of the car, snow bombs hitting his face. Katia had already removed her belt and was attempting to get out of the car by the time he made it to her door.

She said, "I don't want you to leave me."

He heard the fear in her voice but didn't want her to hear his.

He calmed himself before saying, "I'll only be gone a few minutes. Look, there's a fallen tree that will be perfect to hide behind. Jump on my back."

Ivan turned away and squatted down so she could climb onto him. He reached back and hooked his arms behind her knees while she wrapped her arms around his neck and torso. He then hurried down the embankment and up the other side to the toppled evergreen and set her down.

"Okay," he said, wiggling out of his jacket and handing it to her. "Put this on."

"What? No, you need that."

"I'll be moving, generating heat. I'll be fine. But, you won't. You need all the heat you can get. I'll be right back." He didn't wait for a response from her. He kissed her forehead and turned away, making his way back to the car.

Once inside, he put the gear into neutral and guided it backward down the sloped road. Ivan hoped no other cars would come up behind him. Then again, who would be crazy enough to try to drive in this weather? He maneuvered across the Bulchinski Voal Creek bridge and on down the road until he found an adequate location to ditch the car. He stopped and got out of the car, retrieved an emergency pack from the back seat, then pushed it down the slope and out of sight. The bitter cold of the wind and snow made him long for the mass of dryer-tossed blankets he and Katia had cuddled underneath her first night.

Ekaterina

Ekaterina sat in the dark behind the fallen tree where Ivan had left her, the feel of his kiss lingering on her forehead. She realized this was the first time she had been alone since Ivan pulled her from the lake. She recalled the terrifying plane ride and the suicidal jump into the biting cold darkness. Then the all-consuming hyper-cold temperature of the water. This current situation wasn't so bad after what she'd been through. The freezing wind carried enormous snowflakes that slammed into her face and clung to her lashes, but she was able to turn her back to nature's wrath, happy she had the extra layer of protection against the harsh elements. Although she knew her warmth came with a consequence: Ivan would be cold.

Ivan.

Her mind went back to the horror stories she had heard about Crosser homes in Svobodia. Propaganda. The Lazarov family had been nothing but kind and gentle, putting themselves in harm's way to help her—not to mention taking care of the six others who had escaped. How horrible would it have been if they'd been captured or killed because of the heat on her head?

Just a few days ago she had decided that death was better than staying in Bregot. Now she felt glad that option hadn't happened. If she hadn't fought for her life after crashing through the ice, she wouldn't have met Ivan. Too many stars to ignore aligned in the right order for Ivan to come into her life, and her into his. She vowed at that moment she would never again consider death as an option—one never knows what lies just around the corner. For her, Ivan had been just around the corner and she would have missed him.

Headlights lit up the trees like daylight, blinding her. *Did Ivan get the car to start?* she wondered. Relief rushed through her until she realized the motor sounded different. Her chest tightened. She didn't see Ivan anywhere. She ducked her head down behind the snow-covered tree trunk in front of her and listened as the vehicle slowed to a stop, only a few dozen feet away.

CHAPTER 10

Ivan

Ivan flung the emergency pack over one shoulder then pulled the small flashlight out of the side pocket and switched it on. He began to hike back up the road, his muscles feeling the strain of the climb from the previous few days physical exercise. He didn't realize he had rolled the car so far away. He quickened his pace to a jog, which made his heart pump rapidly. The air temperature was cold, but not incredibly so. He'd experienced much colder temperatures, however, the two of them were still a long way from the cabin and until they were indoors, frostbite and hyperthermia were concerns.

He tucked his bare hands, one at a time, under his arms to protect them from the wind as he jogged up the road, back to Katia. He'd nearly reached the spot where the car died, close to where Katia hid behind the fallen tree, when bright lights shined from behind. A vehicle approached. Ivan turned off the flashlight and darted off the road, slipping on the embankment, and rolling down below the road level. He lay flat in the snow and listened as the car slowly drove by. Ivan crawled up to the road and peeked above the snow, his bare hands freezing in the packed snow. His discomfort was all but forgotten when he heard the vehicle come to a stop near the road to the cabin. *Had they seen our tracks in the snow?*

Someone in a large fur-trimmed parka exited the car and hurried toward the cabin road, showing a flashlight on the untouched snow. They angled the flashlight to the left, then the right, dangerously close to where Katia hid. *What if they found her?* Ivan's stomach lurched. He heard the car door slam and the sounds of the tires fishtailing on the slick road. Ivan ventured a peek but couldn't see anything inside the car. Was the man by himself? Had they found Katia and taken her?

Headlights swung his way and Ivan ducked again. Once the car had passed, he released the breath he hadn't even realized he'd been holding, then he peeked down the road and watched the vehicle's taillights disappear around the curve. With quick steps he bolted to the fallen tree.

"Katia!" he hissed in a whisper.

No answer.

"Katia, where are you?" he ventured a little louder.

Nothing.

"Katia!" his voice cracked as he yelled into the forest. Panic coursed through him like a runaway locomotive. She had to be here somewhere. Ivan prayed the man from the car hadn't taken Katia, but he didn't know for sure. Fear rushed into guilt. Could he have hidden her better on the side of the road? That's what she had been afraid of in the tunnel: being left alone, with the threat of capture constantly hanging over her head.

A faint voice sounded somewhere ahead: "Ivan, help."

He looked around, reigniting his flashlight and swinging it wildly. "Katia?"

The harsh wind made it incredibly difficult to hear anything. Her soft voice became audible again between the lulls of the wind through the trees. He moved in its direction and the ground buckled beneath him. He slid down a steep slope and landed in the freezing water of Bulchinski Voal Creek. The swift water pushed him downstream and the biting cold temperature seized his lungs. He needed to get out of the water. Fast. His foot found ground and he pushed his water-soaked body out of the creek, which now seemed strangely odd to be called a creek and not raging river. He looked around and saw Katia, clinging to a tree root at the water's edge.

"Katia!" Ivan watched in horror as she lost her grip and was carried rapidly downstream. As he chased her alongside the creek, she frantically reached for anything she could grab. Ivan knew what lay ahead: certain death. He had to reach her before she hit the steep descent into the canyon.

He crashed into the water as he caught up with her and grabbed her arm. The emergency pack slid off his shoulder and floated away as he struggled to hold her with his other arm. There was no saving the pack and Katia. He could only save one and that choice was obvious. He barely kept hold of the flashlight, his fingertips already numb, while its light shined uncontrolled around him. Katia's water-soaked clothes added an immense amount of weight to be pulled back against the flow of the water. The stream seemed to have a mind of its own with dark plans to separate them. He lost his grasp on her, and she slipped away.

In his mind's eye, he imagined her plunging over the rim of the canyon. The river would be frozen over except for where the falls constantly splashed. If she went over, the current would take her downstream under the ice, and she wouldn't be able to surface.

Adrenaline ignited within Ivan's body as he rushed toward her, splashing through the water as fast as he could, until he caught her by the arm. He readjusted his grip and pulled her toward him. She flung her other arm around his back and took hold, coughing and sputtering water and shaking violently. He struggled to keep his footing as he pulled her out of the biting cold water. They both fell onto the narrow, snowy bank in utter exhaustion.

"Ivan," she whispered. Her teeth chattered.

He turned his head to her. He thought he knew how cold the human body could become. He was wrong. His joints felt stiff and he found it difficult to get moving. With extra effort, he pushed himself up, using sheer will to survive. Even though they were both safe now, their situation would become dire if they didn't get to the cabin soon.

"Come on. Got t-to go." He pulled her upright, and she threw her arms around him. He pressed his face to her forehead and cheeks. "We need to get to the c-cabin. Get on my b-back, I'll carry you." She did so, and he began moving forward. He'd get her to the cabin and they'd be okay. He just needed to keep moving. He lumbered slowly upstream along the bank, past the steep drop where they'd fallen, the thin stream of light from his flashlight a beacon to light their way. Finally, he found a good place to climb up the hill. He trudged through the snow, searching for the cabin road.

Ivan said, "I'm going to set you down a second." He squatted low until her good foot touched the ground. Then he helped her stand. He faced her and unfastened the two coats she wore. "Okay, get on my back again. I'll try to hold the sides of your coat closed with my arms. Our bodies should share heat a little better this way. Try to keep your hands covered."

"Okay." She pulled the coat sleeves over her hands and

climbed on his back once more.

Ivan intertwined his arms behind her knees, clutching his hands together in front of him. He could already feel her warmth radiating against his back.

Ivan plodded on through the snow, stepping over small obstacles and going around large ones, all while trying to keep his orientation in the barely visible landscape. The snowflakes didn't seem to be falling as fast as when they were in the car and the wind had slowed. He began to worry that he hadn't found the road to the cabin yet. Was he walking parallel to the road? He decided to aim slightly to the left in the hopes of reaching the road. What he didn't want was Katia knowing he wasn't sure what he was doing.

His mind swam dizzyingly and he said, "Katia, tell me a story about your childhood."

"I'm too cold."

"That's exactly why I want you to tell me a story," he lied.

"But my teeth are chattering too much. You won't understand me."

"Please try."

A moment of silence. "I only have a few memories of before my mother died, but one of them was that she'd make me animal-shaped hotcakes when I felt sad."

"What would make you sad?"

"The other kids didn't want to play with me, or if they did want to, their parents wouldn't let them. I remember one girl's mom dragging her daughter away while looking at me like I was contagious. My mother told me the dictator was looking for us and the other kids' parents were afraid of being found. I remember asking why we were being looked for and she told me my father was an important man and because I was his daughter, I was important, too."

"She didn't tell you about the whole royalty thing, did she?"

"Not then. That conversation was one of the very last I had with her before she died. Her and my father had been arguing off and on for a few days and as most kids do, I blamed myself. My mother came to me and said, 'You are a *princess*, Ekaterina.' I remember not being surprised to hear the word. My father called me his little princess all the time. She kept saying the phrase, emphasizing the word 'princess.' She also said, 'Never forget it.' She seemed sad when we had that talk. She died a few days later."

Ivan finally found the road. He wanted to express his relief that he knew where they were, but he didn't want to detract from her story. "I'm sorry, Katia. That must have been hard."

"Her death never made sense to me. Afterwards, the Kochev family seemed so nice to us, hiring my father, helping to send me to a good school. I didn't understand my mother's fear of them. Not until after my father's death . . ."

Ivan heard her choke on the word a bit and wondered if there was something more she wasn't telling him.

"Tell me about the cabin, Ivan," she said softly in his ear, obviously wanting to change the subject.

"Well, it's no five-star hotel, so don't get your hopes up. There's a simple supply of food and cooking supplies, a fireplace, a big woodpile chopped and stacked by yours truly last summer, and a comfortable bed."

"Is there a bathroom?"

"No. Sorry. No running water. But we have an outhouse," he said. He picked up his pace as much as he could with frozen stiff jeans and numb feet. The flashlight dimmed, either from low batteries or the dousing in the icy creek, and the ambient light illuminated the snowy landscape only barely. A couple of times, he walked right off the road and stumbled to the ground. Sheer will powered his legs and mind to continue forward.

He didn't know how far away from the highway they'd traveled. At least there weren't any tracks, car or human, on the cabin road for that distance. With Katia on his back, he made a single set of footprints in the snow, which was a good thing in case anyone came looking. He thought about the car that stopped near the turnoff. The body size of the person wasn't a match for his father, so he ruled him out. Maybe the person was lost and was simply turning around—but why would they need to get out of the car? Why did they shine a flashlight down the road? Would Luka have come looking for them? But he should be at the safe-house with the rest of the Crossers.

The outline of the cabin finally came into view in front of him. He nearly collapsed with joy. "Katia, look! We're here."

"Thank God," she whispered.

He climbed the steps to the covered deck and leaned to the side to let Katia down. She sat on the wood porch as he fumbled with numb fingers to find the hidden key in the rafters. He knew exactly where it should be but couldn't tell if he was touching it or not. He swept his hand along the beam to knock the key off, hoping at the same time it wouldn't fall between the cracks of the porch when it dropped.

The key fell safely. He bent down to pick it up but couldn't seem to do so. His fingers wouldn't squeeze hard enough to hold the key. Katia came to his rescue and picked it up for him. He inserted the key in the lock, turned the stiff knob, and opened the door. Then he helped her inside.

The immediate warmth amazed Ivan, even though the cabin wasn't heated. Simply having the wind off them made such a huge difference. Katia sunk into the couch, her eyelids drooping, while he stood frozen in his shoes. He needed to make a fire, warm some water, and keep Katia alert all at the same time.

Ivan flipped the light switch, illuminating the simple dwelling. "Don't fall as-sleep yet. We need to w-warm up f-first. I'll make f-fire." He moved slowly and deliberately toward the door. He did not want to go outside again, but what choice did he have? He pulled the door open.

"Wait!" She exclaimed through chattering teeth. He turned around. She stood and limped over to the kitchen area and pointed to the gas oven. "Does this work? We could light the burners for heat." She picked up the box of matches

"Well, yeah," he said. "That's a great idea." He closed the cabin door and grabbed two chairs from the table and took them to Katia while she lit the burners. He helped her light the oven as well.

She extended her hands above the surface of the stove. "This heat is amazing. I think it takes having suffered from hypothermia to really appreciate warmth." She began removing her arms from the wet coats.

"I agree. I'm going to get us some blankets." Ivan left her, still frozen and numb, but recovering. He hoped his toes and fingertips would fully warm up and not have frostbite. For now, he wasn't sure.

In the bedroom, he stripped the bedding off the bed and opened the closet to retrieve more blankets. The bedding was cold, as was everything in the cabin. He was still relieved Katia thought of turning on the stove versus him trying to start a fire, which would have taken a much longer time to generate warmth.

By the time he made it back to the kitchen, she had managed to take off her shirts and remove the shoe and sock off her good foot. What a sight she was, wearing only a bra and blue jeans, unwrapping the splint on her injured foot.

"I can't get my button undone." She pointed to her waist. A severe shiver wracked through her body at the same time.

Ivan flipped open a blanket and wrapped it around her back, then tried to unbutton her pants. But with his numb fingers, he couldn't get enough of a grip to pull the button out. He looked at her, admittedly shocked at his own lack of ability.

She shrugged her shoulders. "Let's just get as m-much of this wet clothing off as we c-can." She started undoing the buttons on his shirt for him as she could tell his were too numb to manage the detailed work. She worked as quickly as she could and helped him out of the clothing. His own uncontrollable tremors shot through his body, making him move with jerked motions. He bent over and tugged at the frozen laces on his shoes. It was no good, so he kicked his shoes off one foot at a time. He slid his fingers into his socks to inch them off his numb feet. They were so stiff they held their shape once lying on the floor. He wrapped a blanket around his body and turned to Katia.

"Let me try that button again." His fingers were regaining feeling a bit, but with that came incredible burning and pain. He used his fingers to pry and finally slip the button through the hole.

She stood on one leg, held on to her blanket with one hand, and used the countertop nearby to steady herself while he peeled off her jeans. Ivan was sure the pants would be able to stand by themselves, just like the socks.

His blanket fell to the floor and he shivered uncontrollably while he worked her hurt leg out of her jeans as she balanced on her good leg. His eyes zoomed in on the bruises on her leg. He had seen them before, the first night when he'd removed her other frozen clothing, but they didn't look much different, perhaps a little more yellow around the edges. He pulled the pants down to her knee on her good leg and helped her sit back on the chair to remove them the rest of the way.

"You'll warm faster if you take off your underwear, too," he said, then turned his back to her and took off his own pants and underwear. He picked up the blanket and flung it around his back, then turned around and saw her staring at him. His heart thumped hard against his chest wall. She looked away, cheeks blushed, and tightened her hold on her blanket.

Instead of sitting down beside her, Ivan nervously opened a cupboard with one hand while the other held onto his blanket. He removed a coffee pot and a large kettle. Then he picked up the bucket next to the stove and stepped outside to fill it with snow for water. His feet were so numb he couldn't feel the cold of the snow—his heart, on the other hand, hadn't slowed yet from catching Katia looking at his naked body. She seemed uncomfortable and possibly scared when he caught her. Her tight clutch on her blanket made him wonder if she felt unsafe. Ivan decided he'd be more careful. He brought the bucket back inside and emptied the contents into the kettle to begin the melting process.

Katia's own undergarments lay draped across the chair next to her. "I'm so thirsty, Ivan. Can I eat some snow?"

"No, it will be counter-effective to warming up. Let's wait till it melts." He grabbed a can of coffee grounds and thought twice. "Hmm. Maybe we should drink broth instead." *It's what my mother would do,* he thought, which brought his parents and grandmother to the forefront of his mind. He hoped they were okay. Ivan put the coffee away and grabbed the jar of bouillon cubes instead. He'd have to wait to open the foil wrapper until his fingers warmed. He took two mugs from the cupboard and a ladle from the drawer and set them on the countertop. Then he sat on the chair by her.

She scooted closer to him so their blanketed bodies touched.

Ivan said, "I'm really glad you thought about using the stove for heat."

"My mom used to do it when I'd play outside for too long in the cold."

"Oh. My mom would just lecture me on not listening to my body tell me I'm cold, and then she'd make some hot cocoa."

Katia extended her good leg. "My toes are tingling and burning."

"Mine too." He matched her leg extension with his own. Their calves and feet touched skin to skin. "You're warm."

"And you're freezing." She lowered her leg. "You should move closer to the stove."

"I'm fine where I am." He didn't want to move away. Her body heat and nearness warmed him more than any stove could.

Katia asked, "What kind of food does your family keep here?"

"Honestly, not much. Dry stuff, mostly. Some canned items and dehydrated foods. I don't think it's a good idea to eat dehydrated fruit or jerky until we get some water in us."

"How's the water doing?"

Ivan stood and leaned over the pot, then took the ladle and scooped out some precious liquid and poured it in one of the cups. He handed the cup to Katia.

She parted her blanket with one hand and took the offered cup and sipped the life-saving liquid. She made a sound that originated deep in her throat, a moan of pleasure that made Ivan's hair on the back of his neck stand at attention. "Ivan, this is *so* delicious and satisfying. Thank you."

He gave a quick nod and turned to get himself a cup of water. She was right. The water was heavenly. He was filled with hope. They had water, they had heat, although Ivan didn't know how much propane was left in the tank. The fear of running out brought him back to reality. He needed to start a fire in the wood stove to be able to conserve propane for cooking. Then and only then would he be able to relax.

But not yet. He needed to wait till he had feeling in his hands before wielding the axe. The stack of firewood out on the porch was not chopped into kindling, and to start a good fire, he needed kindling.

He topped off her cup and sat down next to her again. "How do you feel?"

"All things considering, pretty good. How about you?"

"Same. I'm hoping my toes don't have frostbite. They're still numb. How's your foot?"

"It aches a little. I wish it was numb like my toes, but it's not."

"And your back?"

"Just another bother to me. Did you hurt anything when you fell down the drop off into the water?"

"Just my pride."

She let out a sigh and dropped her head. "I shouldn't have moved when the car stopped. If not, I wouldn't have fallen into the water."

"I'm glad you moved away. Besides, I fell into the water, too."

Katia sat a little straighter and turned her body to face Ivan. "Ivan, thank you. Truly. If it weren't for you . . . I wouldn't be here. I wouldn't be alive."

How could he respond to that? He felt glad she was alive, too, but something else gnawed at him. He didn't just want her gratitude. He wanted her to care about him, as a person, not just as a protector. Learning about her past, her determination, her strengths, had bloomed a vast amount of respect. He enjoyed being around her, more than just to save her. She made him feel better about himself.

Ivan squashed all those thoughts, believing nothing would ever come from them, and instead said, "I'm happy to help." He stood and checked the water again. Then he inspected his toes and hers for off-coloring. "Your toes have normal color."

"That's good, right?"

"Yes. Mine are white. That's not."

"Is it frostbite?"

"Possibly. I'm going to soak them in warm water." First, Ivan took the empty bucket and went outside for more snow. Then he emptied the melted snow into another pan large enough to dunk his feet. He refilled the melting pot with the new snow and sat on the chair, positioning his feet in the water. "It feels hot, but I know it's not." He bent forward and dipped his fingers in the water.

"Wouldn't they warm faster over the oven?"

"Actually, that can be dangerous. Where my fingers and toes are numb, I wouldn't be able to tell if I was burning the skin."

"Oh, that makes sense. I really hope you don't have frostbite."

"Me too."

"Why don't you have one of those heaters here like you have in your bedroom?"

"The cabin wiring needs to be upgraded. We had one here, but it kept tripping the circuit, so we took it home."

"When are you going to upgrade?"

"It's on the list. Kind of like the completion of the floor and trapdoor in my closet. That only got finished because we needed it. This cabin is not a priority."

"That's too bad for us."

"I talked to my dad about updating the cabin and he said I could spearhead the project after you . . ." he trailed off.

"After I what?"

"Move on." Ivan hated saying the words out loud. He felt a slight flush of excitement when she dipped her chin to her chest, apparently not happy at the idea of leaving either. Did that mean something?

He sat with his feet in the water for a few more minutes, then stood and made them both cups of broth, with her help to unwrap the cubes.

She clasped her hands around the mug and breathed in the

steam with her eyes closed. "This smells like a feast."

After about an hour of sipping warm liquid and breathing in the steam, their shaking bodies were better under control.

He turned off the three burners to conserve propane. "I'll hang up our clothes so they can dry and see if there's anything for us to wear in the meantime."

Ivan returned to the bedroom and pulled the sheets off the bed. He dropped his blanket and wrapped the sheet around him like a toga with one shoulder and arm uncovered. He grabbed his blanket and took an extra sheet out to Katia. "Here. You can wrap this around your body, like I did, then cover it with the blanket. I'm going to go chop some firewood."

He slipped his feet into his shoes and went outside to the wood shed. The cold felt good, oddly enough. It meant he was warming up. He pulled the axe off the hook and chose a small, dry log. The wood cracked apart nicely with a single swing, confirming the log would make great kindling. He went to work splintering off small pieces, then splitting larger logs to feed the fire. While chopping, his mind wandered to Katia's story of childhood and her mother's death. She didn't deserve all that pain. The anger which rose within him helped him split large logs clean with one swing.

He hauled the wood inside and built a fire in the wood stove. Once a strong blaze burned, he turned off the gas oven and helped Katia into the room. Gathering all the blankets, pillows, and couch cushions, he made a comfortable area on the floor in front of the stove so they could be near the heat.

Katia laid down on the make-shift bed while she stifled a yawn. "What's going to happen to us, Ivan?"

"What do you mean?"

"Will someone find us here?"

He pulled a blanket across her, then stood. "There's a phone. I'll call home after a couple days, if no one comes for us."

She propped herself up on her elbow. "A phone? Why don't you call for help now?"

"That could expose our location if the call was traced. We're vulnerable enough as it is. We'll wait."

"For how long?"

"For as long as the food holds out or until they find us."

She paused, then asked while yawning, "A phone? But not running water?"

"Phone lines are easier to install and don't have to be

winterized."

She laid back against the pillows. "This cabin could be so much more."

"Hey, you're not telling me anything new. I'm going to get a bit more wood to make sure we don't run out during the night."

When he came back inside with the first armload of wood, he found her fast asleep. He stared at her, peaceful, safe. He wanted her to be that way always.

After stoking the fire with a few more pokes, he crawled into bed next to her. She moaned in her sleep, draped an arm across him, and a smile touched the edges of her mouth.

Once again, he brushed a few strands of hair off her forehead, admiring her face in the glow of the fire. He placed his own hand on top of her arm, meaning to move it so she wouldn't feel uncomfortable when she awoke, but he felt so warm and sleepy that instead he drifted off.

CHAPTER 11

Ekaterina

Ekaterina awoke to the clatter of dishes and pots in the kitchen area. Ivan was already up and going. She lay for a moment and thought about the events from the day before, taking note that her fingers and toes felt normal. The temperature inside the cabin was warm with the fire Ivan had so diligently tended to the night before. From what she could hear, he was making breakfast. She reached her arm out and felt the existing warmth from his spot beneath the covers. Her skin tingled with the thought of having slept next to him and feeling content enough that she hadn't woken up through the night.

With a delicate touch, she traced the imprint of the pillow next to her. Somewhere deep inside, an idea stirred. She wished she could have awakened up with him still next to her. Her thoughts skipped around, replaying the vivid image of him undressing in front of the stove from the day before, his perfect body in all its splendor. Her own body responded with a chilling buzz that sent a shiver from head to toe. She tightened the blanket over her, relishing the feeling, but a bit afraid of it at the same time.

She sat up and stretched, then rearranged her sheet-toga before standing and hobbling into the kitchen. What she found was a simple stack of hotcakes and a pan with dark liquid she assumed was homemade syrup, based on the aroma, all on a table set with simple plates and utensils.

"Good morning, Katia," Ivan said, holding a spatula in one hand. He wore his clothing that had dried overnight. She suddenly felt under-dressed and looked around for her clothes.

"I should get dressed, too."

"After breakfast. These hotcakes won't taste as good once they've cooled."

"Okay." She pulled out a chair and sat down. Ivan looked right at home cooking over the stove. He was full of surprises.

"Have you ever had hotcakes from a restaurant?"

"Yes."

"Okay. These aren't those."

Ekaterina laughed.

Ivan brought over a fresh-from-the-pan hotcake and slid it onto her plate. "Can you tell what it is?"

"Sorry, what?"

He pointed to the odd shaped hotcake. "Can you tell what it is?"

She looked down and saw he'd made a bear-shaped hotcake. Her heart stopped cold. Memories swarmed of her mother, watching her cook, listening to her read bedtime stories, admiring her smile, hearing her father and mother argue, seeing sadness in her mother's eyes, feeling despair while looking at her mother's still form in a casket, knowing she'd never smile again.

"What's wrong, Katia?"

Ekaterina pulled her attention away from the plate and looked up at Ivan. Tears overflowed and ran down her face as a sob erupted from her throat. She buried her face in her hands and cried. Ivan's arms encircled her and pulled her close to his body.

He caressed her head. "You don't have to eat the bear. I'll make a round one."

She shook her head against his shoulder. "No, it's fine."

"I'm sorry, I thought I'd make you something to remind you of your mom. Only, I imagined a different reaction."

She gulped, trying to find words to the mess of emotions surging through her. "No one has ever done anything like this for me before, other than my parents."

"No one? I find that hard to believe."

His tone was rather accusatory. She pushed back from him with spitfire rising in her eyes.

He sputtered and continued, "What I meant was I can't believe you haven't had others in your life that have done kind things for you. I can't imagine what that would be like."

"Ivan, I think you see me as some sort of princess who had a lavish life with servants and everything. Being a 'princess' meant nothing, except that my life was full of loss. I didn't have anything special. I didn't have any power."

"I'm sorry. Really. I still . . . I don't want to upset you. I thought this would make you happy."

She glanced at the bear-shaped food on her plate, then back to Ivan. "I appreciate your effort and it means a lot to me, however, I still struggle to have happy thoughts when I think of my mother. I've never been given, nor have I taken, the opportunity to properly grieve for her. And now my father is gone, too." Her eyes watered with fresh tears. To fight against them, she sliced off a bit of hotcake with her fork and shoved it in her mouth. It tasted as good as a pancake from a box mix could taste, which wasn't good, but she wasn't going to tell Ivan that.

"I can't imagine not having my parents around."

Ekaterina heard the fear in his voice. "I'm sure they are okay."

"I hope so." He shoveled his own mouthful of food and chewed vigorously.

As they sat at the small table eating their breakfast, Ekaterina asked, "Why doesn't your family fix up this cabin and house Crossers here?"

"My dad says it's too isolated being on a dead-end road. It would be too risky to be cornered here."

"What if some intensive upgrades were made to make it more secure?"

"Like what?"

"Reinforced exterior walls, to start. That would help insulate from the cold. Cement walls would be even better. I think there should be a few weeks' worth of food and necessities, too. Perimeter monitoring like cameras and trip wires would help."

"Sounds kind of like a bomb shelter."

"That's not a bad thought. If someone could hide for two weeks or perhaps longer, it would be a huge security comfort."

Ivan paused, also gazing around the room. His eyes rested at last on Ekaterina's face. "And what about you? Would two weeks be enough time?"

Suddenly the cakes felt heavy in her gut. "Probably not. Boris won't stop until he has found me, dead or alive." She straightened up. "But not all your Crossers are so directly involved with the dictator like I am. One thing's for sure, the whole crossing system will need to change and become more secure, or else the Crosser homes will disappear altogether. Families like yours are constantly in danger. You need better ways to safely move Crosser's where they can stay for longer periods of time, so that the families aren't in as much danger."

"I agree."

She paused. "It must be killing you not to know how your family is doing."

He scratched his fork in circles through the syrup remaining on his plate. "Yes. But it's unlike Boris's men to harm the people housing Crossers. They are Svobodia citizens, and technically the Bregotian patrol has no jurisdiction here. And our police stay neutral unless the patrol breaks the law, like raiding a home."

Ekaterina squirmed in her seat. "Ivan, I hate to interrupt, but I need to use the restroom."

"Oh, right. It's outside. You'll want to get dressed and put on your shoe. Your clothing is in the bedroom. Here, I'll help you in there so you can change."

He offered his arm to her and she stood from her chair. The toga sheet covering her naked body seemed plenty last night, but now in the daylight, with Ivan fully clothed, she felt exposed. He didn't attempt to wrap his arm around her waist like he'd done in the past. Instead, he let her use his arm and body as her own support while she hopped to the bedroom.

He said, once she was in the room, "Do you need my help dressing?" His tone had dropped, almost to a husky whisper.

Her eyes hesitantly met his and she felt the need to clear her throat. "Uh, no, I think I've got this. I'll call for you when I'm ready."

Ivan closed the door and she let out her breath slowly. She heard him clearing the dishes while she slipped into her clothing, her full bladder screaming at her the whole time. She hobbled over to the door and called for Ivan.

After he'd helped her to the outhouse—an experience like none she'd ever experienced, cold wood and all—they came back inside the cabin. She shivered a little and said, "Ivan, it's a little cold in here. Can we start the fire again?"

"I don't think it's good idea to have smoke coming out of a cabin that's supposed to be empty, not during daylight hours, anyway. How about you huddle around the oven until you warm up, and then we'll make another fire tonight. For now, I'm going outside to check the perimeter because, you know, we don't have the fancy cameras or trip wires yet."

Ekaterina sat by the oven for a little while after Ivan left the cabin, thinking about his attempt to cheer her up with the shaped hotcakes. She appreciated that he had listened and remembered what she told him about her mother and wished her reaction had been better. But she'd had no control over the flood of emotions that rushed to the surface when she saw what he'd made for her. The more she thought about it, she realized he handled her melt down quite maturely. He could have become offended, or possibly downplayed her emotions, but he didn't.

After she'd warmed up, she turned the oven off to conserve propane, then searched through the cupboards and found some hygiene supplies. She used some of the water to wash her body and freshen up, bringing a renewed sense of self in doing so. For the first time in four months, she felt independent—well, mostly.

Ekaterina moved over to the window and peered through a slit in the curtains. She couldn't see Ivan. What she saw was a peaceful world blanketed in white, devoid of conflict, political agendas, torture, and misery. She could live here permanently, with Ivan by her side. She wished, anyway. She didn't view Ivan as a hinderance to her independence, but a support. He wanted her to oversee her own life, make her own decisions and consequences. He would prefer to stand beside her, not in front or behind.

Her mind recalled Jovan. He wanted to help her in her dire situation, and help her he had. She would never forget him for everything he'd done for her, and for being her only friend inside the palace. Ivan, on the other hand, wanted to help her live life as a free person. Other thoughts went through her mind as she sat at the window, like how she wanted to operate her own Crosser house someday. She had to do something to fight against the tyrannical reign of Boris Kochev.

But first, she herself had to be free of him.

Ivan

As Ivan approached the cabin after checking the surrounding area, he saw Katia standing at the window, wrapped in a blanket, and his heart leapt into his throat. Would he be able to properly protect her? Would they be able to survive?

He didn't know how to navigate around her traumatic past and unknown future—she was, after all, a princess. He shook his head to try and pull his thoughts together. The princess title was just that: a title. She had reminded him over breakfast when he'd so eloquently shoved his foot in his mouth. Her life hadn't been any more privileged than his. In fact, he'd wager he'd had the better life, even if her last four months weren't considered.

Once inside the cabin, Katia asked, "Any sign of others?"

"No. We're alone. I walked halfway down the road and didn't see any tire tracks or footprints."

"Are your feet okay? You haven't mentioned anything."

"Yes. They're fine. I don't ever want to become that cold again."

"I second that." She pointed to the wash basin on the table. "I found some face and body soap and I washed up. You could do that too, if you'd like. There's fresh water."

"Are you saying I stink?"

"Well, I stunk. So, it's highly likely you do, too. Besides, it felt great to clean up."

He wiggled his eyebrows and dipped his chin. "You just want to see me naked, again."

She let out an exasperated sound and limped to the couch. "Here, I'll move out of eyeshot."

Ivan immediately regretted his flip comment and was about to apologize, but she spoke first, changing the subject. "Would you tell me more about your family, Ivan?"

"What do you want to know?" he began taking off his shirts.

"Your grandma is intriguing. What's her history?"

"Well, I grew up on my Grandma's stories. She was born in Toparti, back when this part of the country belonged to Bregot. She was one of the first women to work with King Dimitar and his security task force. Her position dealt with finding threats to the throne. She felt the Army General as a threat, but King Dimitar refused to believe her." Ivan added some body wash to the water in the basin and swished it around.

"Let me guess. Aleksandar Kochev was the General?"

He drowned a washcloth in the soapy water, then wrung it out and began washing his body. "Yes. Aleksandar advised King Dimitar that selling the top portion of Bregot to Svobodia would be in the best interests of the country, but covertly to the governors and leaders, he degraded the king for choosing to sell off the north section. My grandmother tried to alert the king to Aleksandar's behavior, but King Dimitar didn't believe her. Once it became obvious Aleksandar was feeding the king lies about her and her intentions, she resigned from her role and moved back to Toparti. She'd be the first to tell you she's always regretted throwing in the towel and that she wished she would have remained in Bregot to be a voice against Aleksandar's lies. I know she still feels she could have done more on the other side of the border."

"I don't know. She'd probably have been executed by Aleksandar once he took over."

"She feels she could have prevented the coup."

"Well, there's no way to know if that's how things would have turned out."

"What she did instead was convince as many people as she could to escape Bregot and move to Toparti before the border closed. And, once Aleksandar had successfully ousted the king, he did just that—closed the border. Aleksandar began televising executions of traitors and expatriates and hunting down rebel groups. That was probably the time frame when he began the Cvetkovski hunt you spoke of. My grandfather, Ivan Lazarov—I was named after him—was one of the victims of the dissident raids. He was killed protecting my grandma."

"I'm sorry, Ivan."

He put on his shirts and joined Katia, choosing to sit on the floor in front of her. "You don't need to be sorry. He died before my parents married. My grandma was the target, but he took the bullet. She immediately took her situation to the capital of Svobodia and was responsible for getting the new laws put into place for Toparti and Severni. Up to that point, this was kind of a neutral zone. People didn't really belong to Svobodia, but at the same time they no longer belonged to Bregot either. She raised awareness of how the government of Bregot was killing new Svobodia citizens.

"Svobodia still didn't know exactly what to do, but they came up with a basic set of laws that prevented the Bregotian patrols from operating in Svobodia. Those laws should have been in place from the get-go. New police officers were brought in and Aleksandar's presence in Toparti became less and less. Anyone found housing Crossers was arrested."

"Did your family stop?"

"Have you met my grandma? She had my dad dig a tunnel so they could continue to help Crossers. My dad had just finished his degree in civil engineering and was newly married to my mom. He designed the tunnel and dug it by himself. My mom and grandma hauled the dirt and rocks out bucketful by bucketful for months.

They hauled it by truck to the hills to dump. They didn't want anyone to know what they were doing.

"My grandma was pleased with their new Crosser room and escape tunnel. She felt her family would be safe continuing their business. She had no intention of ever quitting. Not even when Aleksandar began assassinating anyone who had the same tenacity as she did. Boris took over control of Bregot at age thirty-one when Aleksandar died. Grandma didn't know a whole lot about Boris, only that he was Aleksandar's son, so there was no reason to believe he would be any different. She's always believed that a man with complete power will eventually misuse it."

Katia asked, "Do you think every man wants to be powerful?"

"I don't know."

"Do you?"

"I don't want power like that, I just want to leave a mark."

"On what?"

"On the world. Don't you want to do that, too?"

She looked down and pulled her blanket tighter. "I just want to disappear."

"Katia, we might only have one life, one chance to make a mark. Why not have that be something outstanding? Why run from that?"

"You don't know what I've been through over there, Ivan. You don't know why I ran. So, don't judge me."

Oh boy! He couldn't say anything right. "I'm not judging you, or at least I don't mean to come across like that. And, you're right, I don't know fully what you've been through, but I have a pretty good visual of what your life has been like." He motioned with his hand from her head to her feet. "I'm only suggesting that you look deep and see what your strengths are and how you can use them for the betterment of you and those around you."

"Strengths? Okay," —she stiffened her posture and challenged him— "you first. What are your strengths, Ivan?"

He didn't expect that to be her response. He wiped his face with one hand while he gathered his thoughts. "Hm. I see that I'm my best when I'm helping you. I see I was selfish, probably still am, but I'm improving. You've helped me see a bigger world than what I accepted before, an appalling world I don't know I would have ever seen, if not for you. I think more can be done to fight against the Kochevs. Not enough people are concerned, but that can change one person at a time, beginning with me. I guess, deep down, my parents taught me to feel this way, I just didn't want to accept it. Now I do." He pointed to her. "Your turn."

She said, "Yeah, but, maybe—"

He held his hand up and cut her off. "No 'yeah, buts.'"

"What if—"

"Nope. 'What ifs' are not allowed here at the cabin either."

"Are you making the rules as you go?"

"Pretty much." He smiled.

She let out a sigh and leaned forward, resting her elbows on her knees, her hands extended forward and clasped. Her blanket hung off her shoulders. "Ivan, I don't know what my strengths are. I felt like ending my life was the only thing in my control."

"It's important to feel in control of your life?"

"Yes."

"Katia, even if everything around you is out of control, you still control your own happiness. Everything can be taken from you, but you can still find something to be happy about, if you want."

"You've never been in that situation before, so it's easy for you to say those words."

"You're right. I haven't, at least not to the extreme that you have. I like to think I'd be able to find something to be happy about, or at least slightly optimistic if nothing else." He took her hands in his and looked her deep in the eyes. "Promise me you'll think about your strengths."

"Okay. I promise." Her fingers trembled in his grasp and her breathing quickened.

Ivan bent forward and brought their clasped hands to his mouth and gently kissed hers. "I'm hungry. Are you?"

"A little. What is there to eat?"

"Not a whole helluva lot." He stood and walked toward the kitchen area. "How about we order a pizza?"

She chuckled. "Yeah, right. Make sure there's extra pepperoni on mine."

Ivan jokingly grabbed the phone off the hook to play out the wishful thinking of ordering a pizza. He put the receiver to his ear and said, "Hello, Geno's? I'd like to order . . ." He froze. Dread slid down his spine. He didn't hear a dial tone. "Damnit!" he muttered before he could measure his words.

"What's wrong?" Katia asked.

"The phone is dead." He clicked the phone cradle button

several times to see if that would help. Still no dial tone. He checked the plug on the base of the phone and followed it to the jack on the wall. Everything looked right.

Katia didn't respond.

He berated himself for not checking the line when they first arrived. He shouldn't have counted on the phone working in the first place. "I'm going to have to track the wire outside and try to figure out the problem."

Ivan drank down a glass of water and grabbed a stick of jerky, then headed out the door. The storm from the night before had cleared out, but dark billowing clouds to the north threatened to interfere with his efforts to get the phone working.

As Ivan followed the line along the road that led to the main highway, he thought about what other options they had for survival. Maybe they'd have to hike out to the highway and flag down a car for transportation if he couldn't fix the phone. That was too risky, though. Yet, there wasn't much food in the cabin and even with rationing, they'd run out of options within a few days.

Up ahead, Ivan saw that a tree branch had fallen on the phone line. He'd walked past it earlier and didn't even notice the line was down. He trudged into the snow and began pulling on the wire to free it. Once he'd managed that, he moved over to the other end and began pulling the same way, only this line wouldn't budge. He pulled gently, not wanting to snap the cold line any shorter. Still, no luck.

With one hand on the wire and the other moving snow out of the way, he followed the wire to where the tree branch held it trapped. If he could move the branch, maybe he could free the wire. He tugged and yanked on the top end of the branch but only succeeded in snapping twigs off. He'd need to move to the other end. That's when he saw the bigger problem. A pine tree had fallen across the branch, pinning it down. Ivan would have to go back to the cabin and get the axe and chop the branch apart to release the wire.

He walked back to the cabin, hands and feet cold, stomach aching with hunger.

When he entered, he found Katia hovering over a large pile of bags, boxes and cans from the cupboards, doing an inventory. She glanced up at him.

"You've been busy here," he said, stomping the snow from his shoes.

"It gave me something to do. Did you find the problem?"

"Yeah. Tree took the line down. It's stuck. I'll need a few things to fix it."

"Oh."

"Have you come across any black tape?"

"You mean electricians tape?"

Impressed she knew what he was talking about, he answered, "Yes."

She hopped over to a drawer and pulled out a small black roll. "That's the only one I've seen."

"What about a pocketknife or plyers?"

She reached inside the drawer again and produced both.

"Do you have a chainsaw in there, too?" he joked.

She grinned then shook her head. "Ivan, you should wait a while and warm up before going back out there. It's starting to snow again."

"If we're going to get out of here, we need the phone."

"Yeah, but it's not like we're going to starve to death by tomorrow." She waved her hand over the food pile.

"Right now, there's not much snow and a car could drive through it, but what if we get slammed with snow tonight? Fixing the phone line is crucial at this point. I need to find out what my father wants us to do. Should we hike out to the road? Should we stay put? I don't know."

She raised her hands in front of her body. "Okay, Ivan. I understand."

He took a deep cleansing breath.

Katia moved closer to him. "How far away is the break?"

"About a hundred yards down the road, just out of sight of the cabin."

"Okay. I'll make us some food and have some warm water ready for you when you get back."

Ivan nodded and shoved the knife and plyers in his pocket. He went back outside, grabbed the axe, and headed toward the downed tree. Snowflakes swirled threateningly around his head as he thought about Katia's insistence and acceptance of their situation.

He *must* keep her safe.

Ivan chopped at the branch and separated it from the rest. Then he carefully pried it up and freed the phone line. He let out a heavy breath and retrieved the other end of the wire and began stripping the insulation off to expose the tiny wires inside. Then he twisted the two ends together and secured it with tape to waterproof the connection. He gathered the axe and headed back to the cabin through the heavy snowfall.

He found Katia sitting at the table.

He walked directly to the phone and picked it up.

Nothing.

He wanted to slam the phone down, wanted to shout profanities at nothing and no one, just to make himself feel better. Instead, he hung his head down and clenched his jaw, inhaling slowly to calm down. He set the phone in the cradle and turned to Katia only to find her right beside him. Her expression was tinged with pity. He didn't want pity. He wanted success.

"There might be another break in the line," Ivan spoke his thoughts aloud. "Maybe I crossed the wires when I taped it up. I need to go check."

"No," Katia said forcefully. "You need to warm up." She placed both hands on his chest and guided him to the oven where a chair was positioned in front of the stove. "Sit down and take those shoes off."

"Listen, Katia—"

"No, you listen! I need you to be functional more than we need a dial tone! Now, sit."

He sat.

Ekaterina

Getting Ivan to stop and sit felt like moving a mountain. But now she could say she'd moved a mountain. He'd been gone for more than four hours between his two trips to fix the line. His hands shook with cold and his lips were void of color, which worried her. She was right, though. She needed him to be well and strong because she couldn't be at the present.

She sat on the floor and helped him take his shoes and socks off. His fingers were too numb, again. His toes were white and felt like ice cubes. She stood and grabbed the wash basin and set it by his feet, then poured room temperature water in, and he lifted his feet and she pushed up his pants before he set them in the water.

"Let's take your shirts off. Your pants are dry, except for below your knees."

He helped her as best as he could as she removed his arms and pulled his shirts off. Then she opened the oven further and pulled out a turkey roasting pan.

"You baked?" Ivan quipped.

"I baked you a blanket." She removed the lid and pulled the warm wool blanket from the pan and flipped it open, wrapping it around his shoulders. She took the next blanket that she'd folded at the ready and put it in the pot, set the lid on top, and put it in the oven. "I was so comforted by all the 'fresh from the dryer' blankets you kept putting on me that first day, I thought 'how could I replicate that' for you?"

"I think you nailed it perfectly. Thank you, Katia."

She bent forward, her face in front of his. "You're welcome, Ivan." She kissed his lips quickly and pulled back a little to look at him. His eyes were still closed, seemingly lost in his own thoughts.

He opened his eyes and said in a husky voice, "You drive me crazy."

"Sorry?"

He looked down. "I shouldn't have said that."

She lightly touched one finger under his chin and pulled his gaze back up to hers. "You did it first." Then she kissed him again. Both hands cupped his jawline. She swung her leg over his and sat down on his lap. She felt his hands wrap behind her and run all over her back. One hand moved up behind her head and buried into her hair, directing the angle of her mouth on his. His fingers felt freezing, but she hardly noticed. The warmed blanket slid off his shoulders. Without breaking contact, she grasped the edges of the blanket and pulled it back over his shoulders.

His mouth left hers and trailed down her neck, leaving kisses as he went. She was in heaven, in the arms of Ivan Lazarov, the man who pulled her out of the frozen lake and nursed her back to life and opened his world to her. She never wanted to be without him, never wanted to be away from him. She loved everything about this moment.

A loud crash on the porch outside pulled her out of heaven and back into the real world.

Ivan jerked forward and flipped his head in the direction of the door. With little effort, he lifted her quickly off his lap and set her on the floor, pressed a finger to his lips, and then moved slowly toward the door, leaving wet footprints on the floor as he stepped.

Ekaterina's heart raced horribly fast. Who was outside? Had

they been found?

"It's a deer, Katia." He let out a heavy puff of air and dropped his head, arching his shoulders. Then he straightened up and looked like he was regrouping his thoughts.

Ekaterina watched as he slowly turned his head in her direction.

"We can't let that happen again," he said. "Not now. We're not safe. You're not safe."

"I shouldn't have—"

He approached her in three quick strides, taking her hands. "When the time is right and I know you're safe, this will happen if you still want it."

"Why would you even say the word 'if?' Of course I want you!"

"We're on the same page, but I can't do this right now and put you at risk. I'm really glad that was only a deer, though. I was brought back to reality, harmlessly."

"What if I'm never safe, Ivan?" She didn't want to ask the question, but it had been on her mind all day.

" 'Never' is a really long time. I'll do everything in my power to get you to a safe place, not because I want to move forward with you, but because I want you to be safe." He sat down on the chair again and reinserted his feet into the tub of water. Then he pulled the wool blanket over his shoulders. "We're going to get out of this, Katia. One way or the other. I promise."

She wanted to say that promising her safety wasn't in his control, but she didn't. Instead, she simply appreciated his devotion and determination which fueled her own.

After a few hours of warming Ivan's body temperature, feeding him warm liquids, and creating a weird tuna fish sauce over pancake biscuits, they sat on the couch in the front room with a warm fire burning in the wood stove.

"Ivan, what are you going to do with your life after I'm relocated?"

"I thought maybe I'd go north and attend the university, but that was before I met you."

"Me?"

"I draw so much strength from you and your bravery," Ivan complimented her.

"I wouldn't call it bravery. I did what I thought was the only choice."

"Yes, but you acted. You tried to get out of the life that was forced on you in Bregot. You are covered with scars of defiance. You could have perfect, blemish-free skin if you only gave in to the demands placed on you."

Ekaterina felt a knot form in her gut. "You think I don't dwell on that every day? My father could still be alive if only I had said yes to Vladimir. No way! I would never marry Vladimir! But now my father is dead because of my stubbornness."

"Why do you say that?"

"Because when my father came to me and said Vladimir had asked for my hand in marriage, I said I didn't want to marry him. My father took my answer back and was dead soon after."

"Your father's death was not your fault, Katia. Your bravery to say no to the most influential person in the whole country is what motivates me."

"But if I'd said yes, he'd still be alive."

"You don't know that. Maybe he would have died anyway, or maybe Boris would have used him to make you marry Vladimir. Your bravery to defy the wishes of a dictator and his son is monumental."

She hung her head. "I still disagree about it being bravery. It was just common sense. I've heard Vladimir speak of genocide as if it is a reasonable solution to subdue the people, a small price to pay to keep the people under control. I also saw how he treated his mother and how Boris treated his wife. She is a nobody. In fact, I only saw her a couple of times while I was at the palace. I didn't want to become her. I didn't want to become the mother of the next horrible man to take the throne of power. I'd rather be fighting against them."

"Bravery. I rest my case."

"So, you didn't really answer my question. What are you going to do with the rest of your life?"

"I want to spend the rest of my life defying the dictator. I want to be current on all developments in Bregot, to know all about the resistance fighters, and help them if I can. The dictatorship must be brought down, but if I can't bring it down, at least I can help people escape it."

"We want the same thing then." She looked at his lips as she said these words. He had knocked down the last remaining walls around her heart, what was left of them anyway. Knowing the way he truly felt made him all the more attractive to her. She realized that the moment he'd opened up on the first day and shared his fears with her.

She looked up to his eyes and felt her face heat up. Her heart raced so hard she thought it might explode right out of her chest. His eyes were on hers, and his intent in his eyes. He leaned forward and cupped her cheeks with his hands. Gently he pulled her face toward his. Her mouth parted and her eyes closed in anticipation.

She waited for his kiss, but it didn't come. Instead, he pulled her into an embrace and leaned his head on hers.

"Katia, I don't know what I'm feeling for you."

"What do you mean?"

"I don't ever want to lose you. It scared me terribly when I saw you slipping away in the creek, and I had to fight like hell to keep you with me. I want you with me. I want to be with you. There's a difference between those two statements. I would never have thought it possible to fall for someone in only a matter of days, but . . . I mean . . ."

"Maybe you are only drawn to me because of my situation? You saw my injuries and took pity on me. Is that it? You feel sorry for me?" She looked up at him, still in his embrace.

"I do feel sorry for you. I want to protect you. I want to hold you close every night like I already have. With you my life has purpose."

"But Ivan, there's more to life than just holding someone every night and protecting them through the day."

"I want to learn everything about you and show you my world. I've lived a carefree life, exploring and enjoying nature. I want to do that with you. This summer I'm going to show you the magical place where the creek we just about froze in falls into the canyon. I also want to learn what you like and share in your passions. I've had no desire to be close to anyone till now, till you, till I pulled you out of the hole in my closet and you landed on top of me. When that happened, my mind said to me, 'There you are.' "

She stared into his eyes and smiled. His expression of his feelings was all she needed to hear. "Ivan, I want to learn about you, too, and share everything with you. I don't know what that may mean to us, but want to explore all of it."

He swiftly took her mouth in a kiss, stopping her heart altogether. Dreams, aspirations, fulfillment all flooded into her. She wanted every moment to be like this one. Her hands and arms wrapped around his neck, and she deepened the kiss. His hands urgently caressed her back and neck in an uncontrollable fervor. She moved her lips to his cheek and back to his ear, kissing a trail along the way. She began moving her lips down his neck.

He whispered something, and she noticed his body had tensed up. Looking up at his face, she saw his strained expression.

"Katia, we can't do this, not here, not like this." He ran his thumb tenderly down the side of her cheek. "Don't get me wrong—I'd love to—but we can't. Not until you're safe."

Ekaterina sighed, knowing he was right. "Will you just hold me tonight?"

They laid back and he held her close. "We're going to find a way to free you from this unwanted obligation. Then you and I can enjoy life together."

CHAPTER 12

Anton

The phone rang, startling Anton. He picked up the receiver and answered, "Hello?"

"Hello? Who is this?"

"You called this number, man. Don't you know who you called?"

"Anton? Is that you? It's me, Ivan."

Finally! Oh, there is a God! "Yeah man, where are you?"

"Why are you at my house?"

"This whole raid thing turned the entire town crazy. My parents and yours are in the other room talking with the sheriff."

"Can you get one of them please?"

"Yeah, hang on." Anton didn't set the receiver down. He didn't have any plans to go get one of the adults in the other room. After several seconds, Anton cleared his throat and said, as if he'd just come in from the other room, "They're really busy, but your dad says to come on back home now."

"Can't he come to the phone? I really need to talk to him."

"Well, he just went out the front door with the sheriff, but hang on and I'll go try to grab him." Anton stayed silent for a good twenty seconds, cursing under his breath the whole time. If he couldn't convince Ivan to expose himself, he didn't know what he'd tell Vladimir. Anton spoke into the phone. "Ivan, he said to tell you the danger is gone and to come on home."

"The danger's gone?"

"Yeah."

"I sort of can't come back. Our car died."

"No problem, dude. I'll come get you. Where are you?"

Ivan's hesitation to respond spoke volumes. There was no trust, obviously. Finally, Ivan said, "Anton, have my dad call me when he gets back in."

"Oh, all right. What number?"

"He knows the number."

"Okay then, goodbye," Anton said and hung up the receiver. He strode into the front room where Michal, Elena, and Mira sat on the couch. He stood behind them. The two guards across from them held their automatic rifles at the ready. He had to try again to get information out of Ivan's family before Vladimir called.

"Michal, where would your son run to in the event of a raid?"

Michal said nothing.

"That was him on the phone, you know."

Michal glared at Anton and lowered his chin. His lack of cooperation didn't surprise Anton. The last couple of days had been a long, drawn-out stretch of time in defiance.

"Not going to talk? Vladimir's men won't hesitate to pick you three off one at a time to get the answer."

The guard behind Elena pressed his gun barrel against her neck. Anton tensed. He didn't want anyone to get hurt anymore.

Michal lurched forward. "Wait!"

"Where would your son take his Crosser?" Anton asked again, praying Michal would answer so they could all move on with their lives.

Michal sat back, looking defeated. "We usually run to Severni to a hotel there. Of course, it depends on the time of day where we stop to hide."

"What does that mean?"

"If it's early in the day, we drive further up the road."

"Okay then, which hotel in Severni?"

"Grand Executive."

"Room number?"

"It's a private outbuilding around the back. Blue door. But there's no guarantee he's still there."

Anton nodded to the guard to stand down. The he grabbed the phone off the table along the wall and stretched the cord to Michal. "Well, he just called from somewhere. Call him back. Tell him it's okay for me to come pick him up. You'd better sound convincing, too."

"Anton, I need my book of phone numbers."

"Ivan said you know the number to call. Doesn't sound like you need a book for that." Michal didn't make a move. "Look, Michal, I may seem young, but the only way for this to end is to give up the Crosser. She's not worth more than your family."

Anton watched as Michal exchanged glances with the two women. They nodded their approval for Michal to make the call. He dialed the number and waited. Anton moved next to him to hear.

Ivan answered, "Hello?"

"Ivan?"

"Dad, is everything okay?"

"Yes, everything's good. You can bring her back here till we can get some transportation arrangements made."

"Is it safe?"

"As safe as it will ever be."

"Dad, our car died near the cabin. We had to hike in to get out of the storm and now we're stuck here."

"I'll send Anton to come pick you up."

"Anton? Why not you?"

"I'm busy right now. I'll tell him where you are, and he'll be there in about twenty minutes. It will be all right, son. I'll see you soon." Michal hung up the phone.

Anton scooted the phone away from Michal. "Twenty minutes eh? So, he *is* at the vacation cabin."

"Yes."

"There weren't any tracks going in. I had the guard check."

"Anton, sometimes what seems to be isn't what really is."

"What do you mean?"

"Is the road the only way into the cabin?"

"Yes."

"No, it's not."

"Are you saying there is another road in?"

"No. There isn't another road, but when you're on foot, you can walk through the trees. It would seem you made a judgment based on a very narrow assessment. Have you been so narrow in your assessment of the Kochev family, too?"

Anton's breath caught in his throat. "What do you mean?"

"Do you honestly think they will let you live after you turn in Ivan?"

"You're just trying to scare me, and it won't work."

"It's too bad you won't listen, and that you've fallen for the temptation of money."

"What? You think I'm greedy? This money will save my parent's house from the bank! All those Crossers flooding into our town needing jobs, through people like you, put him out of work. Housing Crossers was the only option left to make a living in this damn town, that and the occasional reward money for returning some."

"You're playing with fire, Anton. It's not too late to get out of this unscathed. No one is hurt, no one is dead, but if you go on and finish this, it will be the end of you."

"You're wrong! Plenty of people have turned in Crossers for the reward money and they weren't killed."

"Because they weren't dealing directly with the Kochevs! Do your parents know you've compromised them?"

Anton's chest felt tight. Everything was spinning out of control. "Shut up! Or I'll have the guards shut you up."

"You haven't gone too far, Anton. You can walk away now, and no one needs to get hurt. You wouldn't be in trouble. We wouldn't turn you in or shun your family. We can help your parents save their home, just don't move forward with this foolish choice."

Anton eyed the guards, remembering the look on Vladimir's face when he threatened him with a knife. "Yeah, right. It's too late for that."

Michal gripped Anton's arm, whispering fiercely. "It's never too late. Just go alert the authorities to the situation. These guards could leave before any trouble arrived. They'd be safe, too. No one needs to get hurt. Do the right thing, Anton."

"I am. This is right for my family."

One of the guards shifted. "Let go of the kid," he ordered.

Michal released his hold. "Go on, then. Go pick up Ivan, and good luck."

Anton stormed out of the house, muttering to himself, berating Michal for not understanding his situation. All he needed to do was turn over the girl and Vladimir would give him the reward. Simple. He sped along the roads, inching toward the biggest paycheck of his life, contemplating how he would approach his father with the newfound ability to save the house. Maybe he'd just pay the bank and not tell his father what he'd done. No. Anton wanted his father and mother to know he'd turned in the Lazarov's

Crosser to help them. He felt confident they'd understand. And that they'd be proud of him.

Slowing the car in preparation to turn at the upcoming corner, Anton decided to make the call to Vladimir. He pulled over at the Crossroads Fill-up gas station on the corner and parked near the pay phone. He climbed out of his car and dropped in the necessary coins and dialed.

"You better have good news for me, Anton," Vladimir said.

"I'm on my way to pick them up. How soon can you meet me at the Crossroads Fill-up?"

"Thirty minutes."

"All right."

Anton slowly replaced the receiver on the hook after Vladimir hung up. He really hoped Ivan was in fact at the cabin and that this was not a wild goose chase. Perhaps he should have waited to call Vladimir till he knew for sure where Ivan was. Anton climbed back in his car and peeled out of the parking lot, cutting off a car as he headed west.

Ekaterina

Ekaterina and Ivan sat on the deck waiting for Ivan's friend to come pick them up. Their time at the cabin was coming to an end, however she knew her mind would replay several of the moments they shared together for a lifetime. But what lay ahead? How long would she be at Ivan's home? When would she be able to relocate north?

She glanced out to the lane as Ivan walked through the fresh snow. "Ivan, how deep is the snow? Will a vehicle be able to drive on it?"

"It's only ankle deep, so, yes. Last night's snowfall was only a couple inches."

"I'm really glad you were able to figure out the phone issue quickly."

"Me too. I should have taken a little more time when wrapping the splice so the wires didn't touch."

Anton arrived in his car with the bottom dragging on the snow and his chained wheels spinning, not usually a good vehicle for winter driving.

"Hey guys, get in before you catch your death, as my mother

always says."

Ivan slid into the center position on the front seat. He turned to help Ekaterina into the passenger side.

"Thanks for picking us up, Anton," Ivan said.

"No problem at all, man. Have you guys been here since the raid?"

"Pretty much," Ivan answered.

"Wow. Everyone was wondering what happened to you. The raids must have been successful because the military guys disappeared as quickly as they showed up—oh, and Luka resurfaced."

"Really? Is he okay?"

"He's fine. Oh, damn!"

"What?" Ivan and Ekaterina asked in unison.

"Ah, it's nothing serious. I only need to get gas soon. I don't think I'll make it all the way back on this tank."

Ivan leaned over to look at the gas gauge. "It looks fine to me."

"I overfilled the tank a while back and it messed up my gauge. Empty sits at about a quarter of a tank, now. We'll stop at the Crossroads Fill-up."

The drive there was rather quiet with minimal talking, and Ekaterina felt unnerved. She caught Anton glancing over at her multiple times on the way down the mountain, which didn't help either.

"Here we are." Anton pulled up so that the passenger side of his car was next to the gas pump. He exited the car and began filling the gas tank.

"I don't like this, Ivan." Ekaterina's voice shook slightly as she stared toward the front doors of the convenience store.

"I'm sure there's nothing to be worried about. He'll be done before you know it."

"Ivan, I love that you trust people, but something doesn't feel right about this." She stared out the front window at the large Modry Mountains in front of them. Bregot lay on the other side of the range. Her old life was so near her skin prickled.

"Don't worry. Everything's going to be okay."

Ekaterina heard Anton attach the cap and snap the fuel door shut. He walked in front of the car, his fingers tapping the hood slowly as he passed by. His eyes traveled to hers briefly, then he continued toward the building to pay for the gas. She followed his movement with an increasing sense of unease filling her gut. She watched as Anton pulled open the glass door of the gas station. A man wearing a crisp black suit exited and handed Anton an envelope. Another person came into view causing Ekaterina to shriek, "Vladimir!"

A trap! A well-executed ambush, and Anton was behind it.

"Oh no!" Ivan instantly slid over behind the wheel and reached for where the car keys should be, except Anton had taken them with him.

Soldiers swarmed around the car with guns drawn.

Ekaterina slammed her fist on the door lock before anyone could pull the door handle. Her window was smashed with the butt of military rifle. Ekaterina screamed as glass pelted her body and a gloved hand opened her door. Ivan's unlocked door was pulled open at the same time, and they were both dragged out in opposite directions.

Ekaterina fought hard, only her fight wasn't even remotely fair. Her petite frame and lightweight body were no match for her assailants. She did manage to poke her finger in one man's eye and leave a trail of bloody, lacerated skin down another man's cheek from her fingernails. She tried stomping on toes with her good foot but couldn't do much damage to steel-toed boots.

She watched Ivan fight valiantly, successfully landing hard punches and kicks. But there was no hope in winning. There were too many of them. Then she saw Ivan taken to the ground, and she screamed his name. Simultaneously, she was forced down on her stomach, the right side of her head pressed into the snow and gravel. Her head was held firmly while someone's knee restrained her shoulders.

"Ivan!" she screamed again.

Ivan fought with the five men restraining him to turn his head and look at her for a fraction of a second before someone kicked him in the face, knocking him out.

Ekaterina's face hurt from the freezing snow and her shoulder felt like it was dislocated, but it was nothing compared to the ache of watching Ivan get kicked in the face. He went unconscious immediately, and she cried. She cried even harder as she watched the limited-viewing scene play out under the car. Several booted feet began kicking her precious Ivan in the gut. She screamed for mercy for his sake and was comforted only by the fact that he was unconscious and couldn't feel the pain of the beating. She couldn't stand the thought that she might be responsible for another good man's death.

She heard Anton's voice yelling. "You got the girl! Leave him alone!"

Ekaterina was lifted to an upright position. She couldn't see Ivan any longer, only the men who were still pounding on him.

"Stop! Stop hurting him, please!" she begged.

"Ekaterina." Vladimir came to her side and spoke calmly, "He's an enemy of my father. Any defiance is punishable by death."

"If he dies, then I die."

"How Shakespearian of you. You've always been quite dramatic that way." Vladimir waved his arm, and the men stopped their attack on Ivan. "Now, we leave."

Ekaterina was dragged across the parking lot by two strong men. Her good foot dug into anything and everything to try to stop her advance toward the black limousine that had just arrived. She was pushed into the vehicle, and the door shut before she could get out. She turned in her seat quickly and tried to open the other door. It wouldn't open and she didn't know how to unlock it. Twisting all the way around, she peered through the back window and saw what looked like an argument between Vladimir and Ivan's friend, or more like ex-friend. Anton's arms moved animatedly as he waved an envelope in Vladimir's face. His arm movement and body language made Ekaterina suspect he'd been shortchanged, and he wanted more money. Ekaterina wished she could escape the car and help Ivan, whom she couldn't see from her vantage point. Vladimir walked away and toward the limousine.

The door opened and two guards climbed inside, sitting across from her. Then Vladimir got in. His door was closed by the guard outside the vehicle.

She instantly flew toward Vladimir with the rage of a thousand venomous vipers. She was pulled up short by the body-guard's arms around her waist. "Let me go! Let me kill him! What's the matter, Vladimir? Afraid of a girl? Can't hold your own? Had to have Daddy find me because you can't stand to be abandoned at the altar?"

"Ekaterina, shut your mouth. You're only embarrassing yourself."

"You don't like hearing what I have to say? It must be true then!"

"This little escapade has set our time schedule behind. You and I should have been married already, but if he's already had you, then I don't want you. I'd simply ask, but I can't trust your answer. So, we'll take your little boyfriend with us so that when I find out he took what was mine, I can kill him with my own hands."

"He'll always have my heart, Vladimir, and there's nothing you can do about it." She heard the distinct rip and tear sound that can only come from duct tape. She turned to look, only to be silenced by the sticky tape placed across her mouth. Her hands were also bound behind her.

"I like it when you're quiet." There was a knock on the outside of Vladimir's window. He rolled it down an inch.

"Sir, what should we do with him?"

Vladimir stared at Ekaterina for five long seconds and then turned to the man. "You know what? I've changed my mind. Kill him. I want his parents killed, too."

"No!" Ekaterina tried to scream and moved toward Vladimir, only to be stopped by the two guards. They pushed her down on her side with her face shoved into the leather upholstery. Outside, she heard two gunshots, and she was reduced to tears and sobs for Ivan.

CHAPTER 13

Ekaterina

The convoy reached the palace, and Ekaterina was placed in a secure room with no windows. She assumed it used to be an office of some sorts, now cleared of most furniture, except for an office chair and desk. Boris ordered a guard to stand right inside the door to make sure she didn't try and hurt herself. Her bindings were removed and she was undressed and clothed in a hospital gown before being locked away.

Her thoughts wandered to the little gas station and the memory of watching Ivan being beaten. Grief sunk through her body like a black hole. The gunshots ripped through her memory, almost as if she could hear them echoing through the room. Had anyone collected his body yet? Was he still lying in the parking lot? Did his parents even know, and how would they take it? Had they been killed as well?

Time passed and sobs wracked her body while the guard stood there, unmoved. The reality crashed over her. Ivan was gone. She'd never see him again, never feel him brush the strands of hair from her face. He'd risked everything for her, defying these people, just like her father had, and for what? They were both dead now, because of her.

Guilt melded with her grief and she couldn't understand why she didn't die from the blackness in her chest. She almost wished she would die, just melt away into nothingness, anything for relief.

A sliver of a memory crept into her mind. Ekaterina thought about the conversations she and Ivan had in the cabin and the promise he hoped she'd take. She promised Ivan she'd search for her strengths, that she'd try to find the happiness in any situation.

But how could she find any happiness right now?

Through watered eyes, she looked around the room at the bare surroundings, complete with the unfeeling guard by the door. Something inside her bent. All her grief and guilt twisted into something new—rage. She hated the impassive guard. She hated this palace. She hated Boris and Vladimir. It was *their* fault these people had died, not hers. They chose to discard them like collateral damage, simply to secure their prize: her.

Well, she would give them their prize. She would play the public figure bride they need, but it will cost them, just when they felt secure in their win. She intended to keep that promise to Ivan. She knew her strength: defiance. She would not let Ivan and her father's death be in vain. She would not let anyone else suffer. It was time to bring down these monsters.

Fresh tears trickled down her cheeks, but this time because she knew what she needed to do.

For Ivan.

The door opened and Ekaterina swiped at her tears. Two more guards entered along with Boris Kochev and Dr. Ilievski. Boris walked over to her.

"Ekaterina, I'm so happy you are safe," Boris said, pacing in front of her. "I see you've recovered completely from your attempts to starve yourself, so much so that you were able to pull the wool over all our eyes and flee. I hope you've come to realize you can't escape your duty to this country."

Ekaterina said nothing.

"Naturally, this belligerent behavior on your part won't go without punishment. Judging on your overall healthy appearance, I'd say that punishment should be soon." Boris scratched his head and looked to the side for a moment. "Although, Vladimir probably wouldn't want a broken bride, so we'll wait till after the wedding."

Ekaterina inhaled a deep relieving breath.

Boris narrowed his eyes at her. "Oh, make no mistake, you'll get what's coming to you, whether by me or by Vladimir."

Her mind raced. She looked over to Dr. Ilievski and envisioned him tending to her soon-to-be wounds and fresh injuries at the hands of Boris. She didn't know if she could handle the beatings again. Could she avoid them? Change Boris's mind? Somehow, she needed to convince him not to beat her anymore. Then, her mind opened with possibilities inspired by Dr. Ilievski. She would set her boundaries, play by the rules, even go as far as appear like she was cooperating—all things she'd watched Jovan do in the past few months. His example of how to navigate around Boris while living under the palace roof was motivational to Ekaterina.

Taking a deep breath, and calming her voice to sound submissive and compliant, she addressed Boris, "Sir, you have every right to be angry at my belligerence. What I did was stupid and almost got me killed. I know now that I've taken for granted everything you've offered me here at the palace." She kept her eye contact with Boris so he'd believe she was being truthful, and so she could decipher his reaction to her words. Presently, he looked confused and disarmed. She continued, "I shouldn't have risked my life for the idea of a life of my own. What I found was far from it. Out there is only fear and tough-living. I will be nothing and no one out there. I never realized how much you really protected me. Here, at the palace, is the only place I can truly make a life for myself. My role is to help you and your son with the people of this country.

Boris gently rubbed his knuckles, his brow furrowed. "This is a change from the last time you were here. You wanted to take your own life."

"I understand what you were trying to tell me, but the beatings . . . I could not handle them. They didn't help. Only seeing the outside world, outside of this country, what sort of life they have, made me see the truth. Bregot is lucky to have you taking care of them."

She wanted to vomit after saying the words, but she steeled herself against what her body felt.

Boris's mouth opened, but he didn't speak immediately. He obviously didn't know how to react to her admission.

Finally, he broke the silence. "Am I hearing you correctly? Are you ready to marry Vladimir and will do so willingly, to take your place in front of the public, to show them a unified front?"

"I won't lie," she began, choosing her words carefully. "I don't like Vladimir and would choose not to marry him, but I understand what our union would represent for the people."

"That I can believe. My son is not always . . ." he trailed off, as if catching himself revealing too much. "If you have such a distaste for him, what about an heir?"

Ekaterina saw the gleam in his eye, the hunger. *So, this is what he truly wants. A child he can control. I can't let that happen.*

But how?

She glanced over at Dr. Ilievski, her mind turning wheels faster than she could keep up. A jolt hit her and she returned her focus onto Boris. "We will do this practically. Artificial insemination." Dr. Ilievski's shoulders relaxed and she dared to hope what she planned would be true. If he performed the procedure, he could make sure she never got pregnant. The ruse could buy her a month or more if Jovan lied about her being pregnant, giving her time to escape or bring down Boris and his son.

Boris frowned.

Dr. Ilievski chimed in. "There is a higher chance of success, sir, and we can test sooner to see if the process worked, instead of waiting the entire month."

"Why should I agree to any of this?"

Ekaterina prepared herself for her final statements. Everything depended on her next words. "You need me. And I need you. I don't want to live a life on the run. I want to live up to my parents' name. I want to help the people of our country. I can help with charity work, with orphanages, with hospitals. My life has had no meaning up until this point." She stared him down, her words more truth than she ever thought possible. "I want to help."

"So, you will marry my son, bear his child, and please the public? Willingly?"

"Yes. But there are some stipulations. You can't beat me or hurt me. You can't let Vladimir touch me, either. In any way."

Boris's eyes flashed for a moment. "I will not tolerate disobedience, and you have a track record of disobeying."

"If you'll follow my requests, you won't have any reason to touch me. If nothing else, think of the safety of the child. For me to be able to give birth to a healthy, full-term baby, I need to live in a trauma-free environment."

He rubbed his chin and fell silent.

Ekaterina added, "One more request with this agreement: I want to know what happened to the family that protected me over the border, and if they are alive and okay. I want your promise that they will be left alone and not punished."

Boris eyed her. "Why? I'm not in the habit of letting anyone get away with housing Crossers. Besides, it sounds like you may want options of where to hide if you were to escape again."

"I'm sorry, I'm not speaking clearly. They've suffered enough already because of me. I got their son killed and I feel responsible for their loss. I just want to be assured they are all right."

He grunted. He stared at her, as if calculating any variables he might have missed. Ekaterina knew it was a fair deal and Boris, even through his temper, wanted his plan to work more than anything. "Well, Ekaterina, you paint a tempting picture. I'll need to think on it, but I need something from you to prove you're telling the truth"

She spun through possible acceptable offers in her mind, offers she was okay with. "We can hold the wedding next week in front of the public."

He shook his head. "No. Not good enough. I don't want to give you time to snake your way out of this. Therefore, we'll perform the wedding this evening and tomorrow we'll hold a press conference where you can demonstrate your willingness to cooperate. This will be your test. One slipup on your part and we'll proceed under my conditions, not yours."

"You're not going to have a public wedding?"

"No. The public will understand the risks were too high for an assassination attempt. That's what they were told already. I don't want to wait one more day for this marriage."

"And what about an act of good faith on your part?"

He paused. "You will not be harmed, and I will tell Vladimir the same."

Ekaterina nodded, willing herself to stay strong during these last moments.

Boris turned to Dr. Ilievski. "Have you ever performed and artificial insemination before?"

Jovan straightened his body and cleared his throat. "Not personally, but I know how it's done. I'll order the necessary tools and we'll move forward as soon as everything arrives."

"How long will that take?"

"Two, maybe three days."

"Fine." Boris turned to leave the room, then looked over his shoulder. "Ekaterina, one more thing; who poisoned the food for you? Who helped you?"

She acted confused. "What do you mean?"

"Don't play dumb with me. Who helped you?"

"The Insurgents."

"That doesn't tell me who poisoned the food in the palace."

"I don't know who was responsible for that."

"Well, who helped you escape? How did you know the

poisoning was going to happen?"

Without missing a beat, Ekaterina pulled a lie out of thin air. "A couple of the delivery people are with the Insurgents. They told me when everything would go down. You might want to have better vetting done on all delivery personnel entering the palace."

"So it would seem." Boris left the room, his guards following.

Jovan put his finger to his mouth to give Ekaterina the silent signal. Then he said, "I'll take you to the Infirmary to have that foot x-rayed."

Once Ekaterina was transferred to the Infirmary and the guards were stationed outside the doors with instructions to halt anyone entering, Jovan took her into the x-ray room and closed the door. He pulled her into a tight embrace.

"Oh, Ekaterina! I'm so sorry this didn't work out for you. I'm sorry to hear about the boy dying."

She hugged him back, every emotion fighting each other to reach the surface first. Unable to control anything, she finally broke into tears. "Jovan, it was horrible the way Ivan was beaten. At least he was unconscious when . . ." She couldn't bring herself to say the rest of the sentence out loud.

He moved back from her so he could look her in the eyes. "You knew the risks. His family knew the risks. I'm sorry things didn't turn out better."

She wiped her face. There would be time later, after the wedding, when alone in her room, that she could let everything out. "What have I gotten myself into?"

Jovan smiled, patting her hand. "Are you joking? You are the cleverest young woman I've ever met. You bought yourself time without beatings!"

"But the procedure?" She gulped.

"Not to worry. I won't let anything happen to you and I'll lie, telling Boris you are pregnant. That will buy us plenty of time to get you out of here."

Relief washed over her so strongly she felt dizzy. "I guess I'll just have to play the part until we can figure something out."

"Well . . ." Jovan began.

"Yes?"

"Do you remember the plan I told you about, the one that needed a few more days to finalize?"

"Yes. Is it ready now?"

"Almost. You just need to stay calm, keep up the appearance of appeasing Boris, and I'll see about getting you out once and for all. Now, let's get your foot checked out. How did you hurt it?"

"When I crashed through the ice, I think."

"Through the ice?"

"Yes, it was so thin. I struggled getting to shore. Ivan pulled me out the rest of the way." Her voice choked up, and tears filled her eyes. "He was so kind and caring. He called me brave, but he's really the one who was brave. He helped me realize life is worth living. I'll never try to take my own life again. I'll be brave and live against all odds—for Ivan."

"He must have been something else to change your mindset so dramatically in just a few days."

"He was one-of-a-kind."

Following the x-ray and exam, Ekaterina was taken back to the windowless room. She wasn't surprised to hear her ankle was healing crooked. She wasn't even bothered by the diagnosis. Dr. Ilievski told her she may develop a limp if she didn't have the break rebroken and stabilized. She didn't care. If anything, the lame ankle would be a reminder of her short time spent with Ivan and his family. A reminder to remain strong in the face of oppression.

Several people entered Ekaterina's room, including Boris, Vladimir, two guards, and a priest. She studied the old priest—who looked like he might die at any moment, recognizing him as the same who presided over her father's funeral. He was the royal priest from years back, and now he was being used to perform the merger of royalty with a Kochev.

Vladimir said impatiently. "Well, come on, let's not waste any more time here."

The priest stepped up to the side of the bed and began reciting the verses of the marriage ceremony. When the time came for Ekaterina to answer with "I do," she did so, imagining she was saying the words to Ivan. Vladimir slid a large ring on her finger and gave her a rushed kiss, which she didn't respond to.

The lack-luster ceremony was done.

Vladimir

Vladimir had been informed by his father that Ekaterina was

surprisingly willing to marry him and carry his child. But there would be no sex. And no violence. And no anything. But that didn't make sense. He was supposed to create an heir.

Fury stole through his veins. Not over the terms, but because of how weak his father had become. If Ekaterina was able to bend him to the point of agreeing to fake a marriage, what else was his father about to forfeit?

Vladimir was also angry that his father didn't even ask him how he felt about the arrangement. He simply informed him of it. Like he was only a pawn. Like he had no say in what happened in his life. *Well, we'll see about that,* he thought, as he walked down the hallway to Ekaterina's room.

One of the guards outside the door said, "Sir, you can't go in there."

"Watch me!"

The other guard stepped in front of the door. "We have orders to not let anyone in the room."

Vladimir became enraged. "She's my wife! I can be in the same room as her."

Ekaterina opened the door. "It's okay. Let him in, but I want you two inside the room as well."

"Why? So they can watch?"

"I'm not having sex with you."

He scowled. "You don't have a choice. You're my wife now."

"Just as I thought. You figured marrying you would take all my choices. It seems silly to me that a few words uttered by a man with a priest's collar make it okay for you to take me by force."

"Those silly words make what we do right in the eyes of God and the land."

"Now you answer to God? Or the land for that matter? The only person you have to listen to is your father. He and I struck a deal."

"Look Ekaterina, I don't have to answer to my father. It's you who must. If he finds out you are refusing me, I think you know what you'll have coming. Is that what you want?"

"Your father has agreed to not beat me."

"Yeah, he told me. He also told me the agreement was that you'd produce an heir. That means sex."

"No, it doesn't."

"Uh, yeah, it does."

"Artificial insemination, Vladimir. I never agreed to having sex, married or not. All your father wants is a royal baby with his bloodline. That can all be done artificially—kind of like our marriage. When the baby pops out and has your DNA, voila, I'll have performed what I promised to do. Besides, all you ever really wanted was to possess me so Risto couldn't. Right?"

Vladimir's expression blanked out. Then, he stood taller, straightening his spine. "My father's problem is he's trying to make sure the people approve of him. He's weak. When I'm in power, this country will fear me. I won't be like him."

"You're already not like him, Vladimir."

"Thank you."

"It wasn't a compliment," she muttered. "What about Risto? Do you keep him around so you look better? Does he know he's just your sidekick?"

"I'm not going to listen to you psychoanalyze me. This whole thing is ridiculous!" He took a step towards her.

"Sir! Stop right there!" one of the guards yelled.

Vladimir froze, his body shaking with controlled violence.

"This isn't over," he whispered to her. He turned and stormed out of the room. He needed to vent his frustrations. He needed to hit something, a punching bag, a guard, a prisoner. If she hadn't fled across the border and become so infatuated with the imbecilic boy who emboldened her, she would already be his wife in every sense of the word.

Vladimir started to formulate his own plan of how to get his way in the seemingly out-of-control situation he found himself. He'd already made a few choices unbeknownst to his father, choices he'd keep in his back pocket till he needed to use them for his own gain, or to get the desired outcome.

Ekaterina

The next day at noon, Ekaterina sat alone at the long dining table and pushed the food around on her plate. Two male guards were stationed at the door. Just knowing they stood nearby irked her as she now had no privacy whatsoever.

She stared down at her plate of food and used her fork to flop over the piece of meat. The underside didn't have the fancy grill marks like the top side and didn't look as appealing. The color was dull and gray. She mused to herself that one might think this was an entirely different kind of meat because it was so different-looking than the top. She flipped the meat over again and used the side of her fork to scrape the surface of the charred steak. To her surprise, the lines and coloration were removable as if they'd been painted on. What she had in front of her was nothing more than something dressed up to appear as something it wasn't, to fool the eater into thinking they were eating something of higher quality.

Well, Ekaterina thought to herself, *if that isn't exactly what's going on at the place with the Kochev family, then I don't know what is. Everything here is fake and not what it seems—right down to the food.*

"There you are." Risto entered the room and sauntered over to Ekaterina. He pulled one of the ornately handcrafted chairs out from the table and sat beside her. "See, you weren't gone long. I told you it wouldn't work."

She flipped her steak over to the less appealing side and let out an exhausted sigh. "Why are you bothering me?"

"I have to talk to you, Ekaterina."

"Didn't you get the memo? I'm now Mrs. Vladimir Kochev."

He leaned forward as if what he had to say was significant. A sly smile crossed his face. "I can get you out of here. I have it all figured out. I know how to hide you, protect you, and reinvent you. You only need to come with me, and I'll free you from this life."

"Why should I do anything with you, Risto? Last time Boris caught us together like this, you stabbed me in the back. You did it then, and you'll do it again if you get the chance."

"Don't you see it was for your own good that I said what I said?"

"How was being beaten to within an inch of my life for my own good?"

"It taught you humility."

She crossed her arms. "Leave me alone. I don't need or want you in my life. If you bother me again, I'll take this to Boris myself."

"He won't believe you, but suit yourself. I think eventually you'll come find me and beg me to help you escape."

She sat back in her chair and angled her head as she stared at him directly in the eye. "You know, I don't understand the relationship you and Vladimir have, and I don't think you understand it either. Who in their right mind would continue to hang around the guy who stole his girl? And who with a lick of sense would allow the guy, whose girl he stole, to continue to see her?"

"If you'd leave with me, we could both get out of it."

"You're not being held here against your will, Risto. Last I saw, you can come and go as you please."

"Exactly! I can get you out."

Ekaterina flipped her steak again. "You paint a tempting picture, but I know there's a flipside, a less savory side to your offer."

"If you don't flee with me now, you'll be killed by the Insurgents."

"I've made a deal. It's over. You lost."

Risto stood, roughly pushing back his chair. "You will regret turning me down."

Ekaterina let out an exasperated sigh and shook her head as Risto left the room.

CHAPTER 14

Ekaterina

Ekaterina turned in her seat towards her guards. "Would you call Vladimir here for me?"

After several minutes, Vladimir sauntered in and stood across the table from her. She noticed one of his hands appeared injured. His knuckles looked like he'd fought a brick wall.

"What do you want?" he asked, the corners of his mouth turned down.

"Just a request. Would you tell Risto to stop bothering me?"

"What are you talking about?"

"He was just in here disrupting my meal." She halted her words, not sure if she should say he was trying to persuade her to flee with him.

Vladimir snorted. "Wow! You've really got a sweet deal going on here, Ekaterina. You think you've got everyone under your thumb, but you don't. I won't be ordered around by you on every little detail you don't like."

Ekaterina felt her temper flare, doing her best to keep it in check. "I assumed you'd want him to stop bothering me because he was trying to talk me into leaving the palace with him. I told him to leave me alone. Then I figured since I have no real authority here, I'd ask you. Looks like I was mistaken. Maybe I should take my request to your fath—"

Vladimir cut her off by yelling to a guard at the door. "Get me Risto!"

She laughed. "Risto won't admit he said anything. He'll lie, just like last time. If you want to know what he said, just ask one of my guards. They overheard it."

"Don't tell me how to operate."

Someone needs to. She held her ground, keeping eye contact with him, showing he wouldn't intimidate her anymore. "It was only a suggestion."

Risto arrived in the room looking innocent about the reason he was summoned. Ekaterina listened to the back-and-forth between Vladimir and his so-called friend about how it's inappropriate to be alone with his wife, emphasis on "wife." An obvious jab at Risto. But Vladimir didn't ask if Risto had talked about fleeing together, whether because Vladimir didn't believe Risto would dare do such a thing or because he didn't want to prove Ekaterina right, she didn't know.

After Risto left the room, Vladimir turned back to Ekaterina and leaned forward, placing his palms on the table. "I don't want to hear that you're talking to Risto again. You're my wife. You belong to me."

Ekaterina thrust her chin forward and said, "Only on paper. My heart belongs to Ivan!" Mentioning his name tore at her chest, but she refused to cry in front of Vladimir. He'd taken away her possibility of a real life when he'd murdered Ivan and she hated him for it, but she wouldn't let him see he had any power.

Vladimir sneered and stood. He cocked his neck back and forth and ran his hands down the front of his jacket. Then he set his steely eyes on hers and said, while rubbing his injured knuckles, "Your Ivan *is* nothing but a whiner and a weakling. A pathetic person to waste yourself on." He spun on his heal and stormed from the room.

Is a whiner?

What had he meant by that? she wondered. He must have had a slip of the tongue, saying present tense instead of past. And yet, he'd rubbed the fresh wounds on his hand when he'd said the words. The bottom of her stomach dropped as if she'd just swallowed a bowling ball. Could Ivan be alive and here in the palace? Hope fluttered inside her, but she squashed it down. She couldn't handle the letdown that would most certainly arrive when she learned he was still dead.

A woman entered the room. "Excuse me, ma'am. It's time to get ready for the press conference."

Ekaterina forced herself away from her thoughts. "That's not for a while yet."

"President Kochev wants you immaculate for the photos, and immaculate takes time."

* * *

Boris and his wife sat regally on the thrones in the palace's royal room. Boris took questions from reporters, mediated by General Brankov. His wife might as well have been a mannequin from a shopping center for as much as she participated in the ceremonies. Vladimir stood a couple paces away from his father with Ekaterina by his side. She chose to stand rather than sit, her crutches leaning against the wall behind her.

The reporters zeroed in on her splint and pressed Vladimir for an explanation, which he pushed the question to Ekaterina to answer. She wasn't ready for that. She'd been told she wouldn't need to speak to the reporters. However, being put on the spot, with Boris and Vladimir glaring at her, she told the truth, in a way. She said she'd slipped on the ice and fractured her foot. Boris looked relieved with her answer. Vladimir seemed frustrated. If only the reporters could have seen all the other marks covering her body. Unfortunately, the dress selected for her to wear, elegant as it was with woven white and cream fabrics, stitched together with golden patterns of vines and curls, covered her from neck to floor.

Ekaterina hated everything about the press conference, from the way the old priest had confirmed he'd performed the ceremony the day before, to the way Vladimir kept making physical contact with her while they stood side by side. He kept grabbing hold of her arm or placing a hand on her shoulder, as if reminding everyone of his claim over her. She told herself everything would be wrapped up soon and managed to keep a pleasant smile on her face. She hoped no body language experts were in the crowd to decipher her every move. However, thinking about what someone like that would look for, she decided she should move her body positions to better reflect her "adoration" for Vladimir.

She turned a little toward him and noticed his knuckles again. "What happened to your hand?" she whispered.

"Why do you care?" he responded, keeping his head facing forward.

"It looks like you hit something or someone, which is strange."

He turned his head to her. "Why?"

She saw the glint of impetuousness in his eyes and decided to play with it. Maybe she could get him to reveal his true colors to the crowd.

She tilted her chin up and smiled. In barely more than a whisper, she said, "Because you never lift a finger for anything, dear. Why would you begin now?" She added fuel to the fire by placing her palm on his lapel.

His eye fell to her hand, then back to her eyes. "You think because these reporters are here you can speak to me this way?"

She smiled brightly. "I sure do."

"You're a fraud, *sweetheart.*"

"Excuse me?"

"You aren't going to be able to hold up your end of this agreement with my father."

Through gritted teeth, "I don't know what you're talking about, love."

Flashbulbs began illuminating their faces. The media had picked up on what appeared to be intimacy between the two. Ekaterina's heart raced and her cheeks reddened. *At least the photos would show an embarrassed bride,* she thought.

"Vladimir," a reporter said, "how's married life treating you?"

"Isn't it obvious?" He brought his unmarred hand up and clasped hers that still rested on his jacket. Then, with the other, he reached around and buried it deep into her hair on the back of her head and pulled her head toward his. He brought his lips to hers and pressed harder than he needed to, perhaps to get her to respond negatively.

She was ready for it, though. She knew they'd probably have to kiss in front of the cameras. Thinking about it as an act, like an actress, gave her the strength to keep her cool during the forced kiss. When he didn't pull back, she brought her hand up to his cheek, making it look like she was caressing him, using it as a barrier between the cameras and their lips. Hers had turned tense and her mouth had closed. She was determined to remain calm, with the hopes of having Vladimir reveal his true colors to the media, not that they needed to learn what he was all about. But it was clear he was trying to get her to fold. She wasn't having it.

Finally, Vladimir pulled away and began answering questions. Ekaterina wanted to wipe her mouth with the back of her sleeve. No, she wanted to grab the hem of her dress and wipe her whole face and scrub her lips to rid Vladimir from her skin. Instead, she simply smiled.

Once the press conference completed, the Kochev family left the room. As Ekaterina moved through the doorway on her crutches, she looked back to the reporters and photographers. These people were free to come and go from the palace. These people were free, period. The magnitude of what she'd gotten herself into hit like a sledgehammer as the cameras continued to flash.

The doors closed behind her and she turned forward to find Vladimir in her path, wringing his hands. Boris wasn't far away. She wondered if Vladimir would verbally scold her or possibly strike her. The anger in his eyes made the hair on the back of her neck rise.

Vladimir said, "Don't ever try to embarrass me like that again, *princess!*" His scathing words caught Boris's attention.

"Or what?" she asked in defense.

Boris intervened. "What's going on, Vladimir?"

"Nothing. I need to go punch someone."

Boris pointed to Vladimir's injured hand. "Wear gloves this time when you work out. What did you hit to skin your knuckles?"

"Just a worthless, whining wimp." His narrowed eyes shot to Ekaterina.

Ekaterina's body froze when she heard Vladimir use the description again. She couldn't breathe, she couldn't hear what Boris said in reply to his son's comments due the rushing sound in her head. Feeling faint, she hobbled over to a chair and sat. *Is Ivan alive and in the palace?*

She breathed slowly to regain her composure. Boris and Vladimir finished their conversation and Vladimir left the room. Boris was also about to leave when Ekaterina found her voice. "Sir, may I have a word?"

He looked at his watch and appeared put out. "I don't have time."

"It's concerning our agreement."

His shoulders stiffened while he approached her. "What is it?"

She stood. "I held up my end in the press conference, like I promised."

"And I've kept Vladimir away from you."

"Yes. There's one thing, though. I think Vladimir has Ivan here in the palace. Vladimir has mentioned it twice." She didn't know if it were actually true, but she'd never be able to find out on her own. No one would let her near any prisoners. Her stomach churned while she waited for a response. Boris looked at his watch again. Ekaterina pressed harder. "Part of our agreement was that no harm comes to the family that protected me. Ivan belongs to that family. If he's alive here in the palace and being beaten by Vladimir, our agreement is off."

Boris's attention sufficiently grabbed, he looked at her and said, "Ivan? Is that the boy Vladimir had killed? Why would he bring his body here?"

"I don't know. All I know is Vladimir keeps hinting about Ivan."

"I have an appointment in twenty minutes. After that, I'll look into this."

Desperation flooded her. What if he didn't check or Vladimir found out first and actually killed Ivan this time? "Sir, it will only take a few moments for us to check the cells. Then we will both know for sure. And if Vladimir is going down right now to beat Ivan, he may not leave him alive." She held her breath, the world around her contracting to a sharp focus on nothing but this man's face, on the words that may change her life again.

Boris conceded. "Fine. Let's go now."

Vladimir

Vladimir found himself in a predicament. To remain in line for the leadership of Bregot, he must follow his weak father. His father wanted a royal heir. But the princess didn't want anything to do with him.

Vladimir picked up his pace through the halls of the palace as he made his way down to the dungeon. He had the proper incentive to bend Ekaterina to his will. No more would she run the show, manipulating him and his father. She had some nerve trying to embarrass him in front of the cameras.

His thoughts went to the discussion in the dining hall about Risto. How dare she accuse Risto of trying to flee with her? *Risto knows better than to step on my toes,* Vladimir thought. But a flicker of doubt still caught inside him. He felt as though he was losing control from every angle.

The two men guarding the door to the cell stood to attention as he approached. "Open it," Vladimir barked.

He breezed into the small damp cell. On the floor in the corner, curled in the fetal position, wearing only a pair of jeans, lay Ivan. He appeared to be dead. Vladimir used his foot to push against Ivan's shoulder, trying to rouse him. Beating on an unconscious prisoner was no fun and had no reward or satisfaction.

Ivan didn't wake up.

"Come on, Ivan. Open those eyes. Show me that unending contempt you harbor inside. Let me show you that it doesn't matter."

Boris

Only one door in the dungeon area was guarded. *Damn, that must be the room.* Boris peered through the small window on the door and saw Vladimir facing the nearby corner. A pair of legs in jeans stuck out on the floor from behind Vladimir's frame. His son looked as though he was about to tie into the prisoner. *That better not be the boy,* he thought. He turned to Ekaterina and said to her guards, "Wait here." Then spoke to the cell guards. "Let me in. She stays out."

"But—!" she cried out.

He silenced her with a look.

One of the guards opened the door. Boris took a deep breath and moved into the cell.

Vladimir's head jerked in his direction upon seeing him enter. "What are you doing here?"

"I will ask the questions. What's this all about?" Boris surveyed the unconscious prisoner crumpled on the floor. His bare upper half showed extensive bruising and lacerations, however, he was still breathing. "Who is that?"

Vladimir stood tall and said, "My prisoner."

"I didn't authorize any taking of prisoners."

"I don't need your approval on every single decision I make, father."

"Who is he?" he demanded.

"Ekaterina's kidnapper, Ivan."

Boris's blood boiled within his veins. How could his own flesh and blood be so stupid? He glared at his son, angry at Vladimir's lack of foresight. "Do you realize what you've done?"

"You would have done the same thing!"

"Then you don't understand me at all. You fail to see the danger all around us of coups, Insurgents, and infiltrators. The only way to keep them at bay is to have Ekaterina here at the palace, married to you. Why can't you get that?" Boris hit his fist against the side of his leg.

A flicker of fear flashed through his son's eyes. "Having him here at the palace will help keep her here."

"No. It won't. Now she'll have incentive to flee . . . with him."

"She'll keep following orders if she thinks he'll get beaten," Vladimir said, his voice tinged with pleading.

"You imbecile!" Boris stomped over to the door and pounded on it. A guard outside opened it. "Get me the doctor."

Ekaterina rushed the door, trying to peer around Boris' thick frame. "Ivan? Is it Ivan? Let me see him!"

Boris shook his head and pushed the door shut in her face. Her shouts and pleas were quieted once the door closed.

"You brought her down here with you?" Vladimir's voice cracked with his question.

"I didn't believe my son would be foolish enough to actually bring a prisoner. She needed reassurance. I agreed to keep the family that housed her safe. He's part of that family. You will not touch him again. Do you hear me? You've once again made a mess, only this time I don't know if I can clean it up." Boris began pacing back and forth, rummaging through his mind to find a way to avert an International crisis. His bullheaded son had kidnapped a citizen of another country and brought him across the border and beaten him to what appeared to be within an inch of his life. "The Insurgents are going to *love* hearing this." He rubbed his head.

Vladimir asked, "I don't understand why you don't exert your power to keep them at bay."

"Because you attract more flies with honey than vinegar. If more of the people of this country are in favor of my rule, they will oppose a hostile takeover. I use diplomatic measures whenever I can to demonstrate my willingness to lead the country, not command it."

"But you *do* command it. You should, anyway." Boris could hear the darkness in Vladimir's voice and it worried him.

Before he could delve further, the door opened slightly and Dr. Ilievski, carrying a medical bag, squeezed through before it shut again. Ekaterina's shouts and screams echoed in then abruptly muted when the door closed.

"What's going on?" the doctor asked.

"This prisoner needs your attention." Boris pointed to Ivan. "His life is very important."

Boris watched as the doctor performed a basic evaluation of the prisoner and waited for his medical opinion. Vladimir kept switching his weight from side to side, obviously frustrated.

Boris turned to Vladimir. "What on earth possessed you to decide to bring him over the border? This is worse than if you'd just killed him."

Vladimir didn't respond immediately. His eyes darted back and forth, as if he was trying to come up with an idea. Then he said, "Ivan can expose the locations of all Crosser homes. We can eliminate the network over there and stop the defectors from fleeing."

"Crosser homes don't communicate like that. He wouldn't know any more about other homes than someone off the street."

"Then we could take him to the border and give him back and relieve some of the tension."

"Tension *you* caused by leaving a dead body behind when you kidnapped a Svobodian citizen. I should just give them *you.* Now, none of my men can put a toe over the border or they'll be arrested. You can bet the other side of the border is lined with authorities, just waiting." Boris added, "Besides, we can't take him back now. Ekaterina knows he's here, and I need her to stay. You better hope he doesn't die, Vladimir. If he does, she'll kill herself, then I'll kill you!"

"Sir," Dr. Ilievski stood and said, "I need to perform x-rays. I suspect he has broken ribs."

"Is he going to live?"

"I think so, but he needs fluids and attentive care that I can only give in the Infirmary. He needs to be relocated there."

"No!" Vladimir protested.

"Shut up," Boris hissed. "Doctor, would you tell Ekaterina the young man will survive, but she needs to return upstairs while you take care of him? I don't want her to see him like this."

"Yes. I'll usher her personally and bring back a gurney."

Dr. Ilievski

Jovan couldn't believe what he saw when he entered the cell, moments after Ekaterina pleaded with him to let her come in with him. Boris was wise to not let her see Ivan in this condition.

He exited the cell and looked at her. "Come with me, Ekaterina."

"Is Ivan Lazarov in there?"

Jovan pressed his lips firmly, noting the guards near them. "You need to go upstairs." He motioned for her to move away from the door.

"No. I'm not going anywhere until I see him."

"The *prisoner* is badly hurt. But I can't care for him until you're upstairs, so, please go, Ekaterina." He kept his voice level, but he gave her a look to indicate it was indeed Ivan. Her head swiveled between the door and his eyes, reluctant to obey, yet heavily concerned for the boy in the cell. "The prisoner in there is alive and he needs my help. I'll ask that Boris let you see him once he's transferred."

Her shoulders dropped, revealing her submission. She turned and hobbled on her crutches toward the stairs, her guards following close behind.

Jovan hurried to the Infirmary and released the locks on the gurney's wheels. He pulled a cervical collar off the shelf as he bumped the door open and pushed the gurney into the hallway. His gut roiled with derision for the Kochev family as he rushed to the guarded door.

The door opened and Jovan heard father and son continuing to argue over who was right or wrong concerning the prisoner's care and Ekaterina's future. Jovan asked the guards to come inside and help load up the patient. He directed the careful movement of Ivan's body, keeping the spine as stable as possible and applied the neck collar.

Vladimir let out a scoffing sound. "Is that really necessary?" His finger pointed to the neck collar. "He's a prisoner, not a visiting dignitary."

Jovan ignored him and continued. The guard held the door open as Jovan maneuvered into the hallway. He kept track of the boy's breathing as they rushed down the hall to the Infirmary, Boris and Vladimir followed close behind. First would be an x-ray to check the spine and ribs, then he'd assess the obvious injuries. He'd have to wait for Ivan to regain consciousness to find out what else was damaged.

While Jovan and the guards positioned Ivan on the x-ray table, he worried about bigger problems, being that Ekaterina would not want to leave Ivan behind when he helped her escape in a couple of days. The boy's presence complicated things. Perhaps Boris could be convinced to send the boy back to his own country.

After the x-rays, Ivan was moved to an exam room. Vladimir slouched in a chair against the wall, scratching at his cuticles, while Boris paced. Jovan shoved the films into the lighted board and examined them. The spine looked okay. The ribs were another story. No clean breaks, but obvious fractures. *Poor kid,* he thought. *That's got to hurt.*

He turned to Boris. "He'll live. He's stable enough to transport him home, if you wish."

Vladimir launched off his chair. "What? No!"

Boris whirled on his son. "Sit down. You don't get a say in this." Vladimir sat, looking indignant. Boris didn't speak immediately. After a considerable pause, he said, "The boy stays, just in case Ekaterina decides to renege on her agreement."

Vladimir crossed his arms over his chest with a smug expression plastered on his face. "Good."

Boris pointed a finger at his son. "You won't touch him again. You hear me?"

A slow defeated breath slid out of Jovan's lungs, hopefully unnoticed. His escape plan for Ekaterina would be delayed. Jovan cleared his throat. "Sir, I'd like to keep him here until he wakes up to complete my evaluation and to properly clean his wounds."

"Fine."

Jovan pressed a little more. "Ekaterina will want to see him. She was quite insistent earlier."

"Yes. Wait until he's back in the cell." Boris turned to the guards. "You'll stand guard in here."

Jovan said, "They'll just be in my way. Have them guard the entrance door instead. If I need their help, I'll bring them in. Besides, he's not going anywhere."

"We thought that about Ekaterina, too."

"But we didn't have guards outside the door then. What about the cameras? Aren't they working yet?"

"General Brankov said the new technicians are coming next week to get them online." He paused. "We need to move forward as quickly as possible. Doctor, when will you be ready to perform the artificial insemination?"

Vladimir grunted, obviously disgusted and frustrated.

"Two days."

"And how long will it be until we know if it took?"

"Two to three weeks."

Boris rubbed his face with both palms. "Okay. Let me know when he's awake. I want to talk to him before Ekaterina does."

Ekaterina

As she hobbled away from Jovan with the knowledge Ivan was alive, tears flooded her eyes and her whole body shook. She could only imagine what kind of condition Ivan was in. She didn't want to think about it, but the image of Vladimir's bloodied knuckles pushed its way into her mind. Ivan must be in worse shape than the beating he'd received at the gas station.

But he was *alive*.

Ekaterina tried to make sense of that incident. Vladimir had told his guard that he'd changed his mind and for the boy to be shot. She'd heard two rounds fired off. They must have only shot Ivan's friend, what was his name? She couldn't even remember. But Vladimir must have known he would hurt Ekaterina by staring at her when he told them to shoot the other boy.

Ekaterina made it up the staircase, then found the nearest bench and sat down, or more like fell. Her crutches crashed to the floor and one of the guards rushed to assist her.

"Are you all right, ma'am?"

She pushed his arms away and looked him squarely in the eye. "Did you know Ivan was down there the whole time?"

The guard moved away and didn't answer. She leaned her head against the wall and closed her eyes. Fresh tears slipped down her cheeks, tears of relief of learning Ivan was alive, followed by nausea for the pain he must be suffering from being beaten. She knew all too well.

Ekaterina didn't know how long she sat there, waiting. When the guards stood to attention, she also straightened up, hearing Boris and Vladimir coming up the stairs.

Ekaterina bolted off the bench and limped to the staircase. She confronted Boris, ignoring Vladimir. "Will the deal be kept?

You promised the family would be left alone."

Boris stepped toward her. "He won't be touched again, so long as you hold up your end of the agreement. Vladimir understands."

Vladimir waved his hand dismissively and turned from his father and walked away.

"I need to see Ivan with my own eyes."

"You will, when the doctor finishes evaluating him and he's moved back to his cell."

"Why? What are you going to do with him?"

"That has yet to be decided."

Ivan

Ivan awoke to intense pain stabbing him in the chest with every breath. He tried to move, but the pain caused him to hiss and cuss.

"Keep still, son." A firm hand pressed on his shoulder.

Ivan opened his eyes to see a man in a white lab coat and a stethoscope around his neck. He assumed he was still at the palace, but being treated by a doctor could be a good thing or a bad thing. It either meant his injuries were too severe or that Vladimir wanted him healthy again to be able to withstand a fresh round of beatings. Memories from Katia and the cabin flickered through his mind, though they felt like a lifetime ago. She'd spoken about a doctor, someone who'd helped her. "Are you Dr. Ilievski?" he asked, hoping he'd gotten the name right.

The doctor's eyebrows shot up. "Yes."

Ivan exhaled, but the sharp pain in his chest reminded him he couldn't relax yet. "Is Katia all right?"

"I assume you mean Ekaterina? Her foot is broken and healing crooked, probably because she can't sit still long enough for it to heal."

Ivan smiled. That was Katia, for sure.

"Where do you hurt the most?"

"My ribs. I can barely breathe. It hurts to be lying down like this. Can I sit up?"

Dr. Ilievski pressed the button to move the bed until Ivan indicated he was in less pain. He leaned over, barely moving his lips. "Ivan, you need to listen very carefully to me. I need Boris to keep trusting me. Anything Ekaterina has told you about me needs—no, absolutely *must* be—kept quiet."

"I understand."

"I may be rude to you at times, but I promise I am on yours and Ekaterina's sides."

"My lips are sealed."

The doctor paused. "She thinks the world of you, Ivan."

His smile broadened even further, and his ribs didn't seem to hurt as much anymore.

CHAPTER 15

Boris

Boris entered the Infirmary and nodded to Dr. Ilievski who was attending to another patient. He walked into the exam room where the prisoner was being guarded. The boy, Ivan, sat inclined on the bed with intravenous fluid inserted in one arm. He seemed half-awake.

"So, you're the infamous Ivan that Ekaterina goes on about."

The boy didn't respond.

"I appreciate your willingness to keep her safe while she attempted to escape her duty. This country would have suffered greatly if she had died. She can sometimes be a danger to herself."

Ivan cleared his throat and moved slightly. He winced, then said, "The only danger in her life comes from you and your son."

Boris smirked at the boy's attempt at insolence. "That's where you're wrong. I protected her from the Insurgents. She just couldn't see my intentions were for good and fought against them. But now, she's willing to do her duty, to bear Vladimir's child, and help her country" Boris liked the way Ivan's eyebrows knitted together while listening to the way things are.

"Unfortunately, she thought you were dead when she agreed to comply. Now that you're not, I fear she will resist. I simply cannot have her do that. She's too important to be steered off the rails by someone like you."

"Someone like me?"

"Yes. You are no one. Your family is insignificant. If anything, you are a thorn in my side, an annoyance."

"Well, sir, it would seem I'm enough of something to bother you."

"Yes. Let's just keep it at that. If you'll help keep Ekaterina on track to deliver a healthy child, I'll let you go back to your family. If you resist, your family will suffer. If Ekaterina resists, *you* will suffer."

The boy's face pinched together, but he complied. "I understand."

Boris liked the way he bent so easily, showing he wasn't a threat. Still, Boris would keep him well-guarded.

Dr. Ilievski entered the room. "He's doing much better with fluids."

"Is he ready to be moved back to the cell?"

"Yes. I'll need to check in on him a few times a day at first to make sure his ribs are healing properly."

Boris chewed on the inside of his cheek. "Fine. He's alert and aware of his situation." Boris turned to the guards. "Once he's locked up, bring Ekaterina to see him. I don't want them left alone, and I want to be told if they start talking about escaping." He focused his eyes on Ivan. "You won't be talking like that though, will you?"

Ivan shook his head.

Ivan

Ivan was moved back to the cold cell. The first thing he noticed was a bed had been brought in and pushed into the corner, not a nice one, but better than the stone floor. He carefully sat down on the end of the bed, but when he leaned his shoulder against the wall, pain ripped through his body. Even with the painkiller from the doctor, he could feel every nerve-ending protest.

Dr. Ilievski gave him one of his long-sleeved, button-up shirts to help keep him warm. Ivan had opted not to fasten the buttons to keep the material loose across his painful back. The doctor had said he stitched up some wounds. Ivan wondered what his back looked like if only some of the wounds were stitched. He figured it probably looked like Katia's. His eyes filled with burning tears as he now understood, even if it was only a fraction, of what she'd gone through, except she'd dealt with this kind of treatment for months. If what Boris had said was true, Ivan's cooperation would prevent her from receiving anymore beatings.

His head swam from the medication. Slowly he tried to pull up on the bed, bringing his knees closer to his chest, but a fresh wave of pain struck him. Exhausted, he simply sat, his head and shoulders still resting against the wall. He closed his eyes and let the medication pull him under.

"Ivan," Katia's delicate voice called to him from far away. He imagined they were at the cabin and that he needed to get up and add more wood to the fire to keep her warm. When he tried to move his body, pain ripped throughout his chest, bringing him out of his stupor.

"Hold still," she said, and he felt her hand press gently on his shoulder. The touch sent tingles through his body and he shuddered with pleasure. She was real.

He opened his eyes a sliver to find her face near his, eyes wet with tears. "They won't hurt you again. I promise," she whispered.

"Katia?" He touched her cheek, the skin warm and soft. He reached up a little higher, ignoring the pain, and brushed away some of the hair from her face. "It's really you?"

"Yes." She gripped her fingers around his and brought his hand to her mouth, kissing it roughly.

Vladimir's irritated voice cut through the fogginess. "That's enough. You've seen him. Time to go."

Ekaterina

Once they were outside the cell in the hallway, she awkwardly whirled on her crutches and faced Vladimir. "You're an ass!"

He raised his hand to strike, to which she recoiled. Then he paused and lowered his hand with what looked like the last shred of self-control. "You're just trying to get me to break my father's agreement with you."

"No, that's not why I called you an ass. You really are one, and no one's ever told you that before. I wanted to be the first." She turned around and headed to the stairs.

"If my father heard the way you taunt me, he'd hit you himself."

"Your father feels the same way about you."

"I'd be careful, princess. Your defiance may not be able to be punished directly, but I know how to hurt you indirectly."

She held her composure, even though she panicked inside, and continued to the stairs. When she made it to the main floor, she headed straight to Boris's office and asked to see him.

The male assistant at the desk outside the office said, "Ma'am, President Kochev is in a meeting."

"I'll wait." She sat on a nearby chair and straightened her clothing to calm her nerves.

A short while later, Boris emerged with several men in suits. They shook hands and walked away. Boris turned to Ekaterina. "Is something wrong?"

"May I speak with you in your office?"

He nodded.

Inside the office, she said, "I saw Ivan. He was incoherent and groggy, and in obvious pain. Vladimir only let me see him for a few moments, not long enough to tell whether Ivan is going to be all right."

"Dr. Ilievski has confidence in his recovery. That's enough for me."

"I want to see him again, tomorrow, to see improvement."

Boris's body language told Ekaterina he was growing tired of her demands. She pulled out her trump card. "Just now, Vladimir threatened to beat on him again to keep me under control. I need to see Ivan again to gain reassurance he's healing and not receiving any new injuries."

"Fine."

"Will you talk to Vladimir?"

"Only if he hurts the prisoner again."

Ekaterina decided not to push any further. She accepted his words and left the office.

* * *

The next day, Ekaterina waited anxiously to be able to see Ivan again. She hadn't slept at all through the night. Her mind spun in multiple directions, excited about finding out Ivan had survived, enraged to learn Vladimir had beat on him more, determined to figure out a way to escape, and dead set on making sure Ivan was treated properly.

Following breakfast, she was summoned to the Infirmary. "You asked to see me?"

"Yes. Let's check that ankle."

Jovan flicked his hand to the guards. "You can guard outside the door." After the door closed and the guards were in the hall, Jovan opened a drawer and pulled out a Polaroid camera. "Would you take your wedding ring off?"

She didn't ask any questions and promptly did as he asked, then watched curiously as he photographed her ring from a couple angles and traced the inside of the ring onto a piece of paper.

"Have you seen Ivan today?" Ekaterina asked.

"Yes."

"Has he been injured again?"

"No. He's going to be fine. Here you go." He handed the ring back to her.

"What are you doing?"

"I suspect there is a duplicate in the royal vault, but I don't trust my memory to make sure." He waved the photos back and forth, then placed them in the drawer. "I want you to know I'm working hard to expand the escape plan to include Ivan. Unfortunately, it will take a little more time."

The door opened and two women staff members walked in, ending their private conversation. Dr. Ilievski began his inspection of her ankle.

* * *

After lunch, Vladimir escorted Ekaterina to Ivan. "You can have five minutes. The guard will still be here. No touching."

Vladimir left the room, nodding to the guard on his way out, who closed the door.

Ivan sat at an odd angle with his shoulder resting against the wall. His head hung in defeat, and Ekaterina felt such empathy for him that it brought tears to her eyes. She knew this pose since she had done it herself several times. He had been whipped and must be too sore to lie back. Couple it with his broken ribs, and he couldn't lie on his sides or stomach either. The only other option was to prop himself up against the wall.

"Ivan?" she half whispered and walked slowly to him.

He lifted his head enough to see her and tried to smile. "I'm so sorry, Katia."

"For what?"

"I should have had more pity for your injuries when I found you. I should have tried harder to understand the kind of pain you must have been in."

"How could you have known? You can't really understand until you go through it yourself. Besides, you have no complaints from me on how you cared for me." She let her own mouth turn into a smile.

"Feels so long ago," he whispered.

Ekaterina sat down in front of him. "We're going to get through this, Ivan, and be stronger because of it. Has Dr. Ilievski been in yet to help you?"

"He treated me yesterday."

"I'll get him to give you a painkiller."

"He already did. It's not working."

"Well, for what it's worth, you shouldn't be beaten anymore."

"Really? But I was looking forward to it."

She looked him in the eye to see his pained smile. She laughed a bit. She looked over her shoulder at the guard, who watched with a grimace on his face.

She swallowed, hard. Ivan needed to be updated on everything and she'd rather the update came from her. "Ivan, things have already changed. Boris and I have entered into an agreement. There was a press conference yesterday announcing me as Vladimir's new wife. I represent this country now."

The pain on his face broke her because she knew it was not from his injuries. "You're . . . you're married?"

Her head jerked once in agreement. She couldn't let the guard know any of her displeasure because she knew he'd tell everything to Boris and Vladimir.

"My place is with my people," she continued, willing her voice to remain steady. "But you and your family saved my life when you didn't need to. Boris and Vladimir won't hurt you any longer because of that."

He nodded, but his shoulders dropped a bit in resignation. "What's going to happen to me?"

"That hasn't been decided yet. They will let me see you every day until you are recovered, to prove you aren't being hurt. So, until tomorrow, thank you for saving my life." She took a chance and swooped over to plant a kiss on his cheek.

In that moment, she whispered in his ear, barely making a

sound. "Don't react. I'm here for you. We have a plan to escape."

Dr. Ilievski

Dr. Jovan Ilievski pulled up to the curb in front of the morgue. The streetlights illuminated the sidewalk with a dim glow. He glanced in his rearview mirror, and then out his side windows. Assured no one was around, he grabbed the tied-off black garbage bag from the passenger seat and got out of the car. Looking to the right and left, he walked to the door and entered.

"Jovan, good to see you," Pandil, the morgue director, greeted him.

"You said you found good candidates for me?"

"Yes. The height you ordered for the girl is dead on." Pandil chuckled at the unintended pun. "But the male is a bit short."

"How much shorter?"

"Two inches, but other than that, they should work for you."

"That's fine. They will be lying down, and I don't think anyone will notice the height difference. Are their records clear?"

"Yes, the male is a convicted murderer whom Boris ordered killed yesterday. He hasn't any family to claim his body, and he's on the docket for cremation. The female is a Jane Doe, a street urchin. I couldn't find any information on her, so she's good to go."

"I owe you one," Jovan said as he lifted the black bag to the table. "Will you help me dress them?"

An hour later, the two dead imposters were dressed, and the girl had a splint like Ekaterina's attached to her leg. They placed rings on her left finger matching Ekaterina's new wedding set.

Jovan stared at the two bodies. These people would never know that they'd done so much for their own country in death, even if they hadn't done much in life.

Pandil asked, "Where did you get the ring set? Does it match?"

"It's identical to Ekaterina's set."

"But, how did you get it so fast?"

"I suspected her wedding ring was from the Royal Collection and I was right. Each piece in the collection has duplicates in case the real piece needs cleaning or repair, or if it's accidentally lost. The people are never to see her without that ring. One of the guards on our side retrieved it for me. I'll make the switch-back at the appropriate time and I'll take the real ring from Ekaterina once she's hidden. The guard will place the fake back in the vault and no one will be the wiser."

"Will it survive the heat of the explosion?"

"It's still a quality gold ring, just cubic zirconia's instead of diamonds. I think it will be just fine."

"I've got a guy who will hopefully come by and pick up the bodies later tonight," Jovan continued, handing a thick envelope of cash to Pandil. "For your silence."

"You don't have to do that, Jovan. I mean, I can use the money, but you don't have to buy my silence. It's yours one hundred percent."

Jovan gave his friend a heartfelt hug. "You know once I'm situated, I'll help you and your family cross."

"Thank you. That means so much to me. Oh, Jovan, one more thing. These people you're dealing with, the Insurgents, even though they aren't on Kochev's side, they're not always on the good side either. They draw their own lines in the sand, if you know what I mean."

"I do."

After leaving the morgue, Jovan drove to the address on the note card he'd been given. He parked the car and glanced out at the dark, abandoned warehouses, some partially destroyed, some with broken windows. He looked at the note card again to make sure he was at the right place. The address checked out. He waited in the vehicle as instructed, feeling nervous even though he knew he shouldn't, but it wasn't every night he met with the leader of the rebellion.

Two men in dark clothing exited the building in front of him and approached his vehicle. One was a good six inches taller than the other.

"Dr. Ilievski?"

"Yes."

"Leave the keys in your car and come with us," the taller man ordered.

Jovan did as he was told and got out of the car. He hurried to catch up with the two men who were already halfway to the door they'd exited. They held the door open for him to enter first, and he reluctantly did so. As he stepped into the dimly lit room, he found a plain, empty receiving area with several doors lining the perimeter, all closed. Without warning, the two men behind him immediately took him face-down to the ground.

"What's going on?" Jovan managed to ask.

"We need to make sure you are who you say you are."

"I would have just given you my wallet . . . what the . . ." Jovan was completely shocked that his pants were being removed. He struggled with the men. Footsteps surrounded him.

A voice said, "Look for it on his upper left thigh."

One of the men holding him down announced, "The scar's there."

Jovan had no idea how these people knew he had a scar in that area. Eventually, he was let go, and he quickly pulled his pants up and fastened them. He turned around to see at least twenty men, all carrying automatic rifles. In the center stood a man with a certain air about him signifying leadership, or maybe it was just the fact he was the only one wearing a hat and not carrying a gun. He stood taller than most of the men in the bunch, and his broad shoulders looked like they could handle most anything placed upon them.

The man spoke. "Dr. Jovan Ilievski, Boris Kochev's personal physician. The man who poisoned the entire palace just a week ago, save for a small handful of men who helped clear the way for Ekaterina Cvetkovski's escape. I'm Konstantin Andonov. It's an honor to meet you."

Jovan adjusted his glasses and shook the hand extended toward him. "Is this how you greet all your guests? Public humiliation?"

"I'm sure you must realize how imperative it is that our operations remain secret. I do apologize for any embarrassment you experienced."

"How did you know about my, ah, scar?" Jovan noticed Konstantin had several scars of his own across his face and forehead.

"I know your history, Doctor. I've researched you thoroughly, and in the process, I discovered you spent time in a hospital in Svobodia because of a car crash and needed surgery for your injuries, which included your thigh. In this business, no one's word is good for anything. Identities can be stolen. We need irrefutable proof, and scars are unique."

Jovan cracked a wry grin. "Interesting. I've got something to talk to you about that will make you rethink your methods of positively identifying people. Irrefutable proof will take on a whole new meaning."

"And that's why I've invited you into our circle. Walk with me, Dr. Ilievski."

Jovan followed Konstantin through one of the doors and continued down a long, dimly lit hallway. A staircase at the end of the hall dumped them down a level and into a large room that held several desks and many people. Men, women, and children, all dressed in rags and malnourished, stared at him. Jovan heard several coughs from the sea of faces, which in his medical opinion needed to be evaluated for treatment.

"Doctor, as you can see, we need people like you on our side. Most of the men and women here are wanted by Kochev for some reason or another. They can't afford to flee across the border, like Ekaterina Cvetkovski, or they would."

Jovan didn't like the tone of voice Konstantin used when he referred to Ekaterina, as if she was not worthy of the privilege to escape. They entered a private office of sorts.

"Now, Dr. Ilievski, may I call you Jovan?"

"Yes."

"Jovan, what is your next move, and how may I assist you?"

Jovan didn't waste any time formulating his words. He pulled out a large envelope from his inside coat pocket and handed it to Konstantin, who opened it and pulled out the papers. Jovan said, "I plan on staging the deaths of Ekaterina and a male companion, Ivan. I need a certain vehicle and an explosion to burn body doubles beyond recognition so I can use my medical training to make the identification of the corpses."

"You have body doubles?"

"They are ready to go at the morgue. The director is in league with me."

"What medical records will you use to prove the male's identity?"

"I have x-rays of his broken ribs. They're like fingerprints. Boris trusts me, plus Ekaterina's double will be sporting an identical wedding ring and a splint on her leg. Any male found with Ekaterina would be easily accepted as the Lazarov boy."

Konstantin's head tilted, and his chin dropped to his chest. "Did you say . . . Lazarov?"

"Yes."

"A Lazarov from Svobodia named Ivan. What are the odds of that?"

Jovan hesitated a second. "I'm not sure I follow."

"He's must be related to Mira Lazarov. A grandson perhaps? Mira's husband's name was Ivan."

"I don't know a Mira Lazarov," Jovan admitted.

"And why would you? She would be in her seventies by now. How old is this boy, Ivan?"

"Close to Ekaterina's age."

"What do you know about him? Is he trustworthy?"

"Ekaterina trusts him, and that's good enough for me. Is there more I need to know about Mira Lazarov?"

"Nothing that concerns you at this time. How certain are you that Boris will believe your medical opinion?"

"He didn't suspect me in the poisoning. He allows me full unsupervised contact with both Ekaterina and Ivan."

Konstantin says, "I'm relieved to hear you've broken through Boris's shell. Vladimir is under our control and believes exactly what we want him to believe, but Boris has been a harder nut to crack."

"What do you mean? You think you have control over Vladimir?"

"We have insiders feeding us information."

"And that makes you think you have control over him?" Jovan shook his head. "How many men do you have in the palace?"

"Not nearly enough."

Jovan shifted back and forth on his feet. He'd underestimated the Insurgents reach. And that smelled more of a want of power, not a coup. "But enough to make you think you have control over Vladimir? I'm not sure we're talking about the same person."

"We are. Our people are everywhere in the palace."

"Are they spying on me, too?"

"A little, but it's for a greater cause."

"Your cause? Or the best interests of the country?"

"You don't think our cause is in the best interests of the country?"

"I think the best interests are so far out of reach that you're trying your darndest to keep some kind of involvement and inclusion. I think your intentions are just that, yours."

"You doubt this organization?"

"If I saw actual organization here, I wouldn't doubt it."

"You know, Dr. Ilievski, I'm not sure I get you. You are determined to defy Boris, but you don't want to be affiliated with our group, even though this group is what allowed your first plan to succeed."

"Ekaterina almost *died* crossing the first time, due to thin ice. But now I'm wondering if you knew the ice would be too thin"

Konstantin's eyes narrowed. "You forget that she was not the only one on the plane. Many died to escape Boris. Ekaterina survived. If she had died, we wouldn't be having this conversation right now."

Jovan paused at the heat in Konstantin's voice. He couldn't make the mistake of pushing too hard. "May I ask what your long-term goals are for this organization?"

"Is this an interview?"

"I'm just wondering what your objective is. Are you trying to remove Boris? Are you trying to reinstate the monarchy? Or are you trying to place yourself in the hot seat?"

"We deal with things one situation at a time. Our short-term objective is to get Ekaterina Cvetkovski out of the palace. Our long-term would be to keep her out."

"What have you got against her?"

"She's a Cvetkovski."

"And?"

"The last thing anyone wants, save Boris, is a two-headed indestructible monster. Her presence will undoubtedly elevate Boris far above any level he's imagined. Many people of this country are vacillating between sides. If Boris keeps Ekaterina, we lose those people."

Jovan sighed. "She's already married to Vladimir. Boris already has what he wanted. What are you waiting for? Why haven't you killed her already?"

"I'm waiting for you, Doctor. I want you to join us. And if helping you, once again, to get Ekaterina across the border will secure your allegiance to our cause, then I can handle a couple of days of Boris thinking he got what he wanted. But know this, if your plan fails and she is not transported across the border, or if she is brought back, then yes, we will kill her. This is the last chance."

The door opened and a small boy entered. Konstantin put out his arms to the boy, who climbed up on his lap. Without breaking stride, he said to Jovan, "Ekaterina Cvetkovski residing in the palace as Vladimir's wife is already elevating Boris's rule. I hope for her sake you're able to execute your plan soon. All our lives depend on it, even my son's." Konstantin squeezed the boy on his lap. "If there is any hope to be had for our futures, Ekaterina must disappear, one way or another."

"Do you have any men at the border?"

"We might."

"Well, I may need their help when I get there. The basic plan is outlined in those papers. I'll have to improvise along the way, I'm sure, but any help you can give me would be appreciated."

"Does that mean you'll join us?"

"When Ekaterina is believed to be dead and she is safely relocated, then I'll give you my allegiance."

Konstantin opened a drawer and pulled out a plain white card with a phone number. "Call this number when you're ready to begin. If you find yourself in a jam anywhere along the way, call and I'll see what can be done to help."

Jovan drove back to the palace feeling optimistic. Everything was in place to execute the plan he'd been developing for many months. The only hiccup was he'd be helping two people instead of just one. Ivan's presence was more than just a hiccup, though.

As he stopped at the security gate and had his car searched, he mused how the guards hadn't cared about the contents of his car when he left the palace, but coming back in was something to search. Ironically, the items he smuggled out would have set off alarms and red flags.

When Jovan opened the door to the Infirmary, he froze in his shoes. Boris was there talking to a short bald man in a suit.

"Where have you been?" Boris asked Jovan.

"Excuse me?"

"I wanted you here for the first procedure on Ekaterina." Boris motioned to the man beside him. "Dr. Kranski runs the fertility clinic here in the city. I don't want to waste another day waiting for equipment, nor do I want to risk your lack of experience on the matter being the reason a pregnancy doesn't take."

Jovan inhaled slow and steady. Boris brought in another doctor? His mind reeled, trying to figure a way out of the situation. "When will you perform the procedure?"

Dr. Kranski reached his hand forward for a shake. Jovan took his and shook it. "We've completed this round."

"Already?" The blood drained from Jovan's head with a whoosh. He struggled with his composure. Boris's expression held a bit of suspicion. Jovan thought quickly and added, "I would like to learn in case we need follow-ups."

Dr. Kranski said, "I'll be back tomorrow for another round, even though it's probably not necessary because her temperature was perfect. You can watch and learn then."

Jovan's heart rate increased and he tried not to sound alarmed. "What time? I have some appointments scheduled that I can reschedule if needed."

"After office hours."

Boris turned to Dr. Kranski. "This is priority over your other patients."

Dr. Kranski rested back on his heels. "Sir, increasing frequency only increases risk of infection. Once every twenty-four hours is enough until she passes ovulation. Then we wait. If she doesn't catch, next month we'll treat the sample first and intensify the chances. I also have a medication that she can take to make conditions more favorable. But only if we need to take those measures."

Jovan asked, "Where is Ekaterina now?"

"In the exam room. She needs to stay put for a half hour."

Jovan walked away from the two men with a heavy heart. Their whole plan, the main reason she'd agreed to this, was so that he could fake the impregnation. But now . . .

He knocked lightly on the exam room door and heard her quiet voice tell him to come in. As he entered the room, he placed his finger to his lips and moved his eyes to the side, in the direction of Boris, hoping she'd get his message.

She gave a tiny nod. "Dr. Ilievski, I thought you were going to at least help with the procedure." He couldn't help but notice the tremor in her voice.

He responded with words he knew Boris would like to hear. "So did I. But Boris is right. My inexperience might have botched this up." He closed the door to give them privacy, then brought his hands up and rubbed his face hard. He adjusted his glasses and moved to Ekaterina's side. He spoke quietly. "I'm so sorry."

"Where were you?" She grabbed his arm, clinging to him.

"Securing the final arrangements to get you out of here. I'm so, so sorry."

"Can we do that before tomorrow? I heard the other doctor say he'd be back to run the procedure again." Her face shone white as a ghost.

He peeled her hand off his arm and held it with both of his.

"I'll work as fast as possible. Just keep your strong façade and say a prayer. Say many prayers."

"I don't think that's going to help me at this point."

Jovan, needing Ekaterina to keep her focus for a little longer, said, "Please try not to worry about this." Then he laid her hand on her stomach and lied, "Artificial insemination rarely takes hold the first time."

CHAPTER 16

Dr. Ilievski

Jovan had a restless night, running scenarios through his mind, making sure all his bases were covered for what would be his final attempt to save the princess. He knew once he initiated the plan, there would be no turning back. When he'd helped Ekaterina escape the first time, he'd remained in the castle, continuing the position he'd grown comfortable with. But now . . .

His stomach squirmed, flipping back and forth between excitement and terror at the idea that in a few hours, his whole life would change.

He picked up the phone and dialed the number Konstantin gave him.

"Yes," a gruff voice answered.

"I'm calling to see where we are with the list I gave you."

"Everything is completed and ready for your word to go."

"Good. I almost there on my end. I'll contact you shortly." With trembling fingers, he ended the call. Pausing, he took a deep breath and straightened his coat, then raised his chin.

He could do this.

Ivan

Ivan sat in his room with his back against the wall. His body still hurt in various places from his beatings, but he tried not to dwell on it, knowing eventually he'd heal. Though he could do without the pain in his chest from his mending ribs. To keep himself occupied, his mind continually switched between thoughts of his family and Katia. He worried for their safety and for hers, feeling completely helpless. He thought of Katia's words, that a plan was in action, but he had no idea what it would be or how long it might take. Would he be here for weeks, maybe months?

The loud clunk of the lock turning brought his attention to the present. Dr. Ilievski entered the room and closed the door. The guards remained outside.

"I'd like to have a look at those stiches." Dr. Ilievski moved close to Ivan and whispered, "I told the guards I needed some privacy for your examination. How are you doing?"

Ivan let relief sink in, grateful to have an ally within the palace. "Better, I think. My chest still hurts a lot. Did you see Katia? Is she all right?" Ivan couldn't help but be excited.

"Keep your voice low. Yes, she's fine. She's being treated well. Listen, I've got a plan to get you and Ekaterina out of here. I can't tell you the details, I just need you to do exactly what I ask."

"Absolutely."

Dr. Ilievski moved the shirt aside to look at the wounds on Ivan's back. He continued, "If she had waited a couple more days to flee the first time, I could have used this plan with her. But, she was insistent to avoid being married to Vladimir. I figured it was only a matter of time before she was found and brought back. The offered reward was too tempting."

Ivan scoffed.

"Please don't be offended by that assumption. Her capture had nothing to do with you or your ability to hide her."

"It was my fault, though," said Ivan. "I trusted my friend and he turned us in. I'll never trust anyone outside of my own circle again, well, except for you, Dr. Ilievski. I'll never put her in danger again."

"First let's get you out of here, then we can put that to the test." Dr. Ilievski took a deep breath. "Now, let me paint a picture in your mind. When we know someone is dead, we try to move on, we seek closure, and gradually, over time, we learn to accept that that person is gone. When someone only disappears, we are more likely to spend time searching for them, because we never truly lose hope they are still alive. So, the trick here is to—"

"Make them think she's dead." Ivan began to understand.

"Right. If all goes according to plan, you two will be free in a matter of days."

"Tell me what you need me to do."

"I'll hurry as much as I can for your sake."

"My sake? Do it for Katia's."

"She may have an agreement with Boris, but you are still in danger, more so than she is. Vladimir can't be trusted to keep his temper and he's proven, by bringing you back here, that he's able to do things without his father's knowledge or consent." Dr. Ilievski pulled out a pill of some kind, paused for a moment, then and handed it to Ivan. "Swallow this."

Ivan, trusting Dr. Ilievski, swallowed the pill without water. It stuck for a moment in the back of his throat, but he managed to get it down. "What was that?"

"A narcotic for the pain."

"I'm fine, really."

Dr. Ilievski didn't say anything back, but his face sagged. Ivan wondered what he was thinking.

"When they bring you lunch, you need to pretend to choke. They'll call for me." Dr. Ilievski walked to the door and knocked to signal the guard.

Dr. Ilievski

Jovan forced himself to continue working, waiting anxiously for the moment his door would spring open. He'd given Ivan the pill. There was no turning back now. Ivan would react to the drug and Jovan would need to "save" him. He readied his emergency bag, adding a few syringes and a vial of epinephrine, just in case things turned south.

Thirty minutes later, the door to the Infirmary slammed open. "Dr. Ilievski! The prisoner is choking or . . . something. Hurry!"

Jovan nodded, grabbed his emergency bag, and ran down the hall with the guard.

Another guard stood in the opened doorway to the cell, obviously panicked. "Hurry up! His face is turning blue!"

Jovan entered and found Ivan sitting on the floor, holding his throat, and coughing terribly. Ivan tried to get up and walk, but staggered and fell to the ground. Jovan asked the guard as he rushed to Ivan's side, "What happened?"

"Don't know. He just started coughing and gagging. We tried

the Heimlich maneuver."

Jovan knelt beside Ivan who reached for him with one hand, eyes pleading for help. "He might be having an allergic reaction to the food." Jovan forced his face to stay neutral. Ivan's reaction was much more violent than expected. He reached in his bag, pulled out a vial of epinephrine and a syringe and prepared for an injection. Ivan lost consciousness as Jovan administered the shot. "Help me carry him to the Infirmary. Carry his legs."

The guard asked, "Do we need President Kochev's approval?"

"No time. Boris would want this boy to live, and to do that we need to get him to the Infirmary."

The guards picked up Ivan's legs while Jovan grabbed him under his arms. Together they hauled him down the corridor and put him on the exam table.

"Grab that cart and bring it here," he ordered one of the guards. "Stay with me, Ivan." He took Ivan's blood pressure and lifted his eyelids. Ivan's eyes were rolled back in his head. He gave another shot into the young man's arm and listened to his lungs for breathing sounds. The guards looked on, concerned.

"Should I get Kochev?" one asked.

"Use the phone. I need you to stay here."

Boris

Boris sat at the large dining table with his wife, son, and new daughter-in-law. His family. Thinking about family was new to him, thinking about those who lived before him and those yet to come. He could almost hear the pitter-patter of little feet that would ensure his reign in the history books. Gaining the favor he needed with the influential portion of the population and with countries abroad, he would go on to become the strongest ruler ever.

Pride filled his bosom, and a smile crept over his face.

A servant entered the room and spoke in a low voice to Boris. "Sir, you have an urgent call from the Infirmary. There's a problem with the prisoner."

Boris pushed his chair back so abruptly he startled everyone. "I'll be right back." He ignored Ekaterina's wide eyes. With quick strides he exited the door and took the call.

"I don't know what happened, but he's dying, sir," the guard said on the other end of the line. Boris caught Vladimir's eye at the door and motioned for him to join him. No one, including Ekaterina, missed the urgent tone of the unspoken words. She stood, but Boris pointed at her to sit back down.

Boris and Vladimir moved quickly down the hall in the direction of the Infirmary. Boris hissed, "If this is your doing, Vladimir . . ."

"I haven't touched him."

"But you did. If this is a complication to his existing injuries, your spending allowance will be cut off."

Vladimir snarled as they entered the Infirmary, "You better keep him alive, Doctor,"

"I'm doing my best." Dr. Ilievski injected something into the prisoner's arm, dumping the empty syringe on the tray next to two other spent syringes, then performed CPR. The guard placed the air bag mask on Ivan's face on cue.

Boris realized they'd probably been doing this for a little while already. He watched and thought about the ramifications if the boy died. Ekaterina would be distraught or worse. She'd be an unwilling party in his plan.

Boris turned to a nearby guard. "What happened?"

"It's unclear. He was fine before eating his food, then he began choking. That's when we called the doc."

"I told you I didn't touch him, Father." Vladimir crossed his arms and widened his stance.

"Ivan!" Ekaterina appeared in the doorway. Boris should have known she wouldn't have remained in the dining room. She tried to rush into the Infirmary, but Vladimir intercepted her and held her back. "Dr. Ilievski, what's happening?" she half-yelled, half-cried.

"Get her out of here!" Boris motioned to her guards to assist.

"No!" she protested and fought with the men trying to subdue her. "Ivan!"

She was overpowered and dragged out of the Infirmary. Boris could hear her screaming all the way down the hall and up the staircase. *The boy cannot die! Not yet!* he thought.

"She has too much freedom," Vladimir stated, cocking his head and straightening his jacket.

Boris glared at his son, debating whether to cuff him upside the head.

Dr. Ilievski continued to perform chest compressions, and the guard pumped air into Ivan's lungs.

Boris asked, "Doctor, how long has he been unconscious?"

Dr. Ilievski didn't respond, which only intensified the situation. Boris' trusted physician was panicked. The idea fortified the notion that the boy may not ever wake up.

Then, Ivan's body began convulsing and Dr. Ilievski had the guard remove the mask and turn Ivan's head to the side in time for him to vomit over the edge of the bed. The guard stepped out of the way, and Vladimir let out a disgusted grunt.

"It's common for CPR victims to vomit because of all the air that's been forced into the stomach," Dr. Ilievski said as he wiped his brow with the back of his hand.

"So, is he going to live?" Vladimir asked.

"It's too early to tell." Dr. Ilievski replied, then worked methodically to insert an IV into Ivan's arm.

"What happened, Doctor?" Boris asked.

"I'm not sure. Allergic reaction, I think, maybe to something he ate or touched? I'll have to run some tests."

Boris turned to Vladimir. "Bring Ekaterina back down so she can see he's alive."

Vladimir shifted on his feet. "I'll tell her he didn't die."

"No!" Boris pointed to the ground. "You'll bring her back down."

"Fine." Vladimir whirled on his heel and left the Infirmary.

Boris stood planted in the same spot, observing the doctor and assistant as they continued to work on the boy. Even though the boy was a thorn in his side, that thorn was what Ekaterina clung to. She had no idea how important she was to the success of securing the allies support. Boris prided himself on keeping secret the planned merging of Bregot with Katastasi, the island nation to the south, and with that, the inclusion of military support that would eradicate the Insurgent underground. But to complete the joining of forces, Ekaterina needed to marry his son—already done—and produce an heir, merging the royal line with his. The grand plan was something Boris hadn't discussed with anyone other than the crown prince of Katastasi. There were simply too many untrustworthy individuals roaming the palace.

What Boris didn't need was his son getting his own ideas on how to handle Ekaterina. Boris admired her a small bit for standing tall, for demanding certain stipulations, namely keeping Vladimir away from her. She was smart. Her offspring would also be smart . . . well, if Vladimir's idiotic traits didn't win out. Boris decided that once she was pregnant, she would be locked away from Vladimir and his irrational, unpredictable behavior. Her life and the life she needed to create were far too important. But first, the thorn in Boris' side, laying on the gurney before him, needed to live and Ekaterina needed to see he survived so she wouldn't try to take her life again. As smart as she was, she still had the propensity to harm herself.

Ivan

Ivan lay in the worst pain he'd ever felt, barely able to breathe, unable to move. He couldn't believe it had only been a little over a week since he'd driven around the lake in search of Crossers, bemoaning his pitiful life, wishing he could have more to grasp, more to engage with. He certainly got what he wished for, and boy did he get it good. Luka had warned him not to get attached, his parents had as well, but somewhere in Ivan's mind he had thought they didn't know what they were talking about. Perhaps he was right, still—none of them had ever been taken to the palace and beaten to within an inch of their lives.

Except that didn't explain why he was incapacitated and in his current situation.

He heard a voice say, "Just leave a guard outside the door." Ivan recognized the voice as Dr. Ilievski's.

Boris' voice sounded from nearby. "I'll have General Brankov guard the door. Call me when he regains consciousness, Jovan."

Ivan heard a door close, then the doctor said, "Where are your crutches, Princess?"

"I don't care about that. Tell me what happened to Ivan?"

The beautiful sound of her voice made Ivan's heart rate double. He felt her soft hand take his and press it to her lips and cheek. He could feel her hot breath and skin and wished he could open his eyes or make a sound to let her know he was awake, but his body wouldn't respond.

Dr. Ilievski said, "He didn't handle the drug very well."

"Very well?"

"Okay, not at all. It was supposed to only make him ill. Instead, the drug nearly killed him. Technically, it did. But he's holding his own now and I believe once the sedative wears off, he'll be fine."

"He's going to be so angry with you." She half laughed through her choked sob.

"Yes, he will. Especially because I may have broken another one of his ribs with the CPR compressions. You should return to your room, Ekaterina. Come see him first thing in the morning."

"I want to stay with Ivan."

"No. We don't need Vladimir acting erratic over your attentions to Ivan. Go to your room. In the morning, I want you to wear some specific clothing when you come to visit. Cream pants and a pink blouse. This is crucial to the plan, Ekaterina. I know you have these items in your wardrobe. Please do this."

"Okay."

Ivan felt her kiss his lips gently before letting go of his hand.

* * *

Ivan moaned. His whole body ached, except his chest, which felt like it was being stabbed with bits of fire. He wondered what time it was. The clock on the wall said half past three, but he didn't know if that was A.M. or P.M. There weren't any windows in his room to help with his assessment.

Dr. Ilievski asked, "How do you feel?"

"Bad." His eyes squeezed shut. "Where's Katia?"

"She's gone to bed. She'll come down in the morning. Now that you're awake, I'm going to wheel you into the x-ray room and check out your ribs. Try to relax."

"I feel like I've been run over by a train."

"That's quite a common feeling after having CPR performed on you."

"CPR?"

Dr. Ilievski unlocked the brakes on the bed and wheeled him into the adjoining room. "I drugged you, Ivan, and accidently killed you. But don't worry, I brought you back. No harm, except for the possibility of more damage to your ribs." He moved Ivan directly under the x-ray machine and placed the film canister under him, then stepped behind the wall and took the shot. After repeating the procedure two more times, he wheeled Ivan back to the exam room and helped him sit up.

Dr. Ilievski jammed the developed films up in the lighted board, "I don't see any new breaks, so that's good. You'll have plenty of pain from the compressions for a bit. Sorry about that. I'll get you more medicine."

Ivan tried to find a comfortable position, but each movement brought sharp stabs to his chest. "Why did you do this to me?"

"Because Boris moved up my timeline by bringing in another doctor to perform the artificial insemination on Ekaterina."

"Artificial . . . what?" Ivan gasped as fresh stabs of pain took his breath.

Dr. Ilievski's tone softened. "Look, there's a lot you've missed. Ekaterina is married to Vladimir."

"Yes, I know. She told me."

"Well, the deal she struck with Boris included that she wouldn't rebel so long as he or Vladimir don't lay a hand on her. Boris insisted an heir be part of the deal. She agreed to artificial insemination, to avoid any contact with Vladimir, which I thought was brilliant because I'd be the one to do the procedure. I planned to bluff the situation to Boris while her and I worked on an escape plan. I had already delayed the first procedure by a few days. But that was before we found out you were here in the palace. Boris didn't know about you, either, and boy was he upset with Vladimir. I could tell Boris was worried your presence would threaten the whole agreement he had with Ekaterina. I think that's why he brought in an outside doctor to perform the procedure. He didn't want to waste another second waiting for me. The doctor was here last night. He's coming again tonight. That's why I did this to you, Ivan—for Ekaterina's sake. The first procedure may not have worked, but every time it's done again the chances increase." He placed a hand on Ivan's shoulder. "I'm so sorry."

Ivan couldn't believe what he heard. His thoughts raced back to the last time he'd seen Katia. According to Dr. Ilievski, though, she hadn't been seen by the other doctor at that time. Ivan wondered what she must be thinking. He couldn't imagine the idea that she may be pregnant with Vladimir's child. And yet how much worse must Katia feel? She must be terrified. He closed his eyes and tried to control his quivering chin. If only he'd kept his mouth shut and not told Anton about the kiss, neither of them would have gone through any of this.

Dr. Ilievski took a bottle from the cupboard and tapped two pills into his hand. He continued, "I knew only a serious health situation would get you moved in here. Boris wouldn't have allowed you to stay if your situation wasn't severe. Last night I gathered from his behavior that he *needs* you to live."

"That's good, right?" His words came out scratchy and he forced himself to stay focused on the present moment.

Dr. Ilievski handed the pills to Ivan, then filled a paper cup with water and gave it to him. "Yes, and no. It's good for you, but for Ekaterina it means there's even more pressure to produce an heir. Boris thinks she's cooperating because you're alive. I worry that there's something else going on concerning her importance, and your 'staying alive' is important to making that happen. So imperative, in fact, Boris put General Brankov on guard in the hall."

Ivan tossed the pills into his mouth and washed them down, then asked, "Why did you need me in here?"

"Because this is where the plan hopefully moves forward. For now, you need to try to rest."

Ekaterina

The next morning, Ekaterina stood in front of her closet, sliding through different shirts. She wondered how and why Dr. Ilievski knew about the pink blouse and why it was so important, however, she didn't waste time on the questions. She needed to get down to Ivan. She found what she searched for, slipped into her cream pants and blouse, and opened her door.

"Please take me to the Infirmary."

The guards nodded. She hobbled in front of them, once again leaving her crutches behind. The crutches slowed her down and she didn't want to delay any moment longer in seeing that Ivan was okay.

They passed the dining hall and Ekaterina could see Vladimir sitting with his back to her. Seated nearby was Eva Brankov, General Brankov's daughter who attended school with Ekaterina. Eva's eyes were wide and she sat forward in her chair, as if enraptured by Vladimir's words. Ekaterina shook her head and thought, *She can have him.*

Her personal guards saluted General Brankov as they approached the Infirmary. General Brankov was a military man to the bone. His perfect posture and immaculate uniform were indications of how dedicated he was to his position.

"Good morning, Mrs. Kochev," the general said.

She let out a guttural sound and bit back a retort. "I would like to see Ivan. I assume he's inside, unless you have another high-profile prisoner you're guarding."

General Brankov frowned, then turned and opened the door for Ekaterina. "Dr. Ilievski, is the prisoner awake?"

"Yes. Ah, Ekaterina, come in. Where are your crutches? I'm going to be forced to confine you to a wheelchair if you don't start using them. Is that what you want?"

"No. I've had a lot on my mind, that's all. I forgot to grab them," she lied.

Dr. Ilievski turned to the general. "Your services are no longer needed, General Brankov. I've secured the prisoner."

"Boris ordered me to guard the boy. It's not your place to dismiss me."

"Pardon me, General." Dr Ilievski's tone lightened and became submissive. "I was only indicating you could go and get some rest or food. You must be as tired as I am."

"I'll remain at the door."

"That's your call." Dr. Ilievski nodded toward Ekaterina's guards. "This space is too small. Please join the General outside the room. I will keep them under observation." The doctor closed the door and ushered Ekaterina back to the exam room to Ivan.

She rushed to his side and took his hand. All the emotions swirling inside her broke free. Tears ran freely down her face.

Ivan turned his head slowly. "Hey there."

She kissed his hand repeatedly. "Oh Ivan, I was so scared! You were lifeless. Are you okay now?" She bent forward and kissed his lips.

He brought up one arm and cupped her cheek. His thumb smoothed away the tears that trickled from her eyes. He said, "Don't cry, Katia. I'm all right."

"I can't help it. I thought I'd lost you, again!" Fresh tears flooded her eyes.

"I'm not that easy to kill," he said with a smile. His fingertips traced along her cheek and jaw and she reached up and placed her hand on his. Then his expression turned down.

"What's wrong, Ivan?"

"This is all my fault."

"What? No, it isn't."

"Doc told me what happened to you, how another doctor was brought in and everything. That wouldn't have happened if I'd kept you safe."

She squeezed his hand. "Ivan—"

Dr. Ilievski interrupted, "I know you have a lot you want to talk about, but we don't have time for that right now. How are those ribs feeling, Ivan?" Dr. Ilievski asked.

"They hurt, but they've taken my mind off the other pains in my body. Funny how that works, isn't it?" Ivan kept steady, comforting eye contact with her as he spoke.

Ekaterina sighed. "I know what you're going through."

"Let's see if you can sit up." Dr Ilievski moved to Ivan's side to give him help. "Can you take a deep breath?" Ivan did so and coughed. The doctor listened with his stethoscope. "Your lungs are clear, but that cough could be a problem."

Ekaterina cast a puzzled glance between the doctor and Ivan. She asked, "What do you mean?"

Dr. Ilievski said, "My plan to get both of you out of here requires a stretch of time in silence."

Ekaterina gave a curt nod. "Whatever it takes to get out, we'll do it."

"Well," the doctor said, "for this to work, you both need to be absolutely quiet. No coughing. And for possibly several hours. Also, are either of you claustrophobic?"

Ivan shook his head.

Ekaterina asked, "Why? I mean, I'm not, but why?"

"Because you're going to be in a tight, dark space for at least a day. If you can't handle it, we shouldn't even attempt it. I've worked too hard to have the secret room discovered because of someone coughing or sneezing or panicking."

"You sound like my dad," Ivan said.

"This is all or nothing, Ivan and Ekaterina. There will not be another try. This either works or it doesn't. If it doesn't work, I'm certain Ivan and I will be killed on the spot, and Ekaterina, you would be locked away until you give birth. That's the severity of this situation. I want the two of you to understand. We do this one-hundred percent or not at all."

Ivan reached out for Ekaterina's hand, which she grasped firmly. He said, "I'm in, one-hundred percent."

"Me too. Let's get out of here!"

Dr. Ilievski reached forward and placed his hand on top of hers. "I want you both to know it's been an honor to know you. No matter what happens, I'll never regret becoming involved with helping you survive. If, for whatever reason, this fails, know that I won't hold any ill feelings toward either of you. If this succeeds, I hope we meet again someday."

Ekaterina couldn't speak. She knew what she should say, but somehow the words where caught in her throat somewhere between "everything will be fine" and "thank you." Instead, she flung her arms around him, hugging him tightly. Memories flooded her mind of when she met Dr. Ilievski four months ago, following her first brutal beating from Boris. The doctor's disgusted reaction to her wounds was perplexing at the time. She didn't know if he was disgusted by her or by the injuries. She remembered that over time he became more openly sympathetic to her plight. Now she considered the possibility that he had been converted to her cause from beating number one. And, yes, he'd become a life-long friend.

Once Ekaterina released him, Ivan shook the doctor's hand and said, "We can. We will. Thank you."

Dr. Ilievski dropped his hand and said, "Ivan, lie back down while I tell you about the plan. You should pretend to be asleep, and Ekaterina, why don't you sit on this chair here and hold his hand with a concerned look. This way, if anyone comes into the clinic, like Boris, the stage will already be set."

"Okay." She nodded.

Dr. Ilievski took a deep breath. "I've built a secret space in the storage room of my clinic. Basically, I reduced the overall storage capacity by moving the back wall forward by one meter. I've added a small set of supplies in the corner—a few bottles of water and some granola bars. There's also a bucket with a lid to use as a bathroom. A small bag of peat sits next to it. Sprinkle some when you use the bucket to smother the smell. I plan to hide you in there while the rest of the plan transpires. Once you're locked in, you can't come out unless you're in a body bag."

Ivan says, "Dead?"

"That's the goal."

Ekaterina asked, "What do you mean?"

"We're going to fake your deaths. Convincingly fake your deaths. I have a list of ways to communicate with me if this charade goes on longer than twenty-four hours. The list is posted in the secret room with code names like penicillin for water and insulin for food, and so on. You'll write those on provided slips of paper and slide them under the wall, which I'll keep an eye out for the communications. Do *not* do this until I've indicated we're alone. Make sure you stand and stretch regularly to keep adequate blood flow in your legs. When the coast is clear, I'll let you know in case you need to make noise, cough, or open packages."

She asked the doctor, "How long have you had this room?"

"It's been completed for over a year. I got the idea when I asked for partition walls to create the exam rooms. I figured if I could have enough leftover materials to build another wall, I could create a hidden area inside the storage room. So, I over-ordered lumber and boards and used my spare time to finish the project." He placed his hand on Ekaterina's.

"I had no idea, Jovan."

"I've told no one about its existence before now. If you'd have waited a couple of days the first time you fled, I would have put you in the hideaway and faked your death and gotten you out of the country for good. You would have never been brought back here."

"Yes, but I would have been married to Vladimir and . . ." she trailed off.

Ivan said quietly, "We would never have met if you'd waited."

She smiled.

Ivan asked the doctor, "You said you built it a year ago. That was before Katia came to the palace. So, why did you build it?"

"To help me escape someday."

"But you're not being held captive," Ekaterina stated.

"Yes, I am. Boris lured me into this position with the promise of establishing my medical name. He 'gave me a chance' when no other clinic would take me. However, once I'd joined, he closed off the border, even for me. He won't let me leave the country, except on official business. I've had to witness a lot of pain and hurt at the hands of Boris. I couldn't take it anymore." He looked into Ekaterina's eyes. "You were the last straw." Dr. Ilieveski looked at the clock on the wall. "Now, before we start, I need both of you to use the bathroom."

"I'm fine."

"Me too," Ekaterina said.

"You should try anyway. The longer you can go without using the bucket, the better."

After both had taken turns in the restroom and were resituated in the exam room, Dr. Ilievski had Ivan change out of the exam gown and into an oversized shirt and sweatpants. Ekaterina couldn't help but notice all the markings and bruises on his body that weren't there when the two of them undressed at the cabin. That stretch of time seemed so long ago, even though it wasn't.

"Before we can move forward, I need to make a call. Keep your positions."

Ekaterina sat beside Ivan and lovingly held his hand as Dr. Ilievski talked to someone on the phone.

"I have a setback," Dr. Ilievski said. "The exit isn't clear. Do you have someone on the inside that can distract or remove the blockade? What about the other assets? Good? How soon can your men be ready?" Dr. Ilievski's eyebrows shot up quickly. "Well, then, it's now or never. We go as soon as the path is clear. Hold the line." He put the phone down and slowly walked over to the door. He leaned his ear to the door and waited.

Ivan asked Ekaterina, "What's he doing?"

"I don't know."

Dr. Ilievski made eye contact with Ekaterina and put his finger to his lips.

After a few moments, the doctor hurried back to the phone and spoke urgently. "The path is clear. Start the process in one minute." He hung up the phone and entered the exam room. "It's time. Follow me."

CHAPTER 17

Ekaterina

Ekaterina limped on her splinted leg and Ivan leaned on her for support. Ivan moved fairly well considering everything he'd been through the last couple of days. Hopefully he'd be able to continue to heal in the confined space they were about to occupy. Dr. Ilievski led them into the supply room just off the main exam room. He moved a shelving unit slightly to one side, exposing a narrow opening into the small area he'd described.

"What happens next?" Ekaterina asked him.

"No time to explain. I have thirty seconds to execute the next step. In you go. Silence begins now."

Ivan slid through the narrow opening first. While Ekaterina waited for her turn, she watched the doctor open a couple containers and rip plastic off something flesh-colored and palm-sized. He slammed the strange item onto his forehead and pushed all the edges against his skin. When he removed his hand, she saw what looked like a swollen gash across the top of his face.

Dr. Ilievski noticed her watching and said, "It's theater makeup."

Ekaterina slid through the opening and waited for the doctor to close the wall. He added other effects to his "injury" before coming to close them in. He said, "Remember, silence is imperative. Good luck." He slid the shelving against the wall enclosing her inside with Ivan.

The lighting was dim, mainly coming in through a small gap at the bottom of the wall, with another light source at the other end of the space. The optimal use of the minimal space was astounding to Ekaterina. Three feet wide by ten feet long, two narrow bunks with bedding filled one side of the far end while shelving units attached to the walls above head level held bins and boxes of supplies at the end with the opening. Ivan had already laid down on the bottom bunk.

Crashing sounds from the exam room brought her attention back. She wasn't sure what she was hearing, but knew the doctor was causing the sounds. She pulled the pillow and blanket off the top bunk and sat down on the floor next to Ivan's bed, taking his hand into hers for comfort.

"What if they find us?" she whispered.

"Dr. Ilievski is very smart. He knows what will look suspicious and what won't. An open room with the light on isn't suspicious. They'll be searching the palace and the grounds."

Dr. Ilievski's voice sounded into the room through the closed wall. "Silence. I can hear you."

Ivan and Ekaterina looked at each other, both shocked that even their whisperings could be heard.

The phone in the Infirmary rang, and rang, and rang. Dr. Ilievski obviously wasn't going to answer it. Ekaterina's heart beat faster, knowing any second someone would come to investigate why the doctor wasn't answering the phone. Ivan's body shuddered and Ekaterina looked at him—he appeared to be struggling not to cough. She prayed he could stay quiet.

Five minutes passed in silence.

The door to the Infirmary slammed open.

"What the hell happened in here?" Ekaterina had no problem recognizing Boris's thundering voice. "Doctor, wake up, damn you. Guards!"

"Yes, sir. Oh . . ." the unknown voice trailed off. Several more voices entered the Infirmary. All expressed confusion and questions.

"You there, get me Vladimir! You two, search this area. The princess and the prisoner need to be secured. Don't step in the blood, you idiot."

Ekaterina squeezed Ivan's hand tighter and laid her head on the bed next to his. This was it. The moment where they might be found. Ivan's hand shook in hers as together they heard someone pushing things around in the storage room a mere twelve inches away, on the other side of the fake wall. Then the sounds stopped.

Voices sounded again out in the main area. "Sir, they're not here. I'll contact the gatehouse to lock down."

Boris shouted, "Lock it all down: the border, the airport, set up roadblocks on all roads around the city. No one in, no one out. That girl is as slippery as a greased pig. Where are her guards, anyway? And where the hell is General Brankov?"

Voices barked out Boris's orders, receiving inaudible responses through the crackle of their handheld radios.

Vladimir's voice sounded into the supply room. "What's going on! What happened to him?"

Ekaterina heard Dr. Ilievski moan.

Boris said, "Vladimir, help him sit up. Everyone be quiet or get out."

Voices silenced for a moment.

"Dr. Ilievski, what happened?" Vladimir demanded.

"One of them hit me after I turned my back to put up the x-rays. I fell forward and must have hit my head on the table. How long was I out? Wait, how did they get past the guards?"

"I don't know but someone's neck will be wrung when I find out," Boris answered.

General Brankov's voice sounded. "Sir, I left my post when the girl's guard informed me you wanted to speak to me. He said he'd watch the door. I left five minutes ago. They couldn't have gone far in that amount of time. We'll find them."

Dr. Ilievski responded, "When you find them, bring them to me. I have a score to settle."

"Get in line." Vladimir's harsh voice caused Ekaterina to bury her face further into the mattress. Ivan caressed her head. She didn't believe for one second that if Vladimir found them first he would stick to any deal his father had made.

Boris said, "So, they had help. I want that guard shot on site."

Vladimir said, "He's probably *with* them, so don't shoot unless you have a clean shot."

"I give the orders here, Vladimir!"

"Father, what if they kill Ekaterina by accident?"

Boris muttered acceptance along with a string of cursing, then calmed himself. "Dr. Ilievski, get cleaned up." He almost sounded as if he cared. "We need a description of them. What where they wearing?"

"The boy wore a T-shirt and sweatpants. Gray. The princess wore a pink blouse and . . . not sure on the pants. Light in color though."

"There, we have a description. Get it out to the police and the border," Boris ordered.

The exam room quieted down as most of the voices left the Infirmary. "Dr. Ilievski, may I assist you with your injury?" an unrecognizable voice sounded into the room.

"Yes. Please scoot that cart over to me. Thank you. In the cupboard to the left is a suture tray. It's labeled such. We'll need a cleanup crew, too, for all the blood."

Ekaterina listened with Ivan to the variety of noises coming from the exam room. Small talk between the doctor and his assistant continued for nearly an hour. A cleaning crew arrived at some point and Ekaterina could hear the rhythmic sounds of a mop sloshing back and forth. At one point, Dr. Ilievski instructed the assistant to get some supplies from the room—the very room they were hiding in. They could hear him rifling through containers just on the other side of the wall, not knowing the fugitives were inches away.

Someone entered the clinic and said breathlessly, "They've been spotted!"

Ekaterina's heart jumped into her throat.

"They stole your car, Dr. Ilievski," the voice continued.

A sigh of relief escaped her lips and she felt the tension in Ivan's hand around hers relax.

"What? Are you serious? They must have taken my keys out of my jacket. That's just great! I just paid off the loan! So, where were they spotted?"

"They made it out of the city headed north. They're stupid if they think they can get past the border. Every policeman and military troop is looking for them. They won't get far."

"It would appear they've gotten far enough already," Dr. Ilievski answered back.

Voices on a handheld radio reported in distorted voices, "Suspect's vehicle crashed."

"What location?"

"Three-mile hill. They went over the edge."

"Edge of what?"

"What do you think? The cliff. We're going to need . . . going to need, ah hell, there's no way they survived that." A loud distortion of sound blared through the radio.

Dr. Ilievski asked, "What was that?"

The other voice answered, "It sounded like a—"

The radio's voice was nearly indiscernible. "The car exploded! It's in flames. We need a fire truck." There were a lot of voices in the background. "Cancel that. We're just going to have to wait for the fire to burn itself out."

"How far down is the vehicle?"

"At least five hundred feet," the radio banter continued.

The three men in the Infirmary talked together. Dr. Ilievski said, "Boris is not going to like this one bit."

"Tell me about it. I don't want to even cross his path for fear he'll shoot me just to feel better."

"It wasn't your fault."

"It wouldn't matter."

"How's Vladimir going to take this?" Dr. Ilievski asked.

"Vladimir couldn't care less, I'm guessing. He's been seen several times with General Brankov's daughter ever since Ekaterina's disappearance a few days ago."

"Eva Brankov?"

"Yes."

"Vladimir is a piece of work, really," the third voice stated.

"He's Boris's piece of work, and we all have to live with it," Dr. Ilievski said plainly. "You two better get back to your posts before Boris sees you're gone or I'll be treating you later."

"Um, we realize we don't really have to ask, but can you keep what we just said, you know, confidential?"

"Of course."

The two men left the room and silence settled in.

Ekaterina's muscles unknotted. The first part of the plan had been a success. She quietly climbed onto the narrow bed next to Ivan, burying her head into his chest, relishing his scent and the sound of his heartbeat. The adrenaline in her body slipped away and her eyes drooped. She felt the soft touch of Ivan's fingers running across her forehead and hair. The morning's events washed over and she couldn't resist the lull of sleep.

Dr. Ilievski

No verbal communication between Jovan and his escapees took place throughout the morning and into the early afternoon. Various palace staff members came into the Infirmary with a wide assortment of ailments, as per usual. Everyone voiced their concern for Dr. Ilievski's wellbeing and had their own comments about the situation between Ekaterina Cvetkovski and her mysterious friend. Most of the palace employees felt Ekaterina was right in trying to flee. Jovan found it interesting how willing everyone was to talk openly about the happenings in the palace—and to him, Boris's trusted physician. Did the employees and staff see through his act? Did they trust that he wouldn't rat them out to Boris? Perhaps he needed to tighten down his game to keep Boris unsuspecting of his doublehandedness. Though truthfully, it wouldn't matter for much longer.

At six o'clock, the phone rang. "Dr. Ilievski," he answered.

"Sir, this is the gate house. We have a Dr. Kranski here saying he has an appointment in the Infirmary. Can you confirm this?"

"The appointment has been canceled. Please pass my apologies to the doctor for the last-minute change." Jovan hung up the phone and breathed a sigh of relief. He imagined Ekaterina was doing the same.

A few hours later, the word came in that the bodies of the two escapees were being brought to the palace for identification and to keep their disappearance under wraps. The Infirmary cleared out momentarily and Jovan hurried into the supply room.

"We're alone, if you need to make noise."

He heard several rustlings and then Ivan coughed and cleared his throat.

"How's your breathing, Ivan?"

"Fair," he said, and coughed again.

Jovan scrubbed his face with his hands. "We're almost done. Hang in there." The door to the Infirmary opened, ending their conversation.

Jovan grabbed a box of syringes and walked out of the supply room nonchalantly. He didn't look at the person who entered. Instead he said over his shoulder, "I'll be right with you."

The phone rang. He answered it. "Dr. Ilievski."

"Sir, is General Brankov in the Infirmary?"

"No." Jovan turned his head and found the person who had entered the Infirmary was in fact the general. "Wait, yes. Here he is." Jovan extended his hand with the phone. "It's for you, General."

While General Brankov conducted the call, Jovan busied himself with the box of syringes, feeling relieved he'd decided to bring it with him when he exited the supply room. However, Jovan was also acutely aware of how close they'd come to being discovered. *What if the general had come in a few seconds earlier when Ivan coughed?*

"Burned beyond recognition? Then what makes you think it's them?" General Brankov said to the caller. "Hold the line." The general put his hand over the phone and asked, "Doctor, do you have dental records for Ekaterina and would you be able to make an identification based on them."

"Yes, and yes. What about the boy? Do they need him to be identified, too? Because I performed x-rays on him and could probably make an identification based on those."

The general passed on the information to the caller, then hung up the phone.

"Well, then," Jovan said, "I guess you don't have any reason to stay down here anymore."

"Doctor, I need you to take a look at something."

The general took off his jacket and exposed his forearm. A break in the skin mid arm was obviously infected. The swelling and discoloration radiated away from the wound for several inches. "How long have you had that?" Dr. Ilievski asked.

"A couple of days now."

"What happened?"

"My daughter has a rebellious nature. She didn't like her recent assignment . . . anyway, it doesn't matter. The swelling is climbing."

"I'm not sure I want to know what kind of assignment would result in you getting injured like this. You've got yourself a nasty case of cellulitis. I'm going to give you an injection of antibiotics and some pills, but you'll need to let me check that out tomorrow to make sure it's getting better."

Dr. Ilievski entered the room for supplies. His whole body froze when he heard Ivan cough. Jovan hadn't been talking when the cough occurred, so he could say it was him, if the general asked. Ivan coughed again, harder.

"Dr. Ilievski, are you all right?"

"Yes, it's nothing. I've been fighting off a cold for a while now." Dr. Ilievski returned with a vial and syringe. He wiped the general's bared shoulder and injected the medicine. "There you go. That's a powerful antibiotic. You should see major improvement within twenty-four—"

Ivan coughed again.

General Brankov bolted off the exam bed and pulled his gun.

"Don't move, Dr. Ilievski, or I'll shoot!"

Jovan raised his hands and let the air out of his lungs. This was it. At least he had tried to help the princess. Ivan coughed again, though it sounded more muffled. The general grinned. "What an elaborate plan you've concocted, Jovan. Boris will be pleased to learn the Cvetkovski girl still lives, but it will madden him to no end to learn his trusted physician is a traitor. I should kill you now and save him the trouble, and I should kill the girl too and save the Insurgents the trouble. No," he paused, "I'll call up to Boris. Don't move!"

Dr. Ilievski's knees trembled, and his fingers had gone numb with fear. It had been a good plan, a solid plan. If only he had sound-proofed the cubicle. His eyes darted around the room looking for some type of a weapon. But with a gun barrel staring him down and an excellent marksman behind the trigger, he didn't dare move.

The general picked up the phone and began punching in the four-digit number for Boris: first number, second, third button pressed . . . he stopped and hung up the phone. "Dr. Ilievski, I hope you realize how lucky you are that Konstantin likes you." He un-cocked his gun and put it back in its holster. "I do see his point, though. You will be instrumental when the time comes."

"You and Konstantin?" Jovan's voice nearly burst out of his chest.

"Yes. But don't think for a second I wouldn't kill the girl if she is captured."

"She won't be captured."

"She would have been right now if I was anyone else." General Brankov walked toward the exit.

Dr. Ilievski rubbed his hands roughly over each other and sat on the exam bed with a crunch. "General, don't forget the pills."

"Right, thank you."

"Same. If you don't see improvement by tomorrow night, you'll need another injection."

General Brankov nodded and left the Infirmary.

Dr. Ilievski entered the storage room. "Cough it out, son. We're alone."

"I'm sorry," Ivan said humbly. "I tried holding a pillow over my face."

Ekaterina added, "General Brankov is an Insurgent? Who would've thought that?"

Ekaterina

Late in the night, Ekaterina and Ivan were awakened to the lights being turned on and voices filling the room. Boris, Vladimir, and Dr. Ilievski's voices were easy to pick out. The others must have been guards.

"Place them here," Dr. Ilievski ordered. Dull thuds and chair legs scraped the floor, followed by the sound of zippers being opened.

Vladimir's voice was muffled as if maybe his hand was over his mouth and nose. "Eww, disgusting. That better be the S-O-B." Ekaterina felt Ivan's hand tighten at Vladimir's comment.

Boris asked, "How long will it take you to make the identification, Dr. Ilievski?"

"A couple of hours for a positive ID. I wouldn't stop searching if I were you. This could be a ruse to throw you off their tracks."

"I doubt it. They're not that clever. Besides, that one has a metal splint just like Ekaterina's."

Vladimir's voice sounded somber. "Look at the wedding ring. That's the one I gave her."

Boris asked, "Do you need any assistance?"

"No, but I would like some uninterrupted time. Any medical emergencies can be directed to the hospital, not down here."

"Understood. Let's go, Vladimir."

Vladimir said almost remorsefully, "I'd like to have a moment alone. She was . . . my wife."

A lump of disgust caught in Ekaterina's throat. Ivan's comforting arms wrapped around her.

"Of course. We'll step out," Dr. Ilievski said.

Vladimir's footsteps were heard as he walked around the room. The eerie sound of his voice made Ekaterina's hair stand on end. "I know you can hear me, Ekaterina."

A tremble shook through her. Did he know they were hiding? Ivan held her tighter.

"There's no way you'd do this to me and not be here to gloat. All I can say is I'm happy you're dead. At least Risto can't have you now." The door to the Infirmary opened and then closed.

Ekaterina let out her held breath and pressed her head into Ivan's shoulder. She'd thought for sure Vladimir knew they were in the Infirmary. Come to find out, Vladimir was a believer in vindictive spirits.

Dr. Ilievski came back in and actually whistled while he worked. They heard him breaking bones and wheeling gurneys into the x-ray room. Later they heard the shuffling of files in the filing cabinet. Occasionally Dr. Ilievski would mutter something like, "perfect" or "beautiful." Then he made the phone call informing Boris that he had completed the identification.

A short while later, Boris and Vladimir entered the exam room for the verdict.

"In my medical opinion, based on the evidence, I declare these two corpses are in fact Ivan Lazarov and Ekaterina Cvetkovski Kochev."

"You're one hundred percent positive?" Vladimir asked.

"Absolutely. Do you want to look over my report?"

"No, it's not necessary."

"Really, it's quite fascinating the matching—"

"I said no, Dr. Ilievski," Vladimir rudely cut him off.

"Suit yourself. I have a recommendation to make, if I may, sir."

Boris answered in a much-deflated voice, "Go ahead."

"The body of the male should be returned to Svobodia to keep the tension at a minimum between the two countries, and a formal funeral service should be held for Ekaterina to publicize your willingness to bring her into your family."

"Fine. See that the body is shipped back. But that could pose a problem. Because tensions are still high, my men cannot go across the border."

"Well, sir, since I still retain Svobodian citizenship, I could escort the body and not be arrested. Plus, I would very much like to visit my family. I could take his remains for you and offer condolences on your behalf, if you'd grant me permission to cross the border."

"Fine, I'll give you three days leave."

"Thank you, sir. I'll deliver the princess to the morgue, while arrangements are made for the funeral."

Boris added, "Jovan, retrieve the wedding ring before taking her over."

"Yes sir."

Ekaterina clutched her hand and pulled off the ring, a tightness in her chest easing that she didn't even realize was there, then she looked at Ivan, wondering if he also felt the immensity of the moment, the significance. She was considered dead to Boris and Vladimir, no longer married, no longer a prisoner, no more a refugee. She was free, well, once they'd successfully crossed the border.

The sounds from beyond the thin barrier of the supply room told Ekaterina most if not all the men had left the Infirmary. She wasn't sure who remained.

"Dr. Ilievski," General Brankov said, revealing his presence. "I'll help you with the transfer of the bodies."

"Thank you."

"I suspect this will be the last major action I'll be allowed to carry out unaccompanied by guards not of my choosing."

"What makes you say that?"

"The way Boris looked at me when I explained why I wasn't at the door. It only takes one moment for him to lose all trust. You apparently haven't had that moment yet. That's fortunate for you and your 'dead' bodies. Where are they, anyway?"

Ekaterina tensed and felt Ivan do the same. What if General Brankov wasn't ready to give up his earned trust with Boris? He might use their capture to regain his position.

Dr. Ilievski said, "You know, General, I'd like to keep my secrets in case I need to use them again when I return from Svobodia. You understand, I'm sure. If you wouldn't mind standing guard outside the door, I'll get a couple things ready for your assistance."

"Of course."

The door to the Infirmary opened, then closed. Footsteps sounded inside the supply room.

"Okay, it's time to move. Quickly, into the x-ray room," Dr. Ilievski said as he slid the wall open.

Ekaterina and Ivan moved to the opening, hand in hand.

Ivan asked, "What happens next, doctor?"

"He'll come back in and help the two of you into body bags, then we'll wheel you out to the coroner van in the parking lot. You'll be taken to the morgue for now, away from here at least."

"Do you think you can trust him?" Ekaterina asked.

"We don't have a choice. He's helping because Konstantin wants me to join his cause and I won't do that if anything goes amiss."

"But I was under the impression you weren't going to come back after crossing the border," Ekaterina said.

"They don't know that. Let's keep it that way." Dr. Ilievski closed the wall to the secret compartment and led them to the x-ray room. "I'll be right back." He left.

Ekaterina turned into Ivan, who wrapped his arms around her protectively. She asked, "How are you feeling?"

"Better than ever."

"No, really how are you feeling?" She looked up to his eyes.

"I hurt in lots of places, but my heart is happy because you're safe and whole. And soon we'll be across the border and all this will be in the past."

"What will happen when we get over there? Where will we go?"

"We'll have to move north and get new identities, because, you know, we're dead. My parents know how to make all that happen, and I'm ready to learn. Though I don't know if we should contact them too soon, just in case."

Ekaterina held her breath, afraid of what she must say next. Now that they could have a future, Boris had thrown a curveball by bringing in his own doctor and raising the possibility of a pregnancy. She hadn't been able to talk to Ivan about it due to needing to be completely quiet in the storage room, but that didn't mean it wasn't on her mind. "Ivan, there's a chance I might be pregnant. Dr. Ilievski insists the process probably won't take, but . . ." She let out a sob and held him tighter. "But what if I *am* pregnant? It would be Vladimir's. How would I cope with that?"

Ivan pulled her back and grasped her firmly by the shoulders, staring straight into her eyes. "The doctor told me about the possibility. All I know is, whatever comes next, I want to be with you. No matter what happens, we will protect each other, and if need be, a baby. No one ever needs to know who the father is. Of course, it's your decision. But I'll be there, every step of the way."

"Thank you." Relief warred with the desire to break down into sobs. She didn't know what she wanted concerning a possible pregnancy. She didn't want to think about it, but at least she knew she didn't have to face the future alone.

Dr. Ilievski returned pushing a gurney with a package on top. Behind him stood General Brankov with a stern expression on his face.

Ekaterina raised her face to look directly at the general. "Thank you," she said, then bowed her head.

"Don't thank me yet, Princess Ekaterina. We'll have many eyes on us as we exit the building. If at any time your presence is exposed, I'll act accordingly to retain my position here. You understand."

"Yes." Ekaterina turned to Dr. Ilievski and gave him the ring she had grasped in her fist. "Here." Her tone betrayed none of the turmoil she felt at the gesture. She'd soon be free, but legally and in the eyes of the world, she was Vladimir's wife. She felt Ivan's fingers interlaced with her other hand and realized what she'd gone through had been worth it: she'd get to live her life away from the castle and with someone who truly cared about her. Jovan handed the ring off to General Brankov. "Would you return this to Boris?"

"Yes. But what is the corpse wearing?"

"The duplicate from the vault."

"How in the world did you get into the vault?"

"I didn't. I asked the vault guard to get it for me."

"How did you know he's sympathetic to the Insurgents?"

"How did I know a Crosser plane was going to leave when it did? I have my own web of contacts here in the palace, General."

"I underestimated you, Doctor. I apologize."

Dr. Ilievski turned to Ekaterina and said, "This is the largest body bag I was able to get from the morgue. I hope it's large enough for you both. I know this will be uncomfortable for you, Ivan, what with your ribs, but it's the only way to get you two out of here undetected."

"You don't have to worry about me, Doc."

The bag was opened on the gurney and the doctor and general helped Ivan in first, then they assisted Ekaterina into the bag. She tried not to lie directly on Ivan's chest, but it was near impossible. Dr. Ilievski placed an oxygen tank inside to bottom of the bag and threaded air tubes to Ekaterina and Ivan, which they ran under their noses.

"These bags weren't designed for the living." Dr. Ilievski zipped the bag closed. "While we're wheeling you out, please hold very still. Play dead."

General Brankov said, "Jovan, that doesn't look right. The lump should be centered."

"Let's try this."

Ekaterina felt pressure on the bag as something lightweight

was placed between her and Ivan. She started to have doubts about whether she could do this. But she had to, she knew it. She needed to be strong and courageous. She closed her eyes and tried to imagine the body bag was a cocoon, and when she emerged, she'd have a new life.

"Yes, now we're ready. The van is still parked outside the staff exit," General Brankov said.

"Are you two ready?" Dr. Ilievski asked.

"Yes," Ekaterina and Ivan said together. Ekaterina felt the rumbling of his voice under her ear and smiled.

Yes, she was ready.

Ivan

The gurney began rolling and Ivan took shallow breaths. He didn't want to frighten Katia, but the pressure she exerted caused his ribs to dig in and made him want to cough. He wasn't sure if he could keep his coughing at bay long enough to get out of the palace. If he screwed this up for her, he'd never be able to live with himself.

Katia was obviously uncomfortable, Ivan could tell. He knew she was trying not to put her weight on him, but that meant she was tense and that her muscles would eventually protest and begin to shake, which could give them away. He didn't think they were out of the Infirmary yet so he took a chance and said in as low of a voice as he could, "Katia, relax your body." He felt her melt against him and let out her held breath. The pressure increased, but he willed himself to deal with it. Neither of the two men walking with the gurney commented. They either didn't hear him or agreed.

They turned and the exterior sounds changed to large and echoing. They were out of the Infirmary. Ivan wished someone could tell *him* to relax because he was so tense and scared that they'd be caught, he found it difficult to breathe.

"At ease, soldier," General Brankov said to someone.

A distraught male voice asked, "General, is it true? Princess Ekaterina is dead?"

"It's true, Risto."

"This can't be. I need to see for myself."

The gurney stopped abruptly.

Ivan felt Katia tense again.

Dr. Ilievski responded with, "Son, you don't want your last memory of Ekaterina to be what you'd see inside this bag. Please take my word on it. She's dead."

"No! She can't be dead. I don't believe it!"

General Brankov added sternly, "She shouldn't have ever been put in this situation and you should accept the responsibility of your role in her demise. Now, step aside and show some respect for the dead!"

The gurney began moving once again.

Ivan's entire body was ablaze with the need for oxygen. He didn't realize how long he'd held his breath, scared to death of being caught. Slowly, he exhaled and felt Katia do the same thing which gave him a sense of relief. He inhaled fresh oxygen through the tubing in his nose, ignoring the plastic smell which accompanied it.

They turned again and bumped up and over a threshold. They were outside the palace. Ivan heard the doors of a vehicle open and felt the gurney wheelbase hit into the back bumper, causing them to fold under for ease of sliding into the cargo hold. Then the doors slammed shut, followed by silence.

Neither of them moved or talked. Ivan wondered how long they'd have to hold this position and if it was okay to cough. The urge was killing him, but he would refuse it as long as he could. His body convulsed involuntarily, but the bag's edges didn't move and no sound emerged. *Just a little longer,* he pleaded with himself.

He heard doors open and felt the weight of bodies climbing into the van. He assumed the doctor and general were now inside.

Dr. Ilievski said, "We're alone."

Ivan began coughing before the doctor finished his words. Katia's arm stretched across his body and she gently massaged his chest. After relieving his need to cough, he said, "How much longer, doctor?"

"Five minutes. We are almost finished."

CHAPTER 18

Boris

Boris sat in his high-backed leather chair in his office, sipping a glass of whiskey and staring off into space. Where did it all go wrong? Exactly when had he lost? At least the Cvetkovski girl had been officially married to Vladimir and the press conference had taken place.

Now he'd have to use another excuse to explain her death.

"The damned Insurgents succeeded this time in killing the last Cvetkovski," he spoke to no one. He only wanted to hear how the words sounded.

Yes, the public would buy that. They are all idiots and believe whatever I tell them. Still, all those years of careful planning and plotting to have Vladimir marry royalty were for nothing. It had been so close. Why was the girl so obstinate? Couldn't she see the importance of my overall plan?

Moments ago, he'd watched the monitors in the control room as her body was wheeled out to the coroner's van. He never suspected she'd be so rebellious against the idea of marrying Vladimir or else he wouldn't have been so quick to have her father taken out. At the time it seemed like the best way to ensure she married Vladimir. In hindsight, Boris could see perfectly though. Had he kept her father alive and used *him* as her motivation, she wouldn't have tried to escape. She wouldn't have met the boy. She would be married to Vladimir and, hopefully on her way to producing a royal baby.

Then again, if Vladimir hadn't brought the boy back to the

palace, Ekaterina would have been more malleable.

And yet, there was the other factor in the mess. The Insurgents. They had a firm hold on the workings of the palace, obviously. General Brankov had already rooted out several suspected individuals of whom he'd deal with later, but the fact remained that Boris didn't know for sure who he could trust anymore. Even General Brankov had been conveniently absent at the time the prisoners escaped.

Boris sipped on his drink, then massaged his forehead. He didn't want to think about General Brankov now. He wondered what he'd tell Prince Hector of Katastasi who was going to join his cause based on the union of Ekaterina and Vladimir. Boris needed his help now more than ever to take down the Insurgents before they gained too much power.

Konstantin

Konstantin Andonov sat in the office of the morgue awaiting the arrival of Princess Ekaterina and of his newest member of the underground, Dr. Jovan Ilievski. As far as Konstantin could tell, with the limited intel provided to him, the princess and male companion were considered deceased. The carefully crafted plan was almost completed—the plan being to recruit the doctor. When the news broke that the bodies were being transported to the morgue, Konstantin simply had to be there to welcome Jovan.

Whether or not Konstantin would allow the princess to live remained to be decided. Who was to say whether a freak accident would happen once she relocated across the border? Plausible deniability would be his position should anything unfortunate happen. The fact remained that too many people were aware of the scheme to fake her death and if any of those people spoke up, the search would commence once again. The doctor and general would be removed and/or killed and Konstantin would have to start from scratch. He didn't want to have to do that, not when he was so close to being able to stage a coup d'état.

Headlights shown in the window as the transport van pulled into the garage. Konstantin heard the large door close and he followed Pandil out to the back of the van. Jovan and General Brankov met them at the back doors.

"No time for pleasantries, these two need out," Dr. Ilievski said as he opened the doors. He grabbed the gurney and pulled, allowing the first set of wheels to drop, then the second. He and the general locked them in place and removed the gurney the rest of the way. Dr Ilievski unzipped the bag half-way, revealing two sweat-covered kids.

Konstantin marveled at how young the princess looked. The individual who commanded so much power with Boris Kochev laid an arm's length away from him. Did she know how powerful she was? Surely, she knew.

The doctor helped the princess sit up and get off the gurney. Then he gave aid to the boy, Ivan Lazarov. He listened to the boy's lungs and helped him sit upright, upon which Ivan started coughing. Konstantin reached out and laid his hand on Ivan's back. "Young man, I'm Konstantin Andonov. I'm pleased to meet you."

Ivan turned his head and looked Konstantin in the eye. "So, *you're* the son-of-a-bitch who tried to kill Katia?"

Dr. Ilievski stepped over to Ivan's side. "Konstantin made it possible for us to be here right now. Don't forget that."

"I won't. I'll remember him as someone I don't ever want to meet again."

Konstantin grumbled. "You have your grandmother's mouth, Ivan. And your grandfather's nerve. You be sure to tell her I said that." Konstantin stepped back and said, "I'll leave you to complete the last leg of the plan, Dr. Ilievski. I look forward to working with you when you get back."

"I have a three-day leave," the doctor told him.

"I know." Konstantin grinned, reminding the doctor of how much power and intel he already had in place at the palace. "We will have much to discuss when you return."

Ivan

With slow steps, Ivan followed behind Katia into an office. They both took a seat on a couch while they waited for the doctor and general to go back to the palace and transport the deceased stand-in bodies to the morgue. Dr. Ilievski explained they would stack the two bodies on one gurney with a sheet over top to make it appear as one body being transported.

He hoped that would work.

In the meantime, he was able to sit next to Katia and hold her hand, without worrying how much noise they made or if someone was going to walk in on them. Flashes of the past day raced through his mind—all the fears he had, the people who'd helped them, and of course those who wouldn't have minded seeing them both dead. His thoughts strayed to one person who he hadn't recognized, who'd seemed devastated by Katia's death.

"Can I ask a question, Katia?"

"Of course."

"Who's Risto?"

"He's someone I've known since my family came out of hiding. He was in my class at school, along with Vladimir."

"Why was he at the palace? He seemed really upset to hear you died."

Katia shifted on the couch. "He's Vladimir's friend—sort of. It's a weird relationship that I never understood. I think Vladimir kept Risto around so he could always be above at least one person. I don't know why Risto ever put up with it."

"I guess sometimes friendships are based on selfish desires. Take my friend Anton. I've thought a lot about him, trying to figure out if he was a spy all along, or if he became one somewhere along the way. He always joked how much he hated me. Now I don't know if that was true or not."

"I'm sorry for your loss."

"My loss?"

"He was a large part of your life."

"Yeah, I won't be including him in my life anymore. I bet my dad turns his family in for being traitors."

Katia's eyebrows furrowed. She took his hand in both of hers. "I guess you haven't been told, yet. Your friend was killed at the gas station. I thought they'd killed you when I heard the gunshots, but later Vladimir told me they killed the informant, not you."

Ivan didn't know what to say. He didn't know what to think. So much had happened in the past week since he'd pulled her out of the ice. His entire mindset had changed. His resolve, his passions, his entire life. Anton was dead. The same guy he'd go to *Sophie's* with to hit on the waitresses. The same guy he trusted enough to share his joy about a kiss with Katia. The same guy who'd obviously turned them in to the Kochevs.

The morgue director came in, interrupting their tense moment, and said, "I was able to get a hold of your family, Ivan. They know you're okay and you will be transported back across the border tonight. They'll be waiting for you at this location." He handed Ivan a paper with specific driving instructions.

Ivan glanced at it briefly and recognized the location as the shooting range just outside of town. He pressed the director for more details, "Is my family okay? Is everyone okay?"

"I don't know the answer to that."

* * *

Within the next hour, Dr. Ilievski, General Brankov, Ivan, Katia, and the deceased body double of Ivan approached the border gate. Ivan and Katia were zipped in the large bag just in case one of the guards demanded an inspection. The body double was also in the van and Ivan didn't know what the doctor would say if anyone questioned why there were two body bags when there should only be one.

The vehicle slowed to a stop.

"We must be at the border," Ivan whispered. He could feel her hold her breath.

General Brankov said, "I'll take care of this, Doctor. I look forward to working with you when you return. Enjoy your 'vacation.'"

"Thank you."

The door opened, then closed. Ivan heard the General giving the all clear and ordering the gate be opened for the van to pass. He felt Katia's breath against his neck as she exhaled. They started moving again.

Dr. Ilievski muttered as he drove, "Here we go, crossing over, now we're through. We're through." He let out a loud sigh, then said, "I'll drive for a couple minutes to make sure we're not being followed, then I'll pull over and help you out of the bag."

"Thank you, Jovan," Katia said.

A few minutes down the road, Dr. Ilievski pulled over and opened the back of the van. He climbed inside and closed the door. "All right, let's get you out of there." He unzipped the bag and reached to help Ivan.

Ivan shook his head, "No, help her first."

"Okay. Take my hand."

She did so, and he helped her sit up. She took off the oxygen tube and allowed Dr. Ilievski to mostly lift her out of the bag and set her down by the door.

"How's the leg, Ekaterina?"

"My leg is fine. Ivan's ribs, on the other hand, are probably hurting him."

It was true. Ivan couldn't sit up straight by himself. Dr. Ilievski helped him and then pulled out a couple of pain pills for him to take. "I have a jug of water up front. Let's get you two moved up there."

Katia refused. "I'd rather stay back here, hidden, Jovan."

"That's probably a better idea anyway. I'll get the water, then we'll get moving." Dr. Ilievski opened the back door and jumped out. A strong gust of cold winter air filled the cargo hold.

Katia shivered. "I really hope we don't have car trouble. Neither of us are dressed for this weather."

Ivan wrapped his arm around her shoulders and smiled broadly. "I'm sure we'll be just fine."

She relaxed against him. "Ivan, at the cabin, you made me promise I'd find happiness in any situation." She angled her head up to his.

"Katia, I shouldn't have—"

"Don't speak. That promise helped me keep my head on straight, helped me focus and not melt entirely. You gave me a gift when you had me make that promise; you gave me hope."

Dr. Ilievski opened the door again, handing Ivan a couple pills and a cup of water. He said, "I think I've aged ten years since you came into my life, Ivan."

Ivan swallowed the pills and said, "Sorry, Doc. I'm feeling pretty aged myself."

"Can we please close the door and get moving?" Katia rubbed her arms aggressively. "It's cold and we're still way too close to the border."

"Certainly, Ekaterina."

"Dr. Ilievski, I would like to be called Katia from now on. Ivan and his family all call me by Katia. It's who I am now."

"I wondered why Ivan kept saying that name."

She took Ivan's hand, her cold fingers squeezing his tightly. "Besides, Ekaterina Cvetkovski is dead."

Katia

The van came to a stop and Katia lifted her head off Ivan's

shoulder. "I think we're here, Ivan."

The back doors opened.

"Ivan?"

"Dad?"

"Yes, son. Come on," Michal climbed in and helped Ivan out of the van. Katia followed them with the help of Dr. Ilievski.

Katia saw the small building where they'd stopped: Ludwig Shooting. Michal helped Ivan toward the front doors, a few paces ahead of her and Jovan. Ivan kept trying to look over his shoulder. "Where's Katia?" he asked.

"I'm here, Ivan."

Katia and Jovan entered the small building and found Ivan surrounded by his mother and grandmother. "Oh Ivan, I'm so happy you're alive!" Elena grabbed his head and plastered kisses in his hair. Grandma Mira was right beside her, reminding Elena to be careful of Ivan's injuries.

Katia watched the tender actions from mother to son through watered eyes. She wouldn't have that ever again because of the ruthless Kochev family. Her father had been her life, her strength, and he was gone. She'd never really had a chance to truly mourn his death because of having been taken to the palace directly from the cemetery. Then, shortly after that, Risto's lie landed her in the dungeon which began the cycle of beat down, recovery, rebellion, and back to beat down. But through it all, like a beacon of hope, she had Dr. Jovan Ilievski, who currently held her by the arm, giving her support as her knees shook with elation, anger, and probably a bit of shock. She turned her head to look at Jovan. He had tears on his cheeks, too, as he watched the Lazarov family reunite and express their love for one another.

Katia turned to him and wrapped her arms around his body and let her tears run. Jovan held her as she lost track of time and space in the void of grief. Once Katia lifted her head and wiped her eyes, she found everyone was near her and Jovan.

"Jovan, we owe you everything," Elena said and hugged him tightly. "Thank you for this. Thank you for bringing back my boy."

"You're welcome. Helping Ivan and Katia was my last and final effort to fight against the Kochevs under their own roof." Jovan turned to Mira. "You're Mira Lazarov, correct?"

"That I am, young man."

"A certain individual from the Insurgents doesn't like you very much."

Mira chuckled. "That would be Konstantin, I'm guessing."

"If you don't mind me asking, why the hard feelings?"

"Konstantin has a way of using people for his own gain. He lost his direction many years ago, and I tried to point it out to him. He made a vital mistake, and when his first wife was executed by Boris, he blamed me. It's a typical reaction for any individual who uses people: blame someone else when a plan goes awry. I'm surprised he helped you at all."

"He hoped I'd join his team once I got back to Bregot. In the end, I'm no better than he is, I guess. I used him for *my* own gain, and that of Ekaterina—I mean Katia—and Ivan. Once Konstantin realizes I'm not coming back, well, he won't be happy."

"Understandably so."

"He expressed a great deal of dislike for the Cvetkovski family and promised that if Katia was captured again, she'd be killed."

Mira said, "In my opinion, Konstantin wants the throne. He's placing his people one at a time in the palace so when the timing is right, he can stage a successful coup. If a Cvetkovski remained there, his coup would fail because even his own followers regard the ousted monarchy as being better than him."

"That makes sense and explains more than you know. The question is, would Bregot be in any better hands if he took over?"

"Absolutely not. It would be the same song, different radio station."

"Is there any hope for Bregot's future?"

Mira took a breath. "The Cvetkovski name is the only thing I know of that can help Bregot and bring the Kochev family's rule successfully to an end."

Katia cleared her throat and said, "Too bad the last Cvetkovski died in a horrific car crash."

Ivan smiled at Katia's response. Then he asked, "What happened to Luka?"

Elena answered first. "Luka fled in the middle of the night with his Crossers. Even though it went against what he'd been instructed to do, he probably saved his life and all six defectors. He drove north to a secure location and waited for things to cool down before surfacing."

"Did you get hurt in the raid?" Ivan asked, pointing to each of their cuts and bruises. They nodded. "I'm so sorry."

Michal placed a hand on Ivan's shoulder. "Son, everything happened the way it did without any of us knowing what would come next, that includes you. Wisdom can come from cuts, bruises, and broken ribs. The question is, what wisdom will you gain? While you're thinking about that, consider how Katia's life would be different if the raid hadn't happened. She would always have to be looking over her shoulder, wondering if Kochev's goons were closing in on her. Now she won't have to do that. Everything played out in the best possible way, if you ask me."

"Katia," Elena asked, "what do you plan to do with your new life?"

A surge of warmth and love filled her. Everything happening was real. Her freedom, and life, were now her own. In her heart, she didn't have any idea what to do next. Only one thing stuck in her mind as truth. She turned to Ivan and replied, "Whatever I do, it will be with Ivan."

Ivan's face reddened, even though he smiled, as all eyes moved to him. "For now, we'd better drop off the map entirely."

Mira spoke up. "I couldn't agree more. I'm going to take you two north. Michal and Elena will return home and 'bury their son,' as Boris would expect to see." Mira looked at Dr. Ilievski. "Sounds like you're going to have some heat on your head as well. I'd like to stay in contact with you, but from a distance. You understand."

"Completely. I didn't work this hard on getting the princess out of Kochev's hands just to have him find her because she's too near to me." Jovan turned to Katia. "Sometime in the future, maybe we can work together defying the dictator. Until then, go and live life to its fullest." He leaned forward and kissed her on the cheek, then gave Ivan a careful hug. "Take care of her."

Dr. Ilievski said his goodbyes and left to finish his leg of the journey: to deliver the deceased Lazarov boy to the morgue. Katia felt a sense of sadness with his departure, but knew they had to part ways, like he said, until sometime in the future.

Katia and Ivan were helped into Grandma Mira's backseat and they started their journey north, toward a new life, one Katia never thought she'd get to have. Katia's belongings, including the coat she'd stuffed full of baggies, sat in a box in the front seat. Her thoughts went to the contents. She hoped two specific baggies had survived everything; one which held the dried rose buds from her parents' individual funeral bouquets, and one containing her family lineage documents.

She placed her hand on her stomach and thought about the possibility of a pregnancy. If she was, the baby would never be told of its lineage. The ordeal she'd been through from one power-hungry tyrant was one she wouldn't want anyone else to suffer through, certainly not her child.

Ivan extended his hand to her and they intertwined fingers.

"By the way, I've been wanting to do this for a long time." He pulled her face close and kissed her. Her whole body tingled and she kissed him back, expressing all the love, relief, and gratitude she'd had pent up inside her. Everything around her disappeared and there were only the two of them together, just like they would be the rest of their lives.

They parted slowly, a smile touching Ivan's lips.

"Better than I even imagined."

Katia let out a sigh of contentment and leaned her head against his shoulder. She felt him tighten until he rearranged his body to be more comfortable. She traced her fingertips across his chest, wishing she could undo the pain he'd been through because of her. "I'm sorry your life has changed so much."

"Why? I'm not."

Her fingers paused and she flattened her hand. "But your body is broken, and you'll have scars for life."

Ivan took her hand in his and brought it to his mouth for a kiss. "I'm proud to have these scars, Katia. Every time I look in the mirror, I'll be reminded of the best choice I ever made: to pull you from the ice. That's when my life truly began.

EPILOGUE

Risto

Risto Petkovski stood away from the group of mourners at the cemetery. Snowflakes fell reverently, almost symbolically. The silence of the surrounding area seemed to punctuate the moment. The old priest murmured a prayer or rite of passage for her soul or something like that. Risto didn't care. All he knew was what he felt. He felt empty, stripped of his will to live, tromped on by people more powerful than him, once again.

How had this come to be? How could he have let this happen? Why was he powerless to prevent it? Ekaterina was gone forever now. Gone! This was all Konstantin Andonov's fault. He had pressed Risto to befriend Vladimir, pushed him because there was no one else in the underground of the same age, except for Eva Brankov. Apparently, she'd also been pushed to the forefront, since she currently sat between Vladimir and her own father, General Kral Brankov.

Konstantin's tutoring on how to associate with and act like Vladimir had paid off, somewhat. Vladimir had accepted him as a friend, peculiar as their relationship might be. Risto could see Vladimir's powerful future, and he wanted to be part of it.

Risto was taught how to win over the girls. Vladimir could certainly have any girl he wanted, and if Risto was to be his friend, then he would need to be able to do the same. Risto's outer appearance had been tended to courtesy of Konstantin. The best stylists, top personal trainers, and dieticians all helped him transform into an undeniably handsome man during his teen years. But the one girl he wanted most of all could see through his shallowness. She was the only one who mattered to him; her opinion meant everything. He was hurt deeply to have been rejected by her because of his association with Vladimir, pressured by Konstantin. Now, she lay in the casket before him.

He had been warned not to associate with Ekaterina Cvetkovski. She was off limits. That just made Risto want her more, to show he had at least some power and control over his own life. Konstantin told him any focus on Ekaterina would bring about Vladimir's attentions. Which was exactly what happened. That, Risto truly regretted. But Risto had been torn between love and power. He thought he could have both. He could rise in power beside Vladimir with Ekaterina by his side. Only, the further things progressed, he realized Ekaterina would be by Vladimir's side, not his.

Why wouldn't she listen to him? Why had she hated him so much? He had truly meant it when he told her he could hide her and reinvent her. But she looked at him with disgust in her eyes, and it hurt. That look was the last one he'd gotten from her before finding out the devastating news—she would never look upon him again.

What he wouldn't do to see her eyes again, even if they held loathing for him. At least she would be alive, and he could continue to try to win her over.

Risto blinked back tears. He looked at Eva Brankov's profile, and a flood of hatred filled his entire body. She would now be the star puppet in the show. Her strings would be controlled by Konstantin, and Risto felt sick thinking about it.

Why should Konstantin be allowed to have so much power? Who did he think he was? The only consolation in Risto's mind was that he knew Vladimir's weaknesses, and Konstantin did not. He applauded himself for not revealing these to Konstantin.

The sun shone through a break in the clouds, illuminating the snowflakes as if they had become energized with electricity. Risto's thoughts cleared, and his revenge began to take form. The light illuminating his mind set in motion his plan to rise above all those who had taken everything from him. Risto vowed right there, at that moment, as gentle snowflakes lightly touched Ekaterina's coffin, that he would avenge her death. He would rise above Konstantin Andonov. He would rise above Vladimir. Somehow, someday, he would prevail.

THANKS!

I hope you enjoyed *Royal Refugee*. Please consider leaving a review on Amazon or Goodreads so other readers can learn what intrigued you most about the story. Reviews really matter to independent writers like me, as they help the books rise in visibility where more people can see them and, hopefully, purchase them. That's huge, as it allows me to make enough money to write full time and get more books on the market to readers like you!

Don't know how to leave a review? Send me a message using my <u>Contact Me</u> form on my website and I'll give you instructions. lorenaangell.com/contact-me.html

Sign up for my <u>Awesome Fans Newsletter</u> on my website. Every month I give a $25 Amazon gift card away to a lucky subscriber. Who knows? Maybe you'll be the next winner. Plus, by signing up, you'll receive exclusive offers, freebies, news and updates before the general public does.

Katia and Ivan's story continues in

Book 2: ***Royal Resistance***

Twenty-five years later, their three adult children are no strangers to helping Crossers, having grown up assisting in the effort to help as many people escape the dictatorial rule of the Kochev family. Yet, even with the close proximity to the Underground, Lidja, Andrej, and Deyan have no idea how important their mother is, nor how closely tied they are to the Kochevs, the history of Bregot, and the rightful heir to the throne.

After sending off the latest Crosser cared for by Andrej Mitreski and his family, Andrej looks forward to some time off with his fiancée, Tanja. Housing and hiding border Crossers can be exhausting, yet he's dedicated to continuing in his parent's footsteps. If only his fiancée's attitude matched his. Andrej won't get any time off, however. A critically injured Crosser from the Underground needs help right away and can't wait any longer. Andrej begrudgingly accepts his duty to forgo any intimate time with Tanja to take care of the badly beaten teen boy whose life must be important for the Underground to be involved with his move across the border.

"Eli" arrives beaten and broken and surrounded by mystery. Eli must stay strong and as alert as possible to avoid capture if there's any chance of taking down the Kochev family, namely Vladimir Kochev, the acting leader of Bregot. The information Eli knows will end the authoritarian rule if it can only get delivered to the right ears. However, once Eli discovers exactly who Andrej's parents are, the plan is threatened as important lives are endangered more so than only Eli's.

Royal Resistance is available at all retailers.

About the Author

Lorena Angell is the internationally bestselling author of the YA fantasy series, *The Unaltered*. Inspired by an interview from J.K. Rowling, Lorena began to write and published her first book in 2011. Since then, she's earned over 4,200 reviews (average of 4.5 stars), has been a #1 bestseller in over 11 countries and wants nothing more than to write more books for her readers.

Connect with Lorena Angell at:
www.LorenaAngell.com
Twitter: @LorenaAngell1
Facebook: The Unaltered Diamond Series
Instagram: the.unaltered.series

www.ingramcontent.com/pod-product-compliance
Lightning Source LLC
Chambersburg PA
CBHW021654110726
47902CB00007B/1928